Dahanu
Road

ALSO BY ANOSH IRANI

NOVELS

The Cripple and His Talismans (2004)

The Song of Kahunsha (2006)

PLAYS

The Bombay Plays: The Matka King & Bombay Black

ANOSH IRANI

Dahanu
Road

Doubleday
Canada

Doubleday Canada and colophon are registered trademarks

Library and Archives Canada Cataloguing in Publication

Irani, Anosh, 1974–
Dahanu Road / Anosh Irani.

ISBN 978-0-385-66699-2

I. Title.

PS8617.R36D35 2010   C813'.6   C2009-903964-8

This book is a work of fiction. Names, characters, places and
incidents are products of the author's imagination or are used
fictitiously. Any resemblance to actual events or locales or persons,
living or dead, is entirely coincidental.

Jacket and book design by Kelly Hill
Printed and bound in the USA

Published in Canada by Doubleday Canada,
a division of Random House of Canada Limited

Visit Random House of Canada Limited's website:
www.randomhouse.ca

10 9 8 7 6 5 4 3 2 1

For my father, Adi,

&

for all the Iranis of Dahanu Road

PROLOGUE

Iran, 1920

THE NIGHT BEFORE he was to leave for Yazd, young Shapur was unable to sleep. Thoughts of butter and cream melting in his mouth filled him with delight. After all, his father had promised to take him to the most famed confectioner in all of Persia—Aflatoon of Esfahan. Customers compared his sweets to the poetry of Rumi and Hafez.

Shapur sat up all night dreaming—biting, crunching, savouring, letting chunks of cotton candy remain in his mouth for eternity.

At the slightest hint of light, he was ready.

"You are a true Marco Polo," said his father, stroking the long beard that hung from his chin in an inverted triangle.

Vamog offered his son almonds, but Shapur did not want any.

"We have a long journey ahead of us," said Vamog. "You need to eat."

Shapur gobbled the almonds down, hoping they would not

occupy too much space in his belly. He was only ten, and even though he had the appetite of a man, he was still physically small. He wanted to reserve every inch in his stomach for the creations of Aflatoon.

After trudging through red desert sands and then hitching a ride from a caravan of silk weavers, father and son finally reached Yazd.

They stopped outside a Zoroastrian fire temple. Vamog longed to see the fire that burned in an inner chamber, in a large copper vase, a fire that had been kept alive for over a thousand years. Lovingly tended by a grand priest, it was a symbol of purity and goodness for all members of the Zoroastrian faith.

A bearded angel adorned the yellow entrance, a golden disc in its hand.

"Do you know what that is?" Vamog asked his son.

"A fravashi," replied Shapur. "It will protect me wherever I go, day and night, in this life and the next."

When Shapur had first learned of the fravashis, he imagined a pair of strong golden wings enveloping the domed roof of his house, and it immediately made him feel safe and warm, even on chilly winter nights when wolf howls mixed with the whoosh of the wind to make things so eerie.

Instead of taking his son into the temple, Vamog led Shapur to a well that was outside the temple gates. The old bucket creaked as it rose up the narrow walls, causing the sparrows that stood on the parapet to fly away. Vamog took a mug full of water and held it to his son's lips. Just as Shapur opened his mouth to drink, Vamog emptied the water on his son's head.

A surprised Shapur went into a fit of laughter.

"That's what I wanted," said Vamog. "The prophet Zarathushtra came out of his mother's womb laughing. So one must always be cheerful when standing in front of this place of worship."

Shapur had never heard his father talk about their beloved prophet in this manner. Vamog always spoke of Zarathushtra with such reverence, but now there was an element of mischief in him. Even his long moustache twirled so high it almost reached his cheekbones, as though it were the handiwork of a tiny goblin that had crept into their house the night before.

But Shapur did not want to go inside the fire temple. At least not right now. The fravashi was no doubt close to his heart, but something else was even closer, more alluring.

Vamog detected the eagerness in his son. "Let's go," he said. "Before the great Aflatoon retires for the day."

He soaked his white handkerchief in the mug of water and placed the handkerchief on his neck to soothe the skin that had been burned by the sun. Shapur took one of his slippers off and was about to overturn it.

"Not yet," said Vamog. "The sand must be emptied only when we are *inside* Yazd. That way we are helping the desert claim the city."

Vamog told his son how Yazd was caught between two deserts, the Dasht-é Kavir and the Dasht-é Lut. No matter which desert one crossed to reach the city, a strange magic took place: the moment a man stood still, sand moved towards him and covered his feet, filled his sandals to the brim, in the hope that every grain would be spread throughout the bazaars and courtyards of the city. It seemed that both deserts were fighting for the city's affection, but in the end neither could claim her, and she had to be shared. "It is for this reason," said Vamog, "that Yazd is known all over Iran as 'The Bride of the Desert.'"

Outside the city gates, an old man rubbed his hands together. Shapur thought maybe there was a lamp stuck between them and he was in dire need of a wish. But he soon realized from the man's outstretched palm that it was his way of asking for a tip from travellers.

Around Shapur, tall arched wind-catchers stood erect on domed roofs.

Everyone in Yazd, from the tailor who laid down the most perfect embroidery on silk to the wrinkly grandmother who shared proverbs with her brood, was grateful to the wind-catchers for the way they swallowed the breeze and funnelled it into their homes to keep them cool.

Shapur soon arrived at Persia's sweetest spot.

"Aflatoon's Candy Bazaar." The words shimmered on a green banner. Shapur marvelled at the winding line outside the sweet shop. It coiled just like a candy stick. There was a fragrance in the air, not just the sweetness of pastries but the happiness of customers as well; the fact that they were buying sweets meant they had reason to celebrate. Shapur took in as much as he could, and if there was a special compartment in his nostrils that stored scents, he would store this one for life and take it with him wherever he went.

No one cared about the heat. It was mean and dry, yet people waited with a jovial air. The sun blazed down on everyone, but all it could do was cast shadows on the ground. That was the only darkness in all of Yazd.

"Papa, what do you think Aflatoon's secret recipe is?" asked Shapur.

"No one knows," said Vamog. "When the oldest member of the Esfahan family is on his deathbed, he reveals the secret to his successor, whispers it into his ear so softly that even the wind cannot hear it."

Shapur was impressed. He didn't think anything could stay hidden from the wind.

He wondered if Aflatoon had a son. One day the magic ingredients would be whispered into his ear and he would become Persia's most admired confectioner.

"But if you ask me, I think it's just a ruse to hide the truth," said Vamog. "The real secret is simple. It's the sweetness in Aflatoon's heart. It oozes into everything he touches."

It would soon be their turn to enter the shop, and Shapur could now see the delicacies in a glass case, and samples on the counter, in bright yellows, pinks, and greens, which customers had dipped toothpicks into to show their appreciation, a rating system of sorts.

His father put his hand in his pocket and took out a coin, but he dropped it, and it rolled on the ground, teased him by making a circle. It amused Shapur to see his hulk of a father chase a coin like an eager child whose mother would scold him if it was lost.

His father almost had the coin in his hand.

Almost.

In bending down, Vamog's body cast a shadow on the ground. Part of that shadow touched a Muslim royal.

Shapur saw his father falling. The Muslim royal's henchmen, three of them, kicked Vamog. Shapur ran towards his father, but a hard push from one of the henchmen was enough to send him reeling back.

"You lowly Zoroastrian," they said to Vamog. "You unclean infidel. You have tainted a Muslim royal."

They ripped his shirt open, took the sacred thread that was tied around his waist and noosed it around his neck. Then they paraded him alongside a donkey, calling the donkey the more handsome of the two.

Shapur went numb.

No one from the long, winding line at the sweet shop had moved. There was silence, then a murmur, like the noise of insects flying in groups, and Shapur wanted to move away from them all.

When the henchmen finally left, Shapur watched as his father removed, with shaking hands, the sacred kusti from his neck. For years, his father had kept the soft sheepskin thread completely spotless, and now it was covered in dust.

Shapur could not look into his father's eyes, so with his hands he brushed his father's back, tried to clean the dirt off it. He spotted the coin still on the ground. Shapur went to retrieve it, but his father stopped him.

Vamog just shook his head.

The journey back to their village was solemn.

Sand collected in their slippers, making them heavy.

Shapur wanted to know where his fravashi was and why he did not fly to the bazaar. All he had to do was swoop down from in between the blue minarets that seemed to reach the clouds and help his father.

When they reached home a day later, Vamog told his son that they were leaving Iran for good. But Shapur did not understand. This was the home of the Zoroastrians. "For over three thousand years, we have lived here," his father had once said. A man should not have to leave his own home.

"We are treated like dogs. No, we are worse off than dogs."

Vamog told his son what the Arabs had done to his friend Bizhan, who lived next door to them before Shapur was born. To punish Bizhan, he was tied to a dog, and both were severely beaten, so that the dog, scared and in pain, pounced on Bizhan, shredding his arm, while the Arabs made a sport of it.

"There was a time when if a Zoroastrian was murdered by an Arab," Vamog continued, "the punishment was a mere fine, equivalent in value to the price of a camel."

That was what their life was worth.

"Things may never change," he said. "Our days in Yazd are over. Let us see what India has in store."

They left two days later, on a donkey with a bundle of clothes, oranges, almonds and water, and when Vamog looked back at his home for the last time, he waved out to it, but it was not the mud-brick walls he was waving to—it was his wife, who had died when Shapur was seven.

After an exhausting journey, after the donkey died not even halfway through, after they begged and stole and got rides any way they could for weeks, they reached Karachi, and from there made their way to Bombay, a far cry from the cypress trees and arched streets of Yazd. They found shelter in the fruit orchard of a famous Zoroastrian philanthropist. There, under the shade of a fruit tree, Vamog lay on the ground.

Young Shapur saw the dying light in his father's eyes.

"Ahura Mazda has led us here," Vamog comforted his son. "Ahura Mazda will provide."

Vamog's eyes closed, and Shapur stayed by his father's side for a long time, hoping that Ahura Mazda would show Himself. But there was no sign of the One God.

As Shapur bent to kiss his father's forehead, he saw a small brown fruit near Vamog's hand.

ONE

India, 2000

THE SMELL OF mosquito repellent pervaded Zairos' small room, but he was used to it. Each night his father, Aspi Irani, would come into the room, shut the door and windows, and spray the repellent with great flourish as only an artist would. His father was obsessed with mosquito repellents and owned every brand on the market, from Baygon to Killer. He treated his array of repellents with the kind of passion usually reserved for record collections.

Zairos scratched his thigh and realized that he had been bitten by a monster. A few mosquitoes lay on the ground, some flat on their backs, some sideways, giving the impression that the place had been bombed. But these mosquitoes were part of the everyday death toll in the coastal town of Dahanu. In Dahanu, old-timers high on snuff reminisced about their childhood days in Iran and spoke to themselves in Farsi and Dari; tribal fishermen drowned in the sea, possessing neither the strength nor the will to prevent their boats from capsizing;

retired schoolteachers drank country liquor until their livers understood their plea and put them out of their misery: and the young women who worked in balloon factories became balloons themselves, puffed up, bloated with the air of disappointment.

The bed creaked as Zairos rose from it. He crossed to the porch door and swung it open. His room was on the first floor of his family's home, Aspi Villa, and the branch of a coconut tree reached for him, as it did every morning. The higher branches caressed the red tiled roof, and their leaves always made Zairos think of large eyelashes, as though the tree and the tiled roof were lovers.

Zairos put on jeans and a blue T-shirt and went down the stairs to the living room. His father was seated at the table, cutting an apple, his belly protruding from underneath his white sudreh. The sacred vest had a red blotch, most probably ketchup, on the small pouch at the V that stored the good deeds of the wearer. Zairos smiled at how devout a Zoroastrian his father was—instead of good deeds shining through, there was a blaring ketchup stain.

Knife in hand, Aspi Irani was painfully systematic in the cutting of the apple, accurate in the size of each piece, and not once did he even look at the fruit. An unlit cigarette dangled from his mouth. He used to be a chain-smoker, but when Zairos was a year old, Aspi Irani had dozed off while smoking his last Capstan of the night, and in a stupor flicked his burning cigarette into Zairos' cot, and the horror of the flames was enough to make him quit forever. Zairos was told this little detail when he was ten with the lightness of a fairy tale. "Thank God it happened," said his father. "Otherwise I would be smoking till today." Although he had given up smoking, Aspi Irani had been unable to stop holding a cigarette. That and constantly running his fingers through his salt and pepper hair.

As soon as Zairos was downstairs, Aspi Irani started singing. His songs were a strange concoction indeed, a blend of three languages, Hindi, English, and Gujarati. Zairos always compared his father's songs to country liquor: Use anything you can find—orange peels, battery acid, even leather slippers. Then squeeze hard and let its juice make your head spin. This morning, Aspi Irani's song included two main ingredients— tennis and his old Morris. The two rhymed, and as he sang, the cigarette fell out of his mouth. Then he stopped abruptly and said to Zairos, "I think your mother is having an affair." He said this every other day, whenever Mithoo went to the bazaar.

Theirs was an odd pairing. Mithoo was calm and soft spoken, with a perpetual smile on her face. She spent her time looking after stray dogs and teaching English to just about any child who wanted to learn. As a result, books were strewn all over Aspi Villa, from Wren and Martin's thick dossier on English grammar to books for five-year-olds such as *The ABC of English*. There were times when Aspi Irani would come home and find strange children in his living room, sitting at the dinner table with colouring pencils in their hand and chocolate milk on their lips. "Is this an orphanage?" he would ask his wife. "Can we please give them back, my dear?" Mithoo would pout and wink at her husband, and Aspi Irani would melt, but only for a bit. The moment it got dark outside, he would turn off the lights in the living room, bring out an old rubber skeleton, and shine a flashlight on it, thus ensuring that his wife's students would be terrified of English for the rest of their lives.

Aspi Irani loved the idea of sabotage. He yearned for a situation to ruin, as long as there was no permanent damage. No matter where he went, be it marketplace or wedding hall, he was an imp straight from the underworld, full of guile and mischief. Of course, with his thick forearms and massive calves, he was too large to be an imp, but he had an imp's demeanour, from the sleazy to the sublime. When he was in action, his eyebrows arched like a piece of Mughal architecture; it was the arch of knowing that came upon the countenance of only those who knew secrets, of men who found beauty in the orchestration of disaster.

And it was the arch of his eyebrow, he claimed, that had made Mithoo fall in love with him. Mithoo's parents had died in a car accident when she was fourteen, and she had responded with a bout of silence that lasted four years, until the moment she met Aspi Irani at Café Military in Bombay. "I was so handsome that your mother just *had* to open her mouth and say something," Aspi Irani told Zairos. But then one day at a party, while his father was telling this story for the hundredth time, Mithoo whispered to her son, "I did open my mouth, but only because I was in pain. Your father had worn pointy boots and he stepped on my toe and I howled. But he prefers his version." In any case, they were married six months later. At eighteen, Mithoo was a radiant bride, and Aspi Irani, seven years her senior, continued wearing pointy boots.

In later years, the boots gave way to moccasins. Whenever Aspi Irani went abroad, he came back with five pairs of brown moccasins, "One for each year, until our next holiday in five years' time." At the moment, the moccasins were neatly tucked away in a corner of the living room, while his face was buried in *The Times of India*. "The rupee has hit an all-time low against the U.S. dollar," he grumbled. "What a wonderful way to start the new millennium."

Then he looked up at the silver-framed portrait of Zarathushtra on the wall. "You should become finance minister," he said. "Only a miracle can save us." But the prophet remained unmoved. In his soft and luxuriant beard, a burst of light around his head, palms facing upward, Zarathushtra seemed preoccupied with matters celestial; the plummeting rupee or a foray into Indian politics failed to rouse him.

Aspi Irani turned his affections to the apple he was cutting.

"This apple is raped," he said, pointing to a tiny, almost invisible rotten patch.

The word *rape* was a staple in Aspi Irani's vocabulary. If his wife did not make the scrambled eggs soft enough, he would say, "Mithoo, these eggs are raped." If his back hurt from the long hours of shuttling by train between Dahanu and Bombay, he would say, "My back is raped." Everything was raped. The trees were raped, the walls were raped, the curtains were raped, the shower was raped, the whiskey was raped, the wedding was raped, and finally, if some unfortunate soul made the mistake of asking Aspi Irani for a loan: "Do I look like I want to be raped?"

He offered his son a slice of apple, but Zairos shook his head.

The first thing Zairos did every morning was smoke. He did not smoke at home. At twenty-five he was old enough, so that was not the reason. It just felt awkward, blowing smoke in front of his parents; it took the joy out.

When Zairos was out of sight, he lit up.

The horn of a train echoed off the walls of the bungalow, the sound like a jazz trumpet. It was 8 a.m.—the Gujarat Express had just come in from Bombay, and even though the coconut, mango, and gulmohar trees around Aspi Villa provided it with much-needed privacy, the train station was, as Aspi Irani said, "only a hop, step, and jump away."

"Dahanu Road" read the yellow sign on the station. At one point, that's all that might have existed. A single road. But now coconut sellers in cream dhotis lined the platform, sickles in hand, a pyramid of coconuts in a cane basket by their side. Toddy booths offered salvation to the dry throats of passengers, the palm wine adding sweetness to a sour journey. Vegetable vendors squatted on the ground, cucumbers, brinjals, and cauliflowers sprinkled with water, ready to be cooked at home amidst the chitter-chatter of housewives. Just as fresh as the palm wine and vegetables were the newspapers in the A. H. Wheeler stall. Wafer crisp, the headlines were scoffed at by the drifters, rickshaw drivers, factory owners, and farmers who paraded up and down Dahanu station as though it were a holy ritual.

Soon Zairos would reach his grandfather's bungalow, where he would have his morning tea. But first he had a cigarette to finish, and, more importantly, he had to pay homage to the fruit that had fed his family for three generations. He blew smoke towards the chickoo trees that his grandfather, Shapur Irani, had planted decades ago. It was Zairos' way of greeting the trees. It was the smoke of affection; it was like dew, a first kiss, one he blew their way every single morning.

Sapota. Sapodilla. In other words, the chickoo. Brown in colour, it looked like a potato with a shape so round it reminded Zairos of a woman's bottom. When he bit into it, there was a sweetness that made him want more before he had finished eating what was in his mouth.

The wily chickoo had travelled far and wide. Born in Mexico, it found its way to India, Pakistan, Sri Lanka, Bangladesh (it was a third world fruit), Venezuela, Thailand, Vietnam, Indonesia, Malaysia, and even Brazil and the West Indies. This fruit liked its sunshine and tanned women. It had no patience for snow.

Apart from sapota and sapodilla, it had a bevy of names. In Sri Lanka it went by the name rata-mi; sawo in Indonesia, lamoot in Thailand, nispero in Venezuela, naseberry in the West Indies, sapoti in Brazil, and Zairos' favourite, sugardilly, in the Bahamas.

As he walked the pebbled earth, he threw his cigarette into the cactus fence. His grandfather's bungalow was in view. Even though it had been painted cream only two years ago, heavy rains had lashed the walls, and certain parts were bare again. It had an odd shape, two rectangular blocks at right angles with each other, like displaced train bogies.

His grandfather was on the porch in his rocking chair, still as ever. Even though he sat in his rocking chair all day, he never moved. Movement was the enemy, a thing of the past. And because Shapur Irani rarely moved, he remembered everything. How many trees he had, how old they were, how crisp the air was fifty years ago. More than anything he remembered the love he had for his wife, Banu. He once told Zairos, "If you took an army of starving young men who had not seen their wives for years, and you measured their longing for their wives against mine, it would still come nowhere close to what I felt for your grandmother."

But neither love nor medicine could save his wife. Banumai died of a fever when she was in her late twenties. Zairos wished he could have known his grandmother. His grandfather did talk about her, but he presented her in pieces: she liked to read, she had two younger sisters, twins, she had fair skin, she loved Bombay more than Dahanu, she could bear the pain of childbirth like a tigress, she loved the feeling of morning dew on the soles of her feet, she had once seen a goat being slaughtered and could not eat for three days after that.

Apart from these snippets there were strange utterances, spoken in a haze, phrases such as "Banu, make the water hot," "The gun stays on the bed," "We are not moving to Bombay." Zairos was careful not to let his grandfather know that he heard all these reminiscences, but he put together an image of Banumai; he could smell her bottle of eau de cologne by the bed, he could see strands of her black hair caught in the hairbrush that lay by the mirror, or the sweat on her neck and the paper fan she used to drive the heat away. When it came to Banumai, Zairos was like a thief: he took whatever he could when his grandfather was unaware. But the one thing he did not need to steal, the one thing that was obvious and as deep as the lines that criss-crossed on his grandfather's face, was the love between them.

Zairos climbed the three steps up to the porch. His grandfather called him Zairos the Great. Shapur Irani gave his grandson that name when he saw him walk for the first time.

"He is a conqueror like Alexander," he had said. From then on, whenever Shapur Irani saw little Zairos approach, he would go to the nearest chickoo tree and shake it with all his might. "Be careful," he would say, as sparkly green leaves fell on him, "your strength is making the trees tremble."

But the name had meant something else to Zairos when his Navjote ceremony was performed. On the day of his initiation into the Zoroastrian faith, the head priest, in a white robe and prayer cap to match, admonished the nine-year-old Zairos for using that name, even if it was in jest with his friends.

"Alexander is an enemy of the Zoroastrians," said the priest. "He murdered dasturs like myself and destroyed our holy scriptures."

Shapur Irani was quick to knock some sense into the priest.

"By walking the farm with his head held high, Zairos is reclaiming what Alexander stole from us," he said. "That is a sign of greatness."

Then he bent down and placed his hand on Zairos' head.

"Remember, it is our enemies who make us conquer fear."

Shapur Irani's eyes were closed.

Even though he was ninety now, he was still a big man. Over six foot five, he did not have the hunched look of a person who carried his ninety years in a dhobi sack on his head. He had his teeth, his strong legs and bushy eyebrows, the hair on his chest was white and long, and he shaved every morning at five, even though he never went anywhere.

"Pa," said Zairos as he sat on the porch steps.

Shapur Irani did not respond. His eyes were still closed and his lips revealed the faintest quiver, a ghost language of sorts, which only the dead could decipher. Zairos stared at his grandfather's thick head of hair—slicked back and silver.

"Pa," he said again.

Shapur Irani opened his eyes slowly. If there was one thing that unnerved him, it was light. He did not want the light of the sun to gain entry through his eyes and illuminate the parts of him that were dead and gone. "To look at the past," he once told Zairos, "is like shining a flashlight on a dead body."

Zairos heard the familiar rattle of cup and saucer. His tea arrived magically, as it always did. Lakhu, the male servant who had served his grandfather for years, had strange powers. Perhaps Lakhu heard the cracking of pebbles under Zairos' feet as he walked to the bungalow each morning, and he took it as a sign to boil the tea. It did not matter how Lakhu knew that Zairos was coming. He succeeded in not making Zairos wait for more than a minute.

Zairos took a sip and relished the taste of Brooke Bond, mint, cardamom, and ginger. Ants crawled around his grandfather's feet carrying biscuit crumbs on their backs.

"It's time you visit them," said Shapur Irani.

He was talking about his chickoo trees. They were his children, just as real, and loved, as his three sons, Khodi, Sohrab, and Aspi. Their breathing had kept him alive all these years. Every morning he walked through his fifty-acre farm, with gusto, without a cane, to let them know he was still around. He wanted Zairos to do the same.

"Go meet them," said Shapur Irani.

When the last of the ginger tea was gone, Zairos walked across the gravel and into the farm. The branches brushed against his arm and left their mark. Each day it was a new scratch or two, sometimes on the forearm, sometimes on the wrist, always gentle.

Zairos recalled that the chickoo had been brought to India in the mid-1500s by the Portuguese, and it continued to thrive in its new home long after the invaders had gone. But when Zairos was little, his father had told him that a Mexican gnome named Rose—called that because he had a deformed ear shaped like the flower—walked all the way from Mexico to Dahanu with a chickoo in his hand and, upon arrival, dug a hole and buried the shiny black diamond seed of a chickoo, and himself, in the earth. That was why chickoo trees did not grow as tall as pine trees. They had to restrict their height in deference to the gnome. When Zairos asked his father why the gnome walked all the way to India, Aspi Irani had replied, "He got lost."

Zairos went past the papaya trees that had long ago ceased giving fruit, and over the thick black pipes that ran through the farm like oversized pythons. He took the same route every single time, until he reached the well. It was one of the deepest wells in Dahanu, more than seventy feet deep, with large boulders jutting out from its inner walls, but it gave no water. Old and dry, it was part of the furniture.

He plucked a blade of dry grass from the ground, put it in his mouth, and sat on the parapet of the well. There was an unusual number of crows in the sky. He looked up, tracing the concentric circles they flew in; they were gliding towards something to his left.

Barely had Zairos turned when he saw what the crows were after.

A man was hanging from a chickoo tree. His head was bent to the side, his arms dangling, his eyes wide open.

He resembled a dark puppet.

TWO

"GANPAT," WHISPERED ZAIROS.

There was no movement from Ganpat at all, not a single twitch or half breath.

The rope, thick and strong, had done its job. But its grip around Ganpat's neck was still fierce. It pulled Zairos towards the body. He lightly placed his palm under the sole of Ganpat's muddy, cracked foot.

The smell made him recoil.

He was surprised, ashamed even, at how easily the dead body repelled him. After all, Ganpat was a Warli who had lived and worked on the farm since he was a child. A tribal of the region, he used to be one of Shapur Irani's most trusted workers.

But when he was caught stealing money, he was asked to leave.

Zairos remembered that afternoon ten years ago. Ganpat's eyes were red, and for once it was not the red of liquor but the red of tears, proof that he had betrayed his master. He had to walk away from the farm he had grown up on and was never seen again. Until now.

Ganpat's face had not changed much since that time. His eyebrows were extremely thin, mere lines that had been drawn above his eyes as an afterthought; his moustache was made of small wisps, so frugal, a perfect reflection of his poverty. Only his nose was bulbous, a contradiction to his entire being. His white vest and khaki shorts had small holes in them, the handiwork of rats' teeth. The only thing of any worth on him was a wristwatch.

It was still ticking.

Zairos turned back towards his grandfather's bungalow. Alongside him, water snaked its way on the ground through black pipes that faithfully fed each and every chickoo tree on the farm. A soft wind blew through the trees, waking up the leaves.

His pace was brisk, perhaps a result of the stench, the sheer nakedness of it all.

Soon Zairos was running past a line of cacti that formed the fence of the farm. He was not sure why he was running because nothing could be done to save the man. But it was the natural thing to do. A life had been lost. He could not mourn for Ganpat, but he could show some urgency.

By the time he reached the bungalow, Zairos was panting.

"Pa," he said. "There's . . . do you remember Ganpat?"

Shapur Irani's eyes opened.

"Ganpat hung himself from a tree," said Zairos. "He's dead."

Zairos should have slowed down and regained his composure. He did not want to alarm his grandfather. More than anything, he did not want his grandfather to think he could not handle the situation.

"I'll call the police," said Zairos.

The moment he said it, he knew he had disappointed his grandfather. At a time like this, the police were of no help at all. They would conduct an inquiry and an autopsy, all in the name of securing a heavy bribe. They were cockroaches who had to be kept out.

Zairos waited for a response from his grandfather, but Shapur Irani's face revealed nothing. He might as well be staring at a star in a faraway galaxy.

Then, with a wave of his hand, Shapur Irani said, "Get Damu."

Damu was the Warli who managed the farm. He lived in a thatched hut just behind the bungalow. Only four feet tall, he could be mistaken for a small forest creature. But the workers respected him because he was fearless. He once pounced on a man twice his size and bit his neck.

Damu's five-year-old son was playing outside his hut with the tube of a cycle tire. The moment he saw Zairos, he ran in to fetch his father. While Zairos waited, the aroma of cooking mixed unabashedly with the odour of cow dung. Two large papayas hung from the tree next to the hut. The swell of the papayas made Zairos look away. They reminded him of Ganpat's eyes.

Zairos shuffled his feet, flicked his long hair off his face.

Damu was taking too much time.

A few strands of straw came loose from the roof of the hut. The breeze made a tangled mess of those strands, blew them towards Zairos.

A rooster with a bright red mane was pecking at the soil. It raised its head time and again, unsure and agitated. Zairos stomped the ground and drove it away.

Finally Damu emerged, his hair wet, water on his bare chest, as though he had been washing up.

"Come with me," said Zairos.

Damu scratched his chin, the silver stubble on his cheeks making him look more important than he was. The farm workers always joked that Damu dove into salt pans all over Dahanu to give his stubble such shine.

Shapur Irani's servant, Lakhu, joined them as well. Zairos led the two men to Ganpat's body. He walked slowly this time. He did not want the workers to feel his anxiousness.

By now a crow had perched itself on Ganpat's head. It seemed comfortable there, showing absolutely no respect for human heads. Lakhu was edgy in Ganpat's presence. With no cup and saucer to hold, he did not know what to do with his hands. His knobbly fingers curled even more, but found nothing. After an initial glance, he looked away from the body.

Damu, on the other hand, was studying Ganpat with intensity. Even though they were not related, he saw himself in Ganpat. They both belonged to the same tribe. Their ancestors had stayed at the foothills of the Sahyadri Mountains for generations, and it was a mistake to come down to the plains because the plains had deceived them. The plains had promised a better life, but were full of crevasses, and hundreds of Warlis had fallen through, and Ganpat was the latest casualty.

"Zairos seth," said Damu. "Ganpat has a daughter."

"Where does she live?" asked Zairos, irritated that he had not thought of it himself.

"Not far. Should I get her?"

"Take the tractor."

Even if Ganpat's daughter lived in a nearby hamlet, it would take her too long to walk. Zairos could not change what her father had done, but he could prevent her feet from getting tired.

"Make sure none of the workers come to this side of the farm," he told Damu. "Give them work on the other side only."

Zairos did not want the workers or their children to surround the body and see their tribesman dead in daylight, without explanation. But he was not comfortable with letting the body remain amongst the trees either. Maybe he was being superstitious, but he felt that the trees would suffer. Some force might suck the life out of the trees as well.

It was time for another cigarette. This cigarette would be different from the one he had smoked earlier. There would be nothing celebratory about it. No smoke-kiss to the chickoo trees, no carefree humming to serve as musical accompaniment.

The smoke would be sombre. It would be the smoke of waiting.

The old red Mitsubishi tractor roared on its way up the path that led to the bungalow. More a power tiller than a tractor, it sounded impressive, but was small in size and battered beyond recognition. It had a strange shape—it looked like a jet ski with an open box behind it to transport chickoos to Dahanu station.

Damu stood at the helm, his dark muscles straining to keep the forked handle of the tractor at bay. Behind Damu, two women were huddled together in the open container. They had enough room, but sat close to each other like frightened chickens.

Damu drove the tractor right up to where Zairos was, and the tractor coughed and sputtered. From the blank expression on Damu's face, it was evident that he had not told the two women about Ganpat's death. In fact, all he must have said was, "My master wants to see you," and if an Irani seth wanted to see two Warli women, no explanation was needed. The women must have obediently sat in the tractor with no idea of the sight that awaited them.

When the tractor finally went silent, an old, withered woman with crooked teeth got off first. Her green blouse failed to cover her weary, black skin. Zairos' attention went back to her teeth. They angled in all directions, but with such certainty that they could tear the flesh off bats. One long tooth hung out of her mouth like a hook. If Zairos had seen her as a child he would have thought her a witch. The other woman, however, was a vision. Not a day older than twenty, surely, she got down from the tractor, her waist sliding inwards to provide the most magnificent curve to her hips. Zairos quickly looked away.

Faced with the task of bearing bad news, he went cold.

He had never done this before. Words raced through his mind, but he could not think of a single thing to say. The natural thing to do was to go towards the chickoo trees where the body was placed. Perhaps it was cruel, to give them the news raw and hard, but he could think of no other option.

A stray dog walked with them and Zairos was grateful for the support.

The old woman stepped on the black pipes with an unusual amount of energy, as though the pipes were veins that supplied blood to an enemy.

In a few seconds, the young woman would see her father hanging from a tree.

Initially, neither woman said a word.

Zairos waited for a reaction, but there was nothing. Perhaps it was the sight of Ganpat's bloated face. Or his thin frame suspended in the air like the carcass of a charred bird.

The silence was forcing Zairos to notice the body in more detail. The spittle at the corner of Ganpat's lips. The dark red cut on his right shin, perhaps acquired when he climbed the tree. Even the reek was more pronounced, attacking.

He suddenly felt light-headed, the kick of a hundred cigarettes.

It was the old woman who broke first. Tears streamed down her cheeks, two perfectly shaped drops navigating the crevices on her sagging skin. She took two steps forward, scraping her feet along the soil, and placed her hand on the younger one's shoulder. The moment she did that, the younger one shook. Her mouth opened, she let out a wail, but it broke off midway. On her neck, thick veins throbbed.

Zairos took a step towards her. She seemed to be suffocating.

Her teeth clenched, fingers rolled into a fist, she went to her father's body. She stood below it and looked up at his face the way one looked at an idol in a prayer hall.

"This is Ganpat's daughter," said the old woman. "Her name is Kusum."

The old woman's eyes were red. Fierce and tired, they already contained the smouldering ashes of the dead. The young woman, Kusum, was still gazing at her father. Every breath she took in was deep and angry, wanting to blow out the flames of love and kindness that existed anywhere.

"I was walking through the farm this morning and I saw him," said Zairos.

Zairos wanted to get out of there. Kusum was displaying an enormous amount of strength, and he needed to leave, to allow her to grieve, to heave and sigh as she pleased.

But Kusum did not respond to Zairos' remark. She looked at her feet now, locked in the earth. So Zairos addressed the old woman, so old she could be death's distant cousin.

"Who are you?" he asked. "Are you related to Ganpat?"

"I am Rami," she replied. "Ganpat's sister."

She came closer to Zairos as she said this, and he could smell the tobacco on her breath. He found it strange that a tribal woman dared to come so close to his body. The Warlis always kept their distance. But the shock of the moment could have shaken the fear and respect out of her. When the news settled in, so would the old laws.

"Ganpat was fine when he left the house this morning . . ." said Rami.

When Rami spoke, Zairos felt an old door was creaking open. It was the voice of someone who did not speak much. Once again, she pressed her foot on the black pipes. They were too hard to be crushed, too solid for her to be able to stop anything.

"We can bring the body down now," said Zairos.

He was being clinical on purpose, against his will. He did not want to encourage a discussion. But Kusum, he realized, had other plans.

"This morning my father was on his way to meet Shapur seth," she said.

"Do not mention my grandfather's name," said Zairos.

Zairos knew he was being hard, but it was the right thing to do. Order had to be maintained. In the jungle, the lion was no doubt wise and just, but above all, the lion was feared. Any form of kindness could be viewed as weakness. Kindness could upset the order of things. In a jungle, kindness could lead to revolt.

His sternness made Kusum go near her father's body again. Beauty and grief collided hideously in her face. The chickoo trees offered shade and nothing else. Through the trees, light snuck in. Kusum looked up for a moment and mocked the streams of light. It was a feeble attempt to provide comfort. She took her mouth close to her father's ear. Her mouth was begging him to reveal why he had killed himself.

The first thing Kusum did when the body was lowered was place her hand on her father's chest. Zairos was taken aback by the gesture. It was not that she was looking for signs of life. She just wanted her father to feel the warmth of her palm.

She moved when she saw Lakhu hold a white bedsheet in his hands. He had brought it from the house. He whipped the sheet and let it unfurl. It was too flamboyant, the ballooning sheet. He murmured a prayer as he covered Ganpat's face. But Kusum did not want her father's face to be covered. She slid the sheet off his head until it was just below his chin.

"Let the body stay here for now," said Zairos. "Damu will bring him to you after sundown."

He did not want the body to be taken in the tractor during daylight. A policewala would create trouble. There had been a suicide on a neighbouring farm only recently and the owner had to shell out twenty thousand rupees.

"Damu will take you back," he said. "Use the tractor to collect wood."

"There is no wood," said Rami. "There is no wood anymore."

It was uttered in a trance, as one would an age-old proverb. Sometimes it was hard for Zairos to understand the Marathi of the Warlis. It was a strange dialect that they spoke in staccato, suddenly going out of breath, their sentences amputated.

"Seth, I will pick up rubber tires from the petrol pump," said Damu.

Time and again, Zairos had seen the Warlis line up outside petrol pumps and ask the owners for old tires so that their loved ones could be sent home. If the tires were not given, they were stolen.

Damu started the tractor, turned it around, and waited for the two women.

Kusum stayed near the body for a while. Her eyes were still moist, unlike Rami's, which were now completely dry. Rami had done her share of crying years ago. There was nothing left, no well of tears she could draw from, just dust. She gave Kusum a gentle rub on the back and pulled her up.

They both looked at the ground as they passed Zairos.

The natural order had been restored. They walked with their heads down all the way to the tractor and sat in the back. After a brave and open display of grief, they had become frightened again.

THREE

AS ZAIROS RODE towards the Anna Purna chai stall, he welcomed the sun. He hoped its heat would burn away the memories of the morning. He went past the abandoned train bogies, the bales of straw waiting to be transported to Bombay, the liquor booth where tribals numbed their brains for a few rupees, the collector's office, the furniture shop that sold only mustard benches, the lumber mills with the creepy echo of sparrows, until he hit the main road, which was a dusty, rocky mess. It had been dug up, and bullock carts, trucks, vans, cars, and cycles wove through it, spraying rock debris from under their tires.

After Zairos passed Alan's petrol pump with its wilted array of coconut trees, he turned left and almost ran over Pinky, a six-year-old orphan with an eternally runny nose, who had perched herself close to Anna Purna's to secure her daily dose of Tiger biscuits.

Anna, the owner of the chai stall, was an Indian Clark

Gable: thin moustache, clean skin, hair always set in the most well-behaved manner. No one knew his real name so he was called Anna, or Elder Brother, the title given to any South Indian man who wore a lungi and ran a chai stall. Anna had an old Hollywood charm, but his wife was quite the opposite—dusky, and full enough to be on the cover of *Debonair*.

To the Iranis, Anna's chai stall was one of Dahanu's most prized possessions. It was a beloved meeting place—its hard wooden benches had seated many an overweight Irani over the years—a dingy hole beautifully suited to the hirsute features of the men that frequented the joint. At Anna's, they were like beasts in a cave where they could fart, joke, smoke, abuse, and pontificate. Of course, they did this *anywhere*, but Anna's was the home ground. Each morning, after making a round of their chickoo farms, the Iranis would gather here and drink tea, coffee, or Pepsi. Cigarette smoke gave the place a sinister haze, like fog in a cemetery. Yet the place was alive, full of joy and horniness, and credit had to be given to Anna's steaming chai and his steamy wife.

Anna stood under the sharp white glow of tube lights and poured chai from one steel jug into the other to cool it down. It was quite a show, this hot waterfall of milky tea, and Anna was always guaranteed an audience. There was Merwan Mota, the fattest man in Dahanu, who polished off three omelettes at a time, his little blue diabetes bag by his side; Behrooz, the smoothest bald head in town, who owned the spare-parts shop next door; Keki the Italian, who smoked beedis in a corner and brooded over Camus and Turgenev; and Dara Atom, the town's official god-man-cum-healer, who was only a few chicken breasts away from being just as huge as Merwan Mota.

At its peak, which was from nine till eleven in the morning, Anna's chai stall offered a heady cocktail of languages. Anna spoke softly in Tulu to his wife and loudly in Hindi to the balloon-factory owners; some of the Iranis conversed in Dari just to remind the ones who didn't that they were inferior and had been polluted by India, and the inferior Iranis, who spoke Gujarati, spoke it in a crass manner to make the actual Gujaratis, the Indian ones, feel infuriated that their language was being bastardized in the cheapest way. But in the end, if one kept some distance, one could see the beauty of Anna's, that brothel of languages. All languages knew each other well, were familiar with the twists and turns of each other's bodies, and were not afraid to inhale the pungent smell of each other's underarms.

Zairos heard a sound in the distance, a motorcycle zooming at full speed. Soon, one passed by on the tarmac. It was his dearest first cousin, Bumble. Bumble was his father's brother's son, two years older than Zairos. Bumble's real name was Farhad, but he was called Bumble, as in bumblebee, because he whizzed around on his motorcycle, zigzag-zigzag, without any aim at all. He often overshot his destination because he was going too fast to stop, but he would never admit this. However, he was an expert rider and his bike was a beauty, a red BMW.

This morning, Bumble was dressed in a Santa Claus costume.

And he did, once again, miss his destination. He returned, his cotton-white beard hanging to one side. His Santa cap flopped out of his pants pocket, but his black aviator Ray-Bans balanced perfectly on the ridge of his nose. He parked his motorcycle and walked over to the blue car outside Anna's in which the gamblers of Dahanu were indulging in their favourite, most sacred activity—rummy. Men whose bodies were 70 per cent cards, not water: Aspi Irani looked over his silver reading glasses each time he threw a card on the black suitcase that served as the card table, Kavas Undie left the car, went into the bushes, and returned with his undies worn inside out to bring about a change in luck, and Bumble's father, the left-handed Sohrab Irani, shuffled cards with fervour and dedication that would put any religious man to shame. This hallowed vehicle was known throughout Dahanu as the Mobile Casino.

"How did the party go?" Sohrab Irani asked his son.

"It was good," replied Bumble, "until the children started pulling my beard."

Bumble's nephew was suffering from jaundice, so to cheer the boy up Bumble had thrown an early-morning Christmas party. Christmas was months away, but as Bumble put it, "The children don't know." As he took off his Ray-Bans—an affectation that made him look like a B Division football club owner from Naples—he asked Anna for some chai.

Zairos wished his grandfather would come to Anna's.

Every once in a while, Zairos would ask Shapur Irani to sit with him on the rickety benches, even if he remained silent and just listened to the frying of eggs in Anna's kitchen. Shapur Irani always politely declined. Maybe he thought of Anna's as an aberration, something frivolous.

But on days like this, when Zairos had found a Warli man hanging from a tree, Anna's provided a strange balm, and he could appreciate the lunacy of it all—the humongous Merwan

Mota, highly diabetic, eating strawberry ice cream in dollops; Behrooz scratching his bald skull, gripped by a Hindi graphic novel called *The Day My Wife Bled to Death*; Keki the Italian telling him to read a real writer like Tolstoy, and Behrooz, upon hearing that extraterrestrial name, giving Keki a disgusted look.

Anna's was Zairos' cocoon, and while he sat there, cozy in its extravagance, he thought of Kusum in the back of a tractor with only an old fatigued woman to help her cope with the loss of her father. There was no sugary chai in her world, no air-conditioned car where gamblers hugged their cards tighter than their wives, and certainly no leather wallet, fat with cash, to serve as a cushion when she sat down. As she went home, all she had was the burn of daylight and the roar of a tractor to aggravate the strain on an anguished, racing heart.

Kusum picked up a shovel from outside her neighbour's hut. It felt heavy, the iron handle rusted, extra nails hammered at the base to keep it from coming loose. The sun gave the rust an orange sparkle as though the shovel were at the kiln instead of at the end of its life.

It was only fitting that Kusum was the one who would dig her father's grave.

It was her fault that he killed himself. She had failed to hide the marks on her body from him, ones her husband had made. Perhaps it was the way she walked that had given her away. Or the manner in which her ribs caved when she sat down.

It had made her father go to Shapur seth for money. If her husband was given money, he would grant her a divorce. But she knew the truth. Laxman would not have left her even then. He would have taken the money and kept her.

Into a thicket of trees Kusum went, until she reached the banks of a stream. The monsoon season was a while away, so the stream was dry. She tested the texture of the soil with the shovel. Satisfied, she started digging. When the soil suddenly became hard, she stood on the shovel until it no longer offered any resistance.

In the distance, the hills of Dahanu rose and fell like the very hopes of her people, the Warlis—the Kings of the Jungle. At least that was what the folk tales proclaimed her people to be. That was what the witch doctors, high on daru, always called themselves. If only they had seen her father hanging from a chickoo tree, the folk tales would be revised.

But it had to happen.

The noose had tightened around her father's neck years ago. It was because Ganpat, like his father Vithal before him, was the keeper of his people's stories. Stories whose weight he was not strong enough to bear.

Ever since she could remember, he had been a witness.

It had prevented him from being what a father should be, strong and unafraid.

It confused her, terrified her even, when her father woke in the middle of the night screaming.

She was only a child.

She could not understand why there was so much sweat on her father's face. In the dark, his cheeks had the shine of a rich man who had dipped himself in oil.

Upon waking, upon screaming, he would grab her, touch her, just to make sure she was alive. Then he would cradle her in his arms and rock back and forth, back and forth, until he finally fell asleep again. But the hastiness of his breath, the panic of chattering teeth, the jowls losing colour, all of it would seep into her, create an unnatural music, a steady growl.

Kusum would crawl out of his embrace and go to her mother Kamla, who would say to her, "Your father has visited the time of the screams again."

That was all her mother told her.

She would have to fall asleep listening to the wild dogs outside. Her father's hysteria always got the dogs going. They would stand at the entrance to the hut, the drool hanging from their snarling teeth.

It was only years later that Kusum found out why her father had nightmares.

Now it was almost fifty years since that incident, when the landlords' men had attacked a Warli hamlet. The Warli men, in hundreds, had gone to the beach with red flags in their hands to attend a political rally that promised to put an end to their slavery. Only the women, children, and the very old remained at home.

Ganpat was staying away from the farm he lived on, in a witch doctor's hut, along with his mother and newborn sister. The newborn had a violent cough and the witch doctor had treated her with herbs. Ganpat was only five years old. The witch doctor's wife was asleep in one corner, her eyes half open so that only the whites could be seen like the whites of eggs. Ganpat's mother was asleep in a similar position with the infant next to her on the ground.

The thatched ground was warm. Ganpat loved placing his palms on the warm mud floor, and he felt the slight rumble on the floor caused by the approaching horses.

The infant must have felt a slight tingle in her back, but all she must have done was wiggle her toes in excitement. She must have opened her eyes slowly, seen the sack of grain, the earthen pots, the witch doctor's sorcery paraphernalia, and wiggled her toes once more and drifted back to sleep. Only the witch doctor's wife sensed that something was wrong. But by the time she got to her feet, the landlords' men had entered the hut and begun destroying everything.

Ganpat's mother started screaming because where there should have been her child, there was a sack of grain. Where there should have been her child, there was an earthen pot.

She continued to shriek long after the men left, unable to go near the body, and Ganpat, who was unsure why his mother was screaming so hard, went near the sack of grain and saw his sister's tiny wrist, her curled fingers . . .

It was at this point that he always woke up, covered in sweat.

It did not matter who the men were. It did not matter which landlords sent them—Hindu, Muslim, or Zoroastrian. They were all responsible for her father's death.

With a start like this, what else could her father do but take his own life?

Shovel in hand, she walked back to her father's hut. His body had not yet arrived because the sun was still high. He had to be brought to her after sundown, under the cover of darkness, as though he were something shameful.

But the young Irani seth was made that way.

Just as her back was strong from walking miles, from bending down, from climbing trees, digging holes, and carrying wood, a seth's back was weak from sitting all day, eating chicken and inhaling snuff, counting money and issuing orders. Men who gave orders did not have strong backs.

This was the first time she had seen him in years. She had no idea what kind of man he had turned out to be. She had noticed some trace of kindness on his face when she got into the tractor. Only a trace, faint as a mote of dust. But even that could be a foolish notion.

It did not matter. What mattered was that the sun was still up. She would have to wait.

She stared at the hut she had grown up in. There were eleven other huts like it in the hamlet. They all looked the same except for the one opposite her father's, which sold rice, chana, and peppermints. A black goat rested under its shade, raising its head, then slumping back into the heat.

She would have to go inside the hut at some point.

Her father's rubber slippers were at the entrance, one on top of the other, the blue forked straps wobbly and loose.

Bending her head, she went through the shady mouth of the hut.

Inside, on a clothesline, her father's clothes, some still damp.

She ran her fingers along the line, felt its tautness. One by one, she started taking things down: a pair of khaki shorts, a brown cotton shirt, a red T-shirt.

She was seized by a sudden emptiness, the sharpness of a toothache.

Only one piece of clothing remained on the line, a white vest stretched out of shape. She brought it down, and with it, the clothesline.

When she put the vest against her face, the smell of her father rushed to her, warm and familiar. Soon this smell would disappear, just like her mother's did all those years ago.

Kusum did not want to stay awake.

On the thatched ground she lay, curled into a ball, begging to go back to the womb.

Zairos had to make sure that Damu was not drunk. On most evenings, as soon as the farm labour ended, the workers' drinking began. By sundown, every cell of theirs was soaked in country liquor.

Tonight, Damu needed to be alert.

Ganpat's body was in the back of the tractor, sending out a whiff strong enough to make the stars change positions. The tractor went down the slope, its feeble headlights barely lighting the gravel path.

For Zairos, the day was not over yet.

No matter how late it was he always went to wish his grandfather good night. It was a ritual, a tribute to the nocturnal. For Shapur Irani never slept. He was always in an in-between state, a man who constantly travelled between two continents, except that in Shapur Irani's case those continents were sleep and wakefulness.

The white tube light on his porch was on, surrounded by a swarm of moths. There were days when Shapur Irani sat in his rocking chair with stillness only the dead could possess. But men like Shapur Irani did not die in their sleep. Before going, he would shake the earth, rattle it with all his might to announce his arrival to the heavens.

"I shall warn the angels not to come in my way," he once told Zairos. "Once I have taken flight, I shall go straight to Banu."

When Zairos was little, it was not hard for him to imagine his grandfather flying. To Zairos, he was indeed a superhero, much like the great warrior Rostam in the *Shahnameh*, the Persian Book of Kings, who covered himself in leopard skin, wore a cast-iron helmet, battled dragons and witches, and cut out a demon's heart and liver with his knife.

Zairos would walk about the farm and transform from a boy to a man of six feet five inches and pretend that he was choking enormous snakes with his fist. He would scream, roar, bang his knuckles into the soil, pull out white-haired demons, hold enemy horses by the tail and throw them into orbit until they were singed by the sun.

But what he loved doing most was digging holes beneath chickoo trees because Shapur Irani had told him that's where he used to hide whiskey bottles.

Mithoo would chide her father-in-law: "Why do you tell him these stories? You want him to be a drunkard?" And Shapur Irani would reply, "They are not stories."

At the time Zairos did not understand what that meant, but he did now. Those were not just tales. By sharing his past, his grandfather was sharing blood.

"Pa," said Zairos, "I want to ask you something. It's about Ganpat. His daughter told me that he was on his way to see you this morning."

"He did see me," replied Shapur Irani. "A couple of hours or so before you found him."

"What did he want?"

"Money," said Shapur Irani. "What else do these Warlis want besides money, so they can drink and destroy their livers?"

"But after all these years what made him think that you would give him any? And why did he kill himself after that?"

"Zairos, it is impossible to know the Warli heart."

Zairos wanted his grandfather to go on, but the man did not say more.

Even though Zairos did not have to, he wanted to offer Kusum some sort of explanation. Perhaps he had not done the right thing by letting the body remain hanging from the tree until Kusum got there. But if he had brought the body down, he could have been accused of foul play.

He needed her to know that he was not being callous.

His grandfather would never approve. Masters did not explain things.

Shapur Irani slowly rubbed his right knee through his white pyjamas. Memories were stored in every part of his body, and when they erupted, they had to be soothed. Zairos wondered how his grandfather managed to sit in that chair all day, alone in this bungalow with his male servant. He took a regular morning walk and talked to his trees, and he shared something beautiful with them, but that would never be enough for Zairos.

"In a way, Ganpat is lucky," said Shapur Irani. "I don't think I'm ever going to die. I have the worst luck in the world."

It was strange that he thought of Ganpat's suicide as luck. It reduced Ganpat to a creature with no power at all.

"Zairos, after I am dead, you must never sell this land. Without this land, we are nothing. Even when the British were tearing this country apart, this land was mine. This land was my own country. Do you understand?"

"Yes, Pa."

"There is a tree not far away from here. A mango tree. Do you know which one I am talking about? I was standing under that tree when my first son, your Khodi kaka, was born. Now my son is dead but that tree is still alive. Do you see what I mean? Trees do not get heart attacks. They simply get old, and the older they are, the stronger they get and the deeper their roots go, and the more difficult it is to move them."

Zairos could tell that his grandfather was about to launch into a story.

It always started with the rubbing of knees. Then Shapur Irani would shut his eyes tight, as he was doing now, as though by sheer willpower he would be able to transport his grandson into the past. Slowly the tightness in Shapur Irani's eyelids increased, until they fluttered like the wings of an injured bird, and he took Zairos with him to an older, more promising time.

FOUR

1942

SHAPUR IRANI STARED at the hole he made in the ground. He was satisfied that it was large enough to hide a whiskey bottle. The tool he used for digging was forked like a cobra's tongue. He put it in the pocket of his white trousers and looked to the sky for warplanes. The war was on and India was just a rabbit. It could be shot down at any time by an irate hunter. Even though the country had no role in the war, it was a fear he had, that a great demon would descend from the sky and breathe fire on all his chickoo trees, and his beloved fruit orchard would turn to smouldering ash.

He picked up the whiskey bottle that he had placed on the ground. He unscrewed the cork and took a large gulp. He felt better when the whiskey went down his throat, as though a great river had entered him to give him strength.

Night would fall soon. Shapur Irani always thought of dusk as a beggar. It had no light, it had no darkness; it lived on the scraps that were fed to it by day and night.

He bent down and placed the whiskey bottle in the hole.

Prohibition was a curse from God, and the government was a pawn in God's cruel joke. Perhaps God really cared about his liver, but Shapur Irani did not. This was the thirty-first bottle he had hidden in the ground. He knew exactly where each bottle was, under which tree. There were no markings on the trees, but the shape of their trunks was enough. Some were mere saplings, but the older trees were more or less the same height, and their trunks resembled human legs. They had swellings on them like knees, some puffy, some as smooth as a woman's. He knew each tree in the way he would know a brother, and because he didn't have a brother, he loved the trees even more. After all, he had watched them being born. He had watched them being planted by the local tribals, under his supervision, and he remained patient for years until some of them were finally old enough to give fruit.

Thirty-one bottles of whiskey during prohibition was an achievement. Shapur Irani had made contact with a man named Raghu who worked at the Royal Brewery in Bombay, which brewed special whiskey for the British officers. Raghu stole RB whiskey from the stockroom and sold it to Shapur Irani for a good price. He would also occasionally stay in Shapur Irani's bungalow, take back as many chickoos as he wanted, and drink as much coconut water his bladder could hold.

Shapur Irani breathed in the cool air, which never failed to comfort him.

If only his father were alive. Vamog would be proud to see what Shapur Irani had become. He owned fifty acres of land, he was fit, he had the large forehead of an intelligent man, his black eyes were small like a rodent's so nothing escaped him, and he had the legs of a Persian wrestler.

Look, Father, Shapur Irani would have said. This is your land, all yours, and it does not matter where your shadow falls.

Vamog's thick sideburns would have rushed to meet his beard in celebration, the creases on his forehead would have relaxed, and he would have walked every inch of the farm, praising Ahura Mazda for his benevolence, whispering to the chickoo buds the prophet's teachings, *Manashni, Gavashni, Kunashni.*

Good Thoughts, Good Words, Good Deeds.

There was no doubt that Vamog was in safe hands now.

He had surely been one of Zarathushtra's most loyal followers. Vamog spoke of Zarathushtra with such adoration and respect, it would not have surprised Shapur if his father had served the prophet himself 3,500 years ago.

"In the beginning, no one had faith in our prophet," Vamog told his son. "Except for one man. He was Maidhyoi-mangha, the prophet's cousin. For years, he was the only disciple."

Then Vamog peeled an orange, slipped a juicy slice into his mouth. The tanginess of the orange always gave his eyes a delightful squint. Even though Shapur knew what was coming next, he cherished his father's stories; each time, there was something new to be learned.

"One day Zarathushtra challenged the priests in the court of King Vishtaspa to a spiritual debate," he said. "When he defeated them, those hyenas imprisoned him."

He flung the orange peel over Shapur's head. A moustache of sweat was forming over Shapur's lips in anticipation.

"While Zarathushtra languished in prison, King Vishtaspa's

beloved white horse was paralyzed. Our prophet declared that he could heal the horse. All Zarathushtra did was touch the horse like this"—Vamog placed his hand on his son's shoulder—"and the horse was able to walk again. That was when King Vishtaspa embraced our prophet's teachings and thus started the rise of Zoroastrianism."

Vamog's face went into an exaggerated squirm. He was trying to show his son that he was in deep thought.

"Can you tell me who the hero of this story is?" he asked.

"King Vishtaspa," replied Shapur.

"No," said Vamog. "The king, in my opinion, was not the hero. It was Maidhyoi-mangha. Only he was the true Zoroastrian."

"Why is that?" asked Shapur.

"He did not need a miracle to believe."

Banu could not wait to tell her husband. She could not sit, she could not stand. She was an excited melon ready to burst. The grandfather clock ticked away in front of her, but she knew that time had no meaning in Dahanu. In Dahanu, all that mattered was light. The sun was mighty and its position of utmost importance. Shapur Irani never owned a watch because he felt it was meaningless. Looking at the sun, he would be able to tell the time five minutes this way or that.

The grandfather clock chimed seven times and she knew he would be home soon. Banu did not like him wandering about the farm after sunset. There were too many snakes. Just a day ago, the workers had killed a huge cobra. They beat it to death with sticks. It would be hard to spot a black cobra at night. That is why she always kept all the windows closed. They lived on the farm and a cobra could easily enter the bungalow through one of the windows. But the more she tried to shake off the thought, the more the cobras fanned their fangs before her eyes and danced like banished angels, once having the power to grant wishes and heal, now reduced to creatures that were hunted and burned.

She carried the lantern with her to the mirror and looked at herself. She was a pretty woman, she knew that. She was fair, her black hair was long and wavy, and according to her husband, whenever she looked at him with her brown eyes she made him feel as though he would be forever protected in their glow. He made fun of her smile all the time—he teased her that it was so mischievous, she must have been a nymph in a previous life.

The flame of the lantern shivered, shared her excitement. She wished the cracks in the chalky white walls would disappear. On some days after the cooking was done, after she had brushed her hair and taken her walk, she would stare at the cracks in the walls and cry. She would cry because she had been married to Shapur Irani for five years now and she had not given him a son. Not that he asked for a son, but she knew he wanted one badly. She was twenty-one now, old compared to the sixteen-year-old bride she had once been, and her husband was thirty-two. She was too scared to have a baby in the first year, but as time went on, she realized something was wrong. The fault had to be hers. Her husband was a hot-blooded Irani, and he once boasted that he was capable of producing a baby a day, so he was not the problem.

But all of that was in the past. A baby was about to come into this world, and she would tell him that tonight. Sometimes her husband would put his head on her stomach like a little child, and she could feel the air from his mouth and nostrils, a thin stream of love and assurance. If he did that tonight, she would tell him. Son or daughter, he would be overjoyed, and she would soon have someone in the house with her, someone to look after. She paced up and down the living room, unable to wait. "Chaalni, Shapur," she said out loud. Come on. This was going to be the happiest day of his life.

As Shapur Irani walked, he crushed leaves under his feet. The chickoo trees always shed a carpet of leaves and there were days when he could barely see the soil. He noticed that his white trousers were soiled at the knees from his digging. Shapur Irani always wore white. He never owned anything other than white trousers and white half-sleeved shirts. Even though he could afford almost any clothing he wanted, he kept his attire simple in honour of his forefathers, not allowed bright colours by the Muslim rulers, who believed that the garments of a dull, unclean species had to reflect their stature.

The sun had set completely now, and he had to be careful not to trip over any thick roots. He did not want to disturb his trees. He was respectful of them; they needed rest just like everyone else. When he planted them, some when he was only sixteen, they gave him permission to breathe. Breath that had been stifled in Iran, breath that had barely returned since the day he lost his father.

If it had not been for an Iranian baker named Daryoush, who saw young Shapur walking the streets of Bombay shell-shocked from the loss of the only living soul he cared about, Shapur Irani would not have survived.

Triumph was sacred to Vamog. Triumph of good over evil.

That was what being a Zarathushti was about. "We are not fire worshippers as the Arabs think we are," Vamog used to tell his son. "All natural light is symbolic of Ahura Mazda. That is why we consider fire holy. That is why we pay respect to the sun. These are just vehicles for us to reach Him."

Vamog told his son that Ahura Mazda, Lord of Wisdom, had an arch-enemy.

Ahriman, the Dark One. The further a man moved away from good thoughts, words, and actions, the closer he went towards Ahriman, the more he was aiding Ahriman in his stinking evil designs. The Earth was Ahriman's playground, where he threw pieces of temptation from the skies that the weak gobbled up in minutes, the consequences of which they would experience in the afterlife. "That is why Ahura Mazda has put the sun in the sky," said Vamog. "A reminder for all to choose light instead of what Ahriman throws our way."

But Vamog always made sure to tell his son that the outcome of the fight between Ahura Mazda and Ahriman was predetermined. Zarathushtra foretold a day when Ahriman would be vanquished forever. "But we have to *earn* that," Vamog said, "by using our free will wisely." And then came the part young Shapur relished, where his father became Ahriman and chased him around the house. As Shapur was cornered in the kitchen, Vamog raised his arms and bent his wrists, his fingers turning into Ahriman's claws; he clutched his son by the neck, trapping him in a deadly grip: "I will destroy you, Shapur." Shapur pointed to the sun outside, to the light floating in through the low roof, and said to his father, "You are no match for the light of Ahura Mazda," and Vamog fell to the floor, lay there choking, sputtering, panting.

After his father's death, Shapur Irani would not have believed in light or goodness had it not been for Daryoush the baker. Daryoush was young Shapur's saviour, his archangel, who had a nose like a beak and soft white hair like feathers, whose love for something as simple as bread allowed young Shapur to believe in something as simple as the chickoo.

Early each morning, Daryoush would inhale the scent of warm bread, and paint young Shapur's nose with dough and call him by the name of that great Iranian clown, Khosrow Anushirvan. It was only after Daryoush's death that Shapur Irani realized there was no clown called Anushirvan. There was a king by that name, and perhaps Daryoush's beak-nose could point to the future in which young Shapur would grow into a king who walked on his land with strong strides as he was doing right now, as he was born to do.

The moment Banu saw the dirt on his white pants and the manner in which his shirt stuck to his sweaty chest, she knew what he had been up to. A few strands of his thick black hair were also out of place.

"How many bottles are you going to hide?" she asked.

"I'm doing it for you, my darling," he replied.

"I don't drink, Shapur."

"Sorry, I forgot. For some reason I keep thinking that you are a big drunkardess."

He wiped his face on her shoulder, on the thick strap of her cream nightgown.

"Chee!" she said. "You dirty man."

"Yes, yes, I am dirty. You want to see how dirty I am?"

"No."

"Come on, let me show you."

Then he growled like a tiger, and she knew what that meant. It was a game they played. He called it Tiger-tiger.

He lifted her in his arms and carried her into the bedroom. She loved how muscular his arms were. The old wooden bed was covered by a mosquito net. Shapur Irani hated the mosquito net because he wanted to throw her on the bed, and he had done so once and the mosquito net had ripped, and she had shouted at him, and she was in no mood for any tiger after that.

"You and your mosquito net," he said as he put her down.

"There's nothing wrong with my mosquito net," said Banu as she straightened her nightgown. "I don't like being bitten."

"But which tiger stops when he sees a mosquito net? It doesn't make sense, Banu. You're spoiling it all for me."

"Just wait. Always in such a hurry, you men," she said as opened one side of the mosquito net and let him in. "There, the tiger is in. You can start growling again."

"I don't feel like it now."

"You're such a child."

"And what did you mean when you said, 'you men'? How do you know what men are like? I thought you had only been with me."

"I've been lost in the woods many times, my dear."

And that was enough for him. He put his hand under her nightgown and climbed on top of her.

"Always in such a hurry," she said.

The tiger did not last long. Banu wanted him to go on, to growl and growl, but he had failed her tonight. He lay next to her and was snoring loudly, on this bed that had been in her family for generations. After she got married, she insisted on bringing this bed to Dahanu. Shapur Irani was very uncomfortable with this. "How can we sleep on this bed when your grandmother has slept on it? Do you want me to think of Najamai when I undress you?" Banu insisted that she would not get sleep on any other bed. "But we are newly married. We are hardly going to sleep," he said. The wink made no difference. The bed stayed. She had played cards on this bed with her mother, and she had heard stories from her grandmother Najamai. She always admired Najamai's teeth. For an old lady she had most of her teeth, and Najamai insisted it was because she always tried to speak the truth. "The more you lie, the more your teeth fall out," she used to say.

In the darkness, she snuggled close to her husband, tickled his forearm and listened to the crickets. He was built like a truck, this man, and his skin was reddened by the sun, and when he drank, his face became even redder and his neck looked like it was about to explode. She giggled to herself when she thought of his tomato face. He was eleven years older than her, and she liked that he was experienced. At times she found his strength funny, especially the manner in which he shook her hand the first time they met, as though a colonel was shaking the hand of a soldier—firm, commanding, and awkward. She had laughed out loud and her mother shouted at her for that, but Shapur Irani was amused. He confessed later that he was surprised he was not angry. They met three times after that, always at her house, and her mother would eavesdrop from the other room. Banu had wanted to go for a walk with him alone, but her mother had refused. "It's not what a respectable girl does," she had said. All it took was four meetings and the date was decided, the prayers were said, rings exchanged, promises made, and then she was off to Dahanu. The chickoo farm was a big change from the city, and she missed the bazaars and the trams and the opera houses, but she loved this man, and he loved his farm. "In marriage there is always give and take," Najamai had said. "We are the house-makers and they are the house-breakers." She did not think of her husband as a breaker at all. He was good to her, and even though his snoring prevented her from sleeping, all she needed to do was punch him hard in the stomach and he would wake up momentarily and fall asleep a minute later. She had about five minutes before he started snoring again.

Banu boxed him and he woke up, as always, quite unperturbed. Then she whispered in his ear, "Put your head on my stomach." He was too groggy to understand, so she shook him. "Wake up, Shapur."

"Hah? What is it?"

"What kind of sad tiger are you?"

"I'm tired."

"I have something to tell you."

"Oh no," he muttered.

"I'm not complaining about anything. I just want to talk. Put your head on my stomach."

He groaned and got up from his sleep, then placed his head on her belly. She was naked and she could feel his breath on her skin. That air contained all her husband's hopes and desires, his truth, his love, it contained everything. She remained silent for a while and stroked his hair so that he was comfortable but not asleep. She would write a letter to her mother tomorrow and tell her the news. There would be a lot of excitement in the house, particularly among her sisters. They were twins, only twelve, and she would write in her letter that they were about to become aunties. But before she could write to them, she had to tell her husband.

"Shapur, are you awake?" she asked.

"You know," he mumbled, "I am not a real tiger. I am an idiot who is ruled by his wife."

"That's not true. You are a tiger. And the tiger is about to have a cub."

"What?"

"Yes."

"You mean . . ."

"Yes."

She wanted to say more, but when she saw her husband's reaction, how his small eyes became round as moons, and how he got up from the bed and hugged her hard, she knew what she had said was enough.

Nine months later, Shapur Irani's excitement could still not be contained.

But he tried not to think of his unborn child as he stood under a mango tree and waited for Ejaz. He chose a tree that could not be seen from his bungalow because he did not want to disturb Banu. Ejaz was taking too long. Ejaz, the Pathan. Ejaz, the only man in Dahanu who was the same height as Shapur Irani. Ejaz, all of six feet five inches.

Shapur Irani was having tea at Dahanu station one day when he saw a man alight from the train. He could tell from the man's loose black garb that he was a Muslim, a Pathan. This man towered above everyone, and Shapur Irani and Ejaz locked eyes like two beasts that recognized each other. Ejaz lowered his eyes first because he was the one without work. Perhaps he could tell from the manner in which Shapur Irani stood, tall and uncompromising, that he was a landowner, a man who commanded respect.

Ejaz walked straight up to Shapur Irani and said, "I am looking for work."

It was a moment Shapur Irani would never forget: a Muslim was asking an Irani for work. But Shapur Irani knew that the Pathan was not from Iran. The men who beat his father were not the same as this man. Maybe that was why he felt no disdain for the Pathan.

"Where are you from?" he asked.

"I live in Bombay," said Ejaz. "But my father was from Peshawar."

"Why are you in Dahanu?"

"I am on the run."

Shapur Irani liked the man's honesty. He did not ask what

Ejaz had done. Sometimes men of strength had to do things that went against their conscience.

"Ejaz, you will work for me," he said.

That was eight months ago, and in a short time Ejaz had earned a reputation as the fiercest foreman in Dahanu. When he stared at the Warlis with his black eyes, the men went quiet. All he needed to do was stand over them to make them realize how undernourished and weak they were. He had a long black beard, which he was proud of, and in his first week as foreman, he made himself a weapon that terrified the Warlis—he took a wooden club and hammered nails at one end. He told Shapur Irani that he did not intend on using it on the Warlis. It was just to scare them.

Shapur Irani thought about this first meeting as he waited for Ejaz under the mango tree. He could scarcely wait for the mango season to arrive so he could sink his teeth into that juicy yellow. "The juice of the sun," he would say to Banu. "This is sun juice you're drinking."

Ejaz finally came into sight, dragging a man along the ground. The man was crying and pleading, but Ejaz was a rhinoceros who dragged his victim through the soil. It was one of the farm workers, Vithal. About forty, a man in a white loincloth, with taut stomach muscles, good forearms, thin hair, thin legs, and a deep voice.

"Seth, I did not do anything," said Vithal.

"Did anyone ask you to speak?" shouted Ejaz.

Ejaz led Vithal to the foot of the mango tree. Shapur Irani wiped the sweat off his face with the sleeve of his shirt.

"It was him," said Ejaz. "Vithal is the thief."

"Are you sure?" asked Shapur Irani.

"I'm sure." Ejaz stroked his beard as he said this, as though that was enough.

"Did you find the money in his hut?"

"No, I did not find any money. But don't worry, seth. In a few moments, he will talk."

Shapur Irani wished Ejaz had proof.

By now, three workers had gathered around the tree. Men of similar stature, their heads low, darting scared glances towards Vithal from time to time. They did not have the guts to say anything. Vithal did not look up at Shapur Irani. He lay on the ground face down and stared at the soil.

"Did you take the money?" asked Shapur Irani.

"No, seth," said Vithal. "I did not steal."

"Seth, his wife works on the farm," said Ejaz. "Shall I call for her?"

"Yes," said Shapur Irani.

It would buy time. He hoped that by then the man would confess, and Shapur Irani could go home. He wanted to place his feet in warm water and release all the tension; he longed to smell his wife's hair, especially soon after she had washed it. Violence was not what he wanted on his land. As a landlord, he had never administered a single beating.

Ejaz barked orders at one of the men gathered there. He fled immediately, the power of Ejaz's voice giving him fearful wings. In the meantime, Ejaz tied Vithal to the mango tree. Ejaz's black figure was a complete contrast to the sun and blue sky. Shapur Irani wondered why, even when it was hot, Ejaz wore black.

Vithal kept pleading his innocence. He kept on begging to be released, saying that he did not know what Ejaz was talking about, that the Pathan was a dishonest man, and the seth should not believe the Pathan, and ever since the Pathan came to the farm, the workers had been unhappy and he ill treated the workers and took their wives for his own pleasure.

But that was not Shapur Irani's problem. Ejaz was a lusty man and, who knows, the Warli women might secretly enjoy being taken by a big Pathan. Shapur Irani employed Ejaz because the Warlis were beginning to rebel. They were staging rallies at the instigation of a communist party called the Red Flag and they needed to be taught a lesson. Fear needed to be instilled in them; they needed to be reminded who was king, and the Pathan did a great job of making them fearful. At least four landowners had enquired about the Pathan. They too wanted someone as ferocious as him to protect their land. But the Pathan was loyal to his employer because in his very first week, Shapur Irani had asked him an important question: "How many children do you have in Bombay?" "I have only one child," answered the Pathan proudly. "A son." And Shapur Irani had replied, "From now on, he is my son too."

Within a few minutes, Vithal's wife arrived at the scene. She was followed by most of the workers on the farm— about ten men and seven women. As soon as Vithal's wife saw her husband tied to a tree, she ran to Shapur Irani and fell at his feet.

"Please don't hurt him," she said. "He hasn't done anything."

"I didn't say he's done anything," replied Shapur Irani.

"Seth . . ." said the wife, and failed to add anything else.

"I haven't seen you before," said Shapur Irani. "When did you start work?"

"Just now," she answered.

It was Ejaz's job to employ men and women from time to time, if one worker fell sick or died.

"Seth, she started work two weeks ago," said Ejaz.

"Is this how your husband repays our kindness?" asked Shapur Irani. "We employ you, look after you, and he steals from me? From my own house?"

He raised his voice in an attempt to appear monstrous, so that Vithal's guilt would rush out of his mouth.

"Seth, I did not steal," said Vithal again. "Please believe me."

Ejaz stepped up to thrash Vithal, but Shapur Irani raised his hand, and Ejaz stopped.

"Vithal, I am asking you one last time," said Shapur Irani. "There were ten rupees kept on the table in my house. Someone has taken the money. Was it you?"

Shapur Irani had asked Banu to put the money under lock and key because he did not like money lying around the house. He did not put the money in the safe himself as it was in the bedroom, and Banu was being checked by Jeroo the midwife. So Shapur Irani told Banu that he had placed the money on the table and then gone for a walk through the farm. By the time Banu and Jeroo emerged from the bedroom, the money had disappeared. Ejaz had seen Vithal walk past the house at around the same time.

It was not the loss of money that upset Shapur Irani. What angered him was the fact that someone had had the guts to enter his house. It was a sign that the Warlis were changing. This made him question his future. A child was about to be born and he lived alone on the farm. What if one of his workers, during a drunken fit, decided to harm his wife? He would kill them all. He would have to buy a gun. He despised weapons of any kind. True Persians, true men, were wrestlers. They settled disputes with their bare hands. Weapons were for the weak in spirit and the bodily infirm. A Persian pehelvaan would never carry a knife or gun.

He had also thought that Ejaz might have stolen the money, but then he felt it was not possible. Ejaz was a man of honour. Men who were built like walls did not steal. They broke bones, but they did not steal. It would be too humiliating for Ejaz, too lowly, to enter the house and run with the money. It would diminish him in size instantly. No, Ejaz was not the thief. There was no way he could tell for sure if it was Vithal because no money had been found. But the die had been cast. This was a time for discipline, a time to set a strict example. He had never hit any of his men before, but landowners all over Dahanu were doing it. One of his neighbours, a Hindu land-lord named Ramesh, had a Warli man's wrist broken with a shovel because he ate a piece of fish from the dinner table. It wasn't about the piece of fish. It was about the act.

But Shapur Irani did not want violence.

He was aware that all the farm workers were present too. If he were to let Vithal go, it would send the wrong message. The situation was forcing him to be ruthless. He knew he would not be able to sleep at night. But he was doing this for the safety of his unborn child.

"Did you take the money or not?" he asked again.

If only Vithal would say yes and get it over with.

Shapur Irani's gaze went to Vithal's right hand. The thumb was missing. He had known Vithal for a few years now, and this was the first time he had noticed the missing thumb.

"Did you take the money? I am asking you one last time."

Shapur Irani would have waited a few seconds more, but Ejaz did not.

Ejaz held Vithal's left arm in a wrestler's grip. It snapped like one of the branches above Vithal's head. Vithal's cry was barely audible. He was in so much pain that if that pain were strength instead, he could have lifted the entire tree with it. His wife threw herself at Shapur Irani's feet.

"Let him go," she said. "It wasn't him. It was me. I stole the money. I needed—"

Ejaz pulled her by the hair and slapped her hard. She spat in his face, and that was when Shapur Irani knew that her next few days would be filled with the most searing pain she had ever known. Ejaz kicked her hard and she fell to the ground. Her teeth were on the earth.

"Stop," ordered Shapur Irani.

He could not bear to see a woman being hit. This woman was Vithal's Banu. Shapur Irani's throat was raw. He could barely breathe. Something was coiled around his lungs and it would not let go.

The workers were mostly silent. Shapur Irani thought he heard one woman sob, but he was not sure because of his own heavy breathing.

He needed to get a hold of himself.

This was what he wanted. To set an example. He could not afford to look concerned. He could not appear weak.

Just then the woman's cry became louder and louder, and he soon realized it was not a worker who was crying but the midwife Jeroo. She was running towards them, waving her arms, she was about to say something, but when she saw Vithal and his wife on the ground, she stopped.

She immediately turned away and started walking back towards the bungalow.

Shapur Irani caught up with her.

"What is it?" he asked. "Is everything okay?"

"You have a son," she replied.

"A son!" He beamed. "Is Banu okay?"

"A perfect delivery," she said. "You should be proud."

That night, after kissing his newborn Khodi to sleep, Shapur Irani went to Vithal's hut. He had already instructed Ejaz to provide Vithal and his wife with food and medicine. A doctor had been called to fix the broken arm. Vithal and his wife were told that once they were fit, they could start work again.

When he got to the hut, Vithal's wife was nursing her infant.

Shapur Irani could not bear to look at her mouth, which was bereft of front teeth. Normally it was the Warlis who were afraid to look the landowners in the eye, but at the moment it was Shapur Irani who was standing with his head down.

"What is the child's name?" he asked.

"Ganpat," replied the woman.

FIVE

2000

ZAIROS PARKED HIS black motorcycle outside Anna's, behind a caged rickshaw that was packed with chickens, so overcrowded it would put any peak-hour local train to shame. The cacophony of the chickens, coupled with the muezzin's call, gave Anna's an eerie feel. The rickshaw driver reached into the cage and pulled out a bunch of chickens. Tied in fours, they hung upside down like trapezists. He was delivering them to the Janta Chicken Centre. At least fifty chickens were being sent to their mortuary.

Just as Zairos was about to settle down on one of Anna's green Formica benches, he saw Damu approaching in the tractor. Zairos whistled loudly to get his attention.

"Where are you going?" asked Zairos.

"Ganpat's funeral, seth."

"Funeral? I thought they cremated him a week ago."

"No, seth," said Damu. "It takes time to collect wood, to buy milk, to make other arrangements . . ."

Once again, Ganpat had appeared in Zairos' life.

Even in death, he did not let go, as though he was trying to tell Zairos something. As in fairy tales, Ganpat was leaving a trail, bread crumbs for the lost and lonely. For some reason, Zairos had been thrust into the arc of Ganpat's life, an arc that had started at his grandfather's farm, decades ago. Zairos needed to follow it all the way to the end.

He would go to the funeral.

He was not doing it for Kusum; it was for himself. Maybe his grandfather was too proud, or just too old, to care about such things, but Zairos had young blood in him, blood that was bright and hopeful.

"I will follow you on the motorcycle," Zairos said to Damu.

"No, you won't," shouted Aspi Irani from the Mobile Casino. "I need the bike. I got here walking."

"Don't worry, Aspi Kaka, I'll take you home on my rein-deer," said Bumble, patting the leather seat of his red BMW, still in Santa mode from his Christmas party a week ago.

But by then, much to Damu's surprise, Zairos had climbed into the open box that was attached to the tractor. He used to sit in it as child and have Damu take him around the farm, but he was a grown man now. A seth did not sit in the back of a tractor.

"You're reclining like the Rani of Jhansi," said Bumble.

Even Pinky the orphan was amused. But she had eyes only for Bumble. Enchanted by his BMW, she shyly tugged at his loose white shirt. "Bumble," she said, "I'm hungry." It always tickled everyone when she called him Bumble.

"Anna, get me a packet of Parle-G," said Bumble.

"No biscuits," said Pinky. "I want ice cream."

"This kid is like Hitler," said Bumble.

Bumble started his motorcycle and hoisted Pinky onto the tank. He revved the engine, as was his habit, so as to disturb the whole neighbourhood, especially the patients in the nursing home just above Anna's, who, Bumble had been told repeatedly, woke up with a fright. He made sure he encircled Pinky with his arms so that she would not fall off during the ride.

Both tractor and BMW took off from Anna's at the same time, and Pinky could not contain her excitement as she wiped her nose on Bumble's shirt sleeve, and Bumble scolded her and went faster, and soon it was only Zairos in the tractor, feeling the jerks of the road, every pebble, every stone, eating dust, sneezing, as blue and pink plastic bags from the street flew into his face.

In other words, it was a day just like any other at Anna's.

Too bad that Zairos was on his way to a funeral.

Each time the tractor hit a bump, a current went up Zairos' spine. He had underestimated the treachery of Dahanu roads—the holes, the sharp stones, the thick roots of banyan trees that served as speed breakers, the sudden dips.

He felt ashamed for complaining. He could barely imagine what his grandfather must have gone through as a boy, when he came down the hills of Iran on a mule. "There were days along the way," Shapur Irani told Zairos, "when just the smell of someone's cooking made me faint. I was so hungry. After three or four days of nothing, all we'd get was a piece of naan with some onions."

And now the naan remained, but with it came lamb, chicken, fish, pork, anything the stomach desired. Shapur Irani's mule had been replaced by BMWs, Kawasakis, Hondas, and Yamahas. Whereas Shapur Irani had had to fight for sheer life, his sons Aspi and Sohrab sat in the back of their Mobile Casino, chirping to the rhythm of hearts, clubs, diamonds, and spades.

However, there was no doubt that Aspi Irani was aware of the sacrifices his father had made. But pain had made Shapur Irani serious. He had forgotten that in life a gambler's touch was needed. Shapur Irani had been a valiant gladiator, but the light in him had gone, light that only a clown could resurrect. That was why Aspi Irani was an irreverent prankster. He wanted to impart that lightness to Zairos, something his own father had failed to give him. What was the use of survival if the hardships of the past had so savagely ripped out the smile from one's heart?

That was why, at age twelve, when Zairos had asked his father to tell him where the Zoroastrians came from, Aspi Irani said, "Do you want the religious, historical version, or do you want the truth?"

And by truth he meant, What is history without a little pinch on the bottom?

Zairos was seated at Anna's, as Aspi Irani surveyed his audience. "Put that silly book down," he told Keki the Italian, whose pronounced jaw seemed to be growing in size each day.

"This is *literature*," replied Keki through yellow teeth. "This is Camus."

"By just looking at your face," said Aspi Irani, "the dumb stupor of a retarded person staring at a colourful balloon, I can gather that Camus has not taught you anything."

"Camus is a giant of French literature," said Keki. "He—"

"He's an elf in my book. Now pay attention. I'm talking about the time the Arabs treated us like camel shit."

Then he thumped Keki on the back. This was Aspi Irani's let-me-enlighten-you thump.

"The Muslims had started forcing the Zoroastrians to convert to Islam," said Aspi Irani. "So in 716 AD, many of our ancestors—bless their persecuted souls—fled to India to seek asylum. Quite frankly, I wish they'd gone the other way, to Italy or Spain, but they chose this shithole of a country instead and so be it."

These early settlers were called Parsis because they came from the province of Pars in Persia. The Parsis first landed in Sanjan, in the coastal state of Gujarat: "The state next door to us, son, currently full of moneylenders and men who have black and white chessboard tiles in their living rooms."

The Hindu king of Sanjan, Jadi Rana, was not pleased with this unexpected arrival on his shores, as India was full even back then. So Jadi Rana asked his servant to bring him a jar of milk. Holding the jar of milk in his hand, Jadi Rana said to the head priest of the Parsis, "This jar of milk is filled to the brim."

The Parsi priest replied, "Mohan, I understand what you are saying."

"Why are you calling me Mohan?" asked Jadi Rana.

"Because I had friend in Iran, a Hindu, whose name was also Mohan."

At this point, the Parsis worried that their head priest's faux pas had ruined their chances of getting immigration, and, what's worse, the look on Jadi Rana's face implied that they would be tortured for breakfast, lunch, and dinner.

But then, with the suaveness of a magician, as though he were conjuring red roses out of thin air, the Parsi priest added sugar into the jar of milk.

"This milk, on its own, tastes fine," he said to Jadi Rana. "But add this sugar, and it becomes even sweeter. This is what we will do to your country. We will make it sweeter, and just as the sugar is invisible, you will not even notice our presence."

Jadi Rana was impressed by this quick thinking, and he felt that these people, although completely demented to travel with a burning fire—one they claimed had been kept burning for over three thousand years—would make valuable contributions to their adopted home.

"That's the story of the Parsis," said Aspi Irani. "Did Camus know that?"

"Camus had better things to worry about," said Keki, blowing beedi smoke through the gritted cage bars of his teeth.

"Like what—his accent?"

"You are a philistine," said Keki.

"Ah," said Aspi Irani. "That brings us to the Iranis. We came centuries later. We stayed on in Iran, got abused some more, a few Arab whippings here and there, we ate almonds, and that was it."

Zairos was disappointed. He wanted to hear more about the Iranis. But he was too young to have a voice at Anna's. He was old enough only to listen, not to speak.

Thankfully, Keki goaded Aspi Irani on.

"Come on, Aspi. Tell it for poor, ignorant Camus."

"In that case," said Aspi Irani, "I will oblige."

Centuries after the first group of Zoroastrians emigrated from Iran, another group landed on the shores of India. The

Hindu king, who was the great-great-great-great-grandson of the one whose name was not Mohan, asked the Iranis the same question: "Why should I allow you to enter the country?" The Iranis did not know what to say. They were tired and hungry and horny. They started eyeing the king's servants. "Bring me some milk!" said the Hindu king. The Iranis were even more confused. Why the hell were they being offered milk? Was this king a complete moron?

When the jar of milk was brought, the Hindu king noticed that it had no effect whatsoever on the Iranis. Perhaps they needed a prod in the right direction. So he ordered, "Bring me some sugar as well!" When the sugar came, he offered the jar and the sugar to the Iranis. All they had to do was mix it, and they were in.

Instead, the Iranis asked the Hindu king, "Boss, you got some whiskey?"

"No," replied the king. "We do not drink here. Alcohol is prohibited in the state of Gujarat."

All the Iranis fainted there and then.

By the time they regained consciousness, their boats and donkeys and other modes of transport had disappeared, and they entered the country dejected and full of rage.

"This is how the two kinds of Zoroastrians, the Parsis and the Iranis, came to India," said Aspi Irani. "The Parsis went on to become successful in almost every sphere, from business to cricket. Unfortunately, the Iranis, right from the start, did not understand the concept of work."

When the Hindu king saw them just lounging around, he said, "Why don't you *do* something?" and the Iranis asked him again, "Boss, you got some whiskey?" That is when the king lost it. Even though he was Hindu, saintly and well bred, he abused the hell out of the Iranis—"You motherfuckers, you sons of whores, you lazy cocksuckers!"—and the Iranis whispered into the king's ear, "Boss, you're Irani, aren't you? Only Iranis speak like that." The Hindu king, tired and lost, retreated into his palace and never again emerged.

Then came Aspi Irani's caveat emptor, an insurance of sorts in case the story were to be repeated outside Anna's walls, and some self-righteous Zoroastrian, the kind Bombay's high society was full of, decided to take offence: "I would like to add that not all Iranis are foul mouthed and ill mannered," Aspi Irani said. "Some are quite polished indeed—none live in Dahanu, of course, the majority live in Bombay—their English is impeccable, their clothing immaculate, their knowledge of the stock market insurmountable, their love of classical music obvious, and so on. These are souls who *contribute* to society."

There. He had done his bit to satiate the purists. Now it was time to poke them in the bum again.

"But I always believe that lurking within these well-mannered souls is a true Irani beast waiting to unleash itself. We are exhibits to be put in cages, dissected and studied. We may not have discovered the wheel, and we may not have conducted stem cell research or any such activity connected to plants, but we are unique. We are pioneers because in an age when everything seems to be moving forward, we simply refuse to evolve. We are not new-and-improved versions. We are just as disturbed as our fathers. We are fish in a pond, with no obvious beauty, and our true story shall never be known."

Then, as a final flourish, Aspi Irani picked up Camus' *The Outsider* and threw it in Keki's face.

Zairos smiled as he remembered that day. In the eighth grade, when he was in private school in Bombay, his English teacher, Mrs. Costa, asked the class to write an essay based on their family history. Zairos wondered what would happen to Mrs. Costa if he were to write things as his father had told him. Mrs. Costa's long black hair would freeze. But even though Aspi Irani's tales were just that, mere tales, there was an underlying truth to them.

On the one hand, there was Zairos' father, free to follow the twists and turns of his imagination, redrawing, retelling the history of his people, with a pinch of salt and chili sauce. But there was also Ganpat, who was not as lucky, who had been asphyxiated by his own history, and perhaps even if he had not found a rope to hang himself that day, one would have materialized from the desolate, unforgiving loops of his own life.

The tractor came to an abrupt halt.

They had arrived at Kusum's hamlet. Damu got off first and waited near the open box for Zairos to get off. Damu always waited. There were times when Zairos would forget that Damu was near him, so artful was he at making himself invisible.

About twenty Warlis, men and women, surrounded the funeral pyre.

Unlike at the farm, Kusum and Rami seemed more powerful here, amid their own kind. The dry stream with burning grey stones, the date palm trees, the thorny twigs that lay on the ground, the brown soil, made Zairos realize that these women were of this place. Their feet had roots that went deep into the earth, and if distance could be measured in years, their roots were thousands of years deep.

Zairos was face to face with Ganpat again.

Ganpat had been wrapped in a new white cloth. His face was smeared in ghee, and there was a red mark on his forehead, a short streak that had been made with someone's thumb. The village elders, men with white stubble and only a few wisps of white hair, stood close to the wooden pyre.

Old Rami was hunched near a small cactus bush with a vessel of milk in her hand. One of the elders, in dusty brown shorts, went near the pyre, opened Ganpat's palms, and put one-rupee coins in them.

Zairos knew he was being stared at. Especially by Kusum.

Twice she looked at him, then away, as though he were some apparition created by the heat and dust and the imminent burning of her father's body.

Slowly she walked towards him, her head down, glancing sideways at the elders, then at the hot ground again. As she came closer, Zairos was once again struck by her beauty. She was shorter than most Warlis, but also rounder, fuller. For a woman who was meant to be in mourning, she had a surprising amount of colour on her—a pink blouse, a red ribbon tied in her hair, which was combed back into a bun.

Zairos realized he needed to say something to her. She had been standing in front of him with her head down for quite a while.

"Look at me," he said.

He had no idea what possessed him to say that. That was how the Warlis always stood. Subjugation was as natural as a sunset.

She looked up at him and quickly lowered her eyes again.

In that one short glance, Zairos caught her brown pupils moving, floating in a white lake. His gaze then went to her waist. How narrow it was, how her hips curved.

The sun was making his white T-shirt stick to his chest with the possessiveness of a lover. The sudden movement of orange bangles on her wrist sent out a tinkling sound in the air.

It was a mistake to come here.

The blood of a landlord was swirling inside him, questioning him.

Still, he had to say something. Not an apology, not even an explanation, just a pure statement. By keeping Ganpat's body at the farm until sundown, he had denied her the last few hours to be with her father. By the time the body was brought to her, Ganpat was a stinking corpse fit for a morgue, not for the crying arms of a daughter.

But instead of words, he gave her paper.

A thousand rupees in all, removed from the back pocket of his blue jeans with sleight of hand only a landlord possessed. More than an explanation, she needed money.

She took the money, held it in her hand.

He wanted her to go back to the body. There was nothing he could do for her. It was vain of him to think so.

"Seth," she said. "I want to ask you something."

He was surprised by the low timbre of her voice, the gentle strength in it. There was no tremble, neither anger nor sorrow, even though her father's flesh would soon melt away before her eyes.

"Did Shapur seth say anything about my father?" she asked.

"He wanted money," said Zairos. "My grandfather refused."

She opened her palm, looked at the hundred-rupee notes now dampened by her sweat.

"If Shapur seth had given the money," she said, "my father would still be alive."

Years of observation had made Zairos think that these people were taught not to feel. They were numbed by history, their hearts trained not to ask questions.

Zairos' face hardened, a sign of his masculinity and power. He needed Bumble's black aviators, whose metallic sheen would create enough distance between him and Kusum.

His eyes had failed him. They were brown, just like hers.

He would not stay and watch the funeral. By coming here, he had upset the order of things.

≈≈

He did not remember her. But Kusum knew there was no reason he would.

He was a landlord's son, and the broad shoulders and muscular legs of his forefathers would not allow him to remember.

At one time, though, he did possess gentleness.

That was years ago, when white lilies grew on the farm, row upon row in between the chickoo trees, lilies wet with morning dew, so soft she hated plucking them. While her father plucked chickoos, she plucked lilies. That was all they did. They took things that were living and snapped the life out of them.

Then, at night, her mother would give her raw mahua flowers to eat.

Kamla would show her daughter how to extract oil from the mahua, which could be used for cooking. Sometimes there was dry fish and chana as well, and on days when Ganpat had not spent all his wages on liquor, he would bring her sweets, round white balls with black stripes on them.

Even though she did not like the taste of raw mahua, Kusum loved eating flowers. If she ate a flower, something would change in her, something of the flower would become hers.

But the mahua was not as pretty as the lily. Not even close.

So one day at the farm, as thousands of white lilies sparkled in the sun, she stopped plucking and stood up.

"I am going to eat you all," she said to them.

She crouched back down, tore one lily away from its stem, and was about to put it in her mouth when a boy appeared on his blue cycle. She had never seen that kind of blue before, shining like teeth in the night. She quickly threw the lily away. The boy was not a Warli; he was one of *them*, the other, the strange one. Older than her, but not by too much, he towered over her.

Then the strange one spoke: "That's not for eating," he said.

He spoke her language, but he spoke it like an idiot, a complete buffoon, a boy whose brain had some disease, a lizard brain or, even worse, a combination of a donkey and a reptile. She tried not to laugh and she was glad she didn't.

"Why are you laughing?" asked the boy.

She looked down, worried that he might hit her or scream at her because the blue of his cycle was so unusual only witch doctors could make a colour go that crazy.

"Speak," he said.

She could not understand the tone of his voice. Even though her eyes were on the ground, she knew that he had gotten off his cycle and was standing right next to her. Then, the strange one did something truly strange. He crouched down beside her.

"Were you going to eat this?" he asked.

She nodded fast-fast-fast because she wanted him to go. She wanted him to get on that witch doctor cycle of his and leave.

He was going to strike her. She was about to eat his lilies, and he had to be a witch doctor otherwise how would he know she was going to eat *all* of them?

"Lilies are used in weddings," he said. "We put them on strings and hang them all over the wedding hall to make things look pretty."

Then he picked up the lily she had torn, the one she had tried to steal-eat.

He was keeping it as proof. He would take it to his elders and that would be the end of her. She would be beaten, or thrown into a pot and made into the colour blue. Oh, that was how he did it. The sparkle in the blue was brought by dead Warli children like her.

"You can also put it in your hair," he said in his best broken Marathi.

He brought his hand close to her and her eyelashes flittered a thousand times because he was going to slap her.

He tried to stick the lily in her hair, but he could not find a way. He almost touched her face, but then decided not to. Instead, he just left the lily on *top* of her head and she stayed crouched in that position for a long time, afraid that if she dropped the lily he would come back. After a while, her eyelashes continued to flitter, but it was not out of fear anymore, it was something else, and now, years later, Kusum realized she had never felt anything like it again.

That night, as Aspi Irani sang "There's a hole in the bucket, dear Mithoo, dear Mithoo" to distract his wife from studying for her Montessori teacher training exam, Zairos sat on the porch and had a glass of whiskey.

He understood a man's desire for whiskey. It was, after all, an antiseptic. As it slid down a man's throat, it numbed his internal cuts and wounds. But Zairos did not understand his own need for whiskey. He had not undergone trauma or loss of any kind. Still, wounds opened up inside him naturally, like flowers did on grass.

He listened to the sounds the night brought him—the howl of dogs, the blare of the train as it sped past, the cough of a sick man in the darkness, the prattle of a thousand crickets. He picked up the flashlight that lay next to him on the floor. A thick, steady beam of light travelled towards the stars. For once someone was sending light to them. Mosquitoes spun in and out of that light wondering where it led. He thought of searchlights in war movies and how to prisoners light meant death, a reversal of laws.

What if that was the case with Ganpat's suicide?

In all probability, it was a simple act of desperation, the only swan song Ganpat was capable of. The only statement of revolt the poor could make was to put an end to their own misery. It happened all the time—men lay themselves on train tracks, hanged themselves from trees, consumed rat poison, and women set their kerosene-soaked bodies alight in front of their husbands. These were blazing ends to insignificant journeys. But in all this, there was always one man who, in that final gush of blood, in that final breaking of neck and bone, set things in motion.

Zairos knew it was the guilt talking.

But it had no business being there in the first place.

It was not up to him, or his grandfather, to submit to the demands of every single Warli. How was his grandfather to know that his refusal would result in asphyxiation?

Zairos followed the beam from his flashlight as far as he could. A Zoroastrian priest had once told him that prayers were rays of light that travelled upwards. Up and up they went, beams full of hope and desire, until the light hit an angel's wings, made them flutter, so the angel had no choice but to pay attention.

But Zairos had absolutely no idea what to pray for.

The sun created a furnace that burned the workers' skin while Zairos stood in the shade and smoked. It was noon, the only time of day when the Iranis took any interest whatsoever in farming, a time all farm owners cheerfully referred to as "bathtub time." Each day, after the chickoos had been plucked, they were washed in bathtubs. Old, grimy bathtubs, the kind that were found in American motels. The chickoos made a *dub-dub-dub* sound as they hit the bottom of the empty tubs. Then, a thick pipe spurted water into these tubs, covering the chickoos, until they floated around like naughty children in a swimming pool. That was when the fun began. That was when Aspi Irani made a statement that would, in his opinion, have filled any Greek philosopher with pride. "Poverty's greatest gift to the rich," he declared, "is no bra."

Warli women could not afford bras, much to the delight of every farm owner in Dahanu. However, they did wear a blouse, a cheap, handmade version, which benevolently displayed their breasts. As they bent down and pushed the chickoos to and fro creating waves in the tub, the Iranis went into waves of ecstasy. Such was their fervour that they praised Ahura Mazda for this great mercy. Apart from Ahura Mazda, they praised one mortal—Aspi Irani.

He was the first to use bathtubs because he knew it would make the women bend low, and all the Iranis grudgingly admitted that it was a stroke of genius, and Aspi Irani, who lacked humility in the way people lacked calcium, accepted the compliment and threw it back in their faces by saying, "Someday you too will get a stroke."

But as Zairos watched the women wash the fruit, he realized that while their breasts brought a song to Irani lips, the workers themselves never sang. They did not speak much either. He wondered if the silence symbolized something—the women were reminding the chickoo that they were not its friend. He had once asked Damu if the Warlis ever ate chickoos, and Damu had replied, "Rarely." Damu was going to say something else, but stopped. It was clear that the chickoo was the fruit of his bondage.

Just then Damu showed up with Kusum. In the sunlight, his salty stubble acquired the sparkle of diamonds. The moment Zairos saw him, Damu went his way.

As Kusum walked towards Zairos, he could tell from the sway of her hips that this was no ordinary woman. She was an enchantress in command of her skin, and of the moment. The closer she came, the more he sensed his own lust. Pure, unadulterated, it was honey straight from the hive. His eyes navigated every surface of her, from the blossom of her lips to that flat, smooth belly, until he noticed something that should not have been there, something that disrupted the sweet brown of her skin.

A blue-black mark on her rib cage.

"Seth," she said. "I . . ."

She put her head down, more than usual, and touched the sole of one foot to the instep of the other. This was one of the signs Zairos had learned to read. Whenever the Warlis did this, it meant they wanted something, something they were ashamed to ask for. In most cases, it was money.

At the funeral, he had already given her some. She was here to extort more.

"Seth," she said. "I want work."

Once again, he was taken by surprise. But, unlike at the funeral, she was in his territory now.

"What kind of work?" he asked.

"I will work on the farm."

"You want to work on the same farm on which your father killed himself?"

It made no sense, her wanting to see those trees again. Or even him.

"Seth, we all have to work and we all have to die," she said.

Reminders existed everywhere. A few trees could do nothing. He could do nothing.

"But you must be having a job already," he said.

"At a balloon factory, seth. But I lost that job a week ago."

"I have enough workers," he said.

She kept quiet but did not leave. For a while, both of them listened to the flutter of sparrows, that fast whipping of wings, the futility of small creatures trying to put their stamp on the world. Zairos did not like these silences, this lull in power. If his words stopped, and neither of them spoke, the silences seemed to be supporting her.

"Seth," she said again.

The softness in her tone was a way of asking for permission to speak. He raised his head, just a fraction, which allowed her to carry on.

"My father wanted money to free me from my husband," she said.

The mention of her husband made him feel clumsy. But it was not something he would allow her to detect.

"My husband beats me, seth. For me to leave him, I have to give him whatever he spent on our marriage."

The blue-black mark was the handiwork of her husband. That did not surprise him. He knew that these women were beaten by their men. It was inevitable, like gravity. Hands rained down on these women. Some of the women struck back. When the men were drunk and weak, unable to speak or strike, the women beat them with sticks.

Maybe she had children too, but he was not going to ask. The children would assume this was how life worked. Man beats woman, woman beats man, man beats woman again, stronger, harder, woman understands the futility of fighting back and waits for her face to be slit by lines of age, line after line etched deeper with each beating so that when man and wife reach the heavens a count has been kept, and final retribution begins. At least that is the woman's only hope.

"Seth," she said. "I just wanted you to know why my father was asking for money."

She turned, started walking away.

He let her go. He wanted those hips to get away from him. They were made of a substance that drove men to the edge of madness.

And that blue-black mark was not his problem. It was just a mark, no more, a blow to the ribs the gods had to stop. It had nothing to do with him or his grandfather or his chickoo trees.

He was glad that she did not turn back to look at him. She did not beg or cajole.

The further she walked away from him, the more uneasy he got. A few seconds more and she would go out of view; then he would never have to see her again.

The very shape of her made him believe that she would be better off away from him.

He wished she had begged for a job; some histrionics, even a tear or two.

He went behind her, dragging his slippers through the grass, ensuring that she would hear him and turn.

Slow, wasteful, still mulling over how to say it.

"You can start work" was all he said.

Even in her grief she was striking. Her hair, raven black, her poise, that of a dancer. He wondered how hot her breath would be as it came through those slightly parted lips.

Later that afternoon, as Zairos rode towards Anna's, he spotted his father in jeans and white sudreh, hiding in the tall bush of dried grass just opposite the train tracks, with a wooden sling-shot in his hand.

Aspi Irani was squatting, peering this way and that, and before Zairos could stop his motorcycle and approach his father, Aspi Irani took aim, and with a healthy *twang* let go of the thick black rubber band and disappeared. A yelp came from that same bush, from a man who was clearly disoriented, scared stiff in fact, because he had been stung by a stone in his naked bottom. The man was not a tribal but a bhaiyya from Uttar Pradesh who sold coconuts at Dahanu station. Even though the station had a toilet, the man was defecating in the bush, and since there was no government regulation against this, at least none that could be enforced, Aspi Irani had decided to take matters into his own hands. He continually complained about this "special brand of manure" that would one day be the downfall of his fortunes if he ever wanted to sell his home. "How can I call it Aspi Villa?" he screamed one day. "What kind of villa carries the aroma of shit?"

Zairos quickly rode away, not knowing if he should bless his stars for giving him a father like that or question the entire galaxy for the insanity of it.

At Anna's, an old favourite had returned.

With a beard thick as the jungles of Vietnam, puffy cheeks and a paunch to match, Hosi was Zairos' other cousin, ten years his senior. Hosi was priceless, a family heirloom. No one in Dahanu wanted Hosi to die because if he did, the Irani race would lose a grand specimen. People spoke about his death because that's all Hosi ever spoke about. Whenever he met someone for the first time, he would be cordial, charming even. Then, just as he would shake the person's hand to say goodbye, he would say, "I don't think you'll see me again. My time has come." He had been doing this for the past ten years. His most fatal problem was dandruff.

The other thing Hosi did was hug priests.

So as soon as Jamshed Moped showed up at Anna's, smelling fresh as the sandalwood he fed daily into the temple fire, Hosi pressed his nose into the priest's chest and inhaled deeply. Hosi was addicted to the smell of sandalwood and frankincense.

"Jamshed Moped," he said, "you smell sweeter than a newborn."

It was Aspi Irani, of course, who gave Jamshed that name. Instead of rightfully calling the priest a mo*bed*, Aspi Irani called him Jamshed Mo*ped* because that's what he rode.

"So you're back," said Jamshed Moped, adjusting his glasses, dabbing his thin moustache into his skin, worried that it was going to fall off. He looked more like a chartered accountant than a priest.

"Yes," said Hosi, releasing Jamshed Moped from the bear hug. "One horse has a disease and they stop everything."

Hosi had returned from Bombay because the racing season had been cut short. It was one of his darlings, Black Leila, who had fallen ill. Hosi's life was full of mares with names such as Athena, Red Dawn, Chagall, Hazel Head, and Supreme Sword. They were his true loves, the only Juliets he was willing to die for. Otherwise, no woman was good enough for him.

"With the season stalled, what will I do in this depressing town?" he asked.

Of course, Hosi knew exactly what he was going to do. Until the horses were back, he would spend his days at Anna's, trying to bed his sultry wife, who flirted with Hosi, teased him to the point of madness, sent him up and down like the graph of a cardiogram, but never let him touch her.

Zairos watched Anna's wife too, and something rose inside him, but it was lust of a different sort, of wanting to leave Anna's, of wanting to do something, but he did not know what.

Leaning against the wall, he thought about Kusum.

He did not like how she occupied his mind. She had the power to intrude. Like lightning or thunder, she did not ask permission.

Night was a time for answers.

Zairos stared at his grandfather, a man of no movement who spoke about things in no order. Chronology, sequence, logic— only puppets ventured there, men and women who had not suffered. Shapur Irani had suffered, the past swirled inside him, and the moment it found a tear in his skin, it erupted.

Tonight Zairos wanted to direct the course of the conversation.

But Shapur Irani did not give his grandson the chance. "Damu told me that you allowed Ganpat's daughter to work here?"

"Yes, Pa."

"Do you know why she wants to work here?"

"No," said Zairos.

Shapur Irani took in a deep breath. It meant that he would exhale something, some sort of truth that Zairos was not aware of. His nostrils flared, his eyebrows rose, and he rubbed his right knee as though that jogged his memory.

"You are a good man," said Shapur Irani.

Zairos knew what his grandfather was hinting at. *You are a good man, but if there is one thing I do not like, it is weakness.* And Shapur Irani had a pair of antennae on his head that could detect this flaw in others every single time.

"Both my sons are well settled now," he continued. "They have their own land. They are landlords in their own right. Initially, I wanted to distribute this land between my three grandsons— you, Bumble, and Hosi. That was my intention. But things have changed now. I want to leave this land only to you."

"But, Pa . . ."

"This land is mine. I can do with it as I wish."

It was perhaps the only explanation he would receive from his grandfather. If a man could live in solitary confinement on fifty acres of open land, he could build walls around anything.

"Part of this land belonged to Ganpat's father," said Shapur Irani. "His name was Vithal."

Zairos became just as still as his grandfather.

"When I moved to Dahanu at the age of fifteen, I started a liquor stall. I gave Vithal liquor on credit, and when he could not pay I had to take his land. That is why Ganpat came here before his death. He wanted money. He said this was his father's land. I told him he was right. It *was.*"

Zairos wondered if Kusum knew this. Of course she did. That was why she could stand tall in front of him. She thought of him as a thief.

"Zairos, I will tell you all I know about this land," said Shapur Irani. "I will tell you everything because only then will you be man enough to own it. Goodness will not take you far, my son. Only courage will. I know what you are thinking. If this land belonged to Vithal, then how can it ever be mine?

It is *always* somebody else's land. We were chased out of Iran. That was our land. What about that?"

What had his grandfather meant by *part* of this land? How much of it had actually belonged to Vithal?

"I did not cheat Vithal," said Shapur Irani. "I was young then. I was poor too. I had to take the land when Vithal was unable to pay me. I was . . . it was soon after the death of Daryoush the baker."

It was a time when Shapur Irani had become raw all over again.

For five years, Daryoush had looked after Shapur like the boy was one of his own. While Vamog used to slip slices of orange into his son's mouth, Daryoush favoured apricots and pomegranates. If Vamog was big and booming, Daryoush was dainty and lush. When he spoke, Shapur sank into the softness of that voice like a body into a leather couch. But the two men, Vamog and Daryoush, had something in common. They instilled in Shapur a strong moral sense, the foundations of which were as solid and muscular as his legs.

"Your strength is not for you," Daryoush would say. "It is there to serve others."

At first, Shapur took this literally. "What do you want me to lift?" he asked.

"You are indeed Anushirvan the Clown. Now bend down. You have become too tall for me."

So Shapur bent down, and Daryoush put some dough on his nose. But Shapur was determined to put into practice what Daryoush had mentioned. He saw an opportunity a few days later, when he found out that the old lady who lived above their bakery could not walk anymore.

So Shapur went to her small room, picked her up, carried her downstairs, and placed her on a chair outside the bakery, so she could hear the trams, smell the warm bread, and watch a woman thread garlands out of magnolias and lilies, which temple-goers used to buy every single morning.

Shapur knew he had done well when he saw the beam on Daryoush's face. It had the contentment of one who owned kingdoms.

Perhaps that was why Daryoush left.

One day, after Shapur had gone upstairs to bring the old lady down, he came back to find no one behind the bakery counter. This was unusual because a customer was waiting. And whenever there was a customer, Daryoush's head was always there, just a couple of feet above the glass.

When Shapur lifted the wooden counter to enter, he found Daryoush on the ground. Shapur's thick legs gave way.

He did not want his grandson to feel pain like that.

Ever.

He had made the mistake of softening up to Daryoush, to his dough, to his meaningless theatrics about clowns. That day Shapur Irani realized that softness did not take a man far. It brought a man close to happiness, just inches away, only to tear him apart soon after.

Shapur Irani could see that same softness in Zairos. The willingness to believe in life, the notion that goodness took a man places. Once and for all, he would tell Zairos what this land had done to him, what it had made him do, and all along he had convinced himself that he was working from a place of conscience, an inner voice, which had failed to give him any solace at all.

SIX

1945

WHEN THE WAR ENDED, there was elation all over. It
came in through the radio, waves of relief, frenzied announce-
ments that lifted Indian spirits even though they had no real
stake in the war. When Shapur Irani went to Bombay to visit
Banu's mother, the city's mesh of two-wheelers, trams, and
cycles was dizzy with excitement; perhaps even India's fortunes would change and the country would gain indepen-
dence. But there was also fatigue from what seemed to be an
unending struggle—the freedom marches, the bombs, and
lathi charges.

Shapur Irani had remained far away from it all.

The British were too large an entity for him to think of. His
mind was on another revolution, another war. The War of
the Warlis.

For years the Warlis had endured the beatings, the loss
of their land, and the hunger in their belly like one giant
knife wound. The gods, it seemed, had taken everything

from them, but they had also left them with a gift—endurance.

The Warlis would have continued to endure had it not been for a woman from Bombay who was known as the Lady of the Red Flag. The landowners failed to realize that their cruelty was serving as inspiration; not inspiration in the way sunlight was inspiring, but in the way a dead baby could cause a young mother to scream.

For the first time, the Warlis were united. They had a voice, they were being educated, and they were being reminded that they were humans, not animals. They were being taught self-respect.

"This woman from Bombay is raising their hopes," Shapur Irani told Banu. "She is putting them in more danger. Nothing is going to change. Only blood will be shed, that is all, and it will be Warli blood."

"Shapur, please don't talk like that in front of Khodi."

"He's not even three. He doesn't understand what we're saying."

"Look, I know you are worried, but calm down."

"You don't understand, Banu. The Warlis have attacked a landowner. They have invited trouble."

A week before, Pestonji and his friend Noshir Irani, owners of adjoining farms, were returning home after attending the wedding of a forest officer's daughter. It was midnight, and their breath was heavy with country liquor made from jaggery and battery acid, a poisonous brew that hit them so hard they almost ran into the tribal running away from their farm with stolen coconuts.

Pestonji caught the tribal by the neck so tight and deep it felt as though he was looking for a vein. Noshir Irani took a cricket bat made from the finest English willow and hammered it into the tribal's chest.

Ribs cracked. They asked him his name.

With cracked ribs, it was hard for a man to remember his name.

They wanted his name as though that would solve anything. His name could have been Sukhla, Ravi, Lakhu, Patlya, or Navsia. It would not have quenched Pestonji and Noshir Irani because the battery acid from the liquor had singed their hearts.

They were sick of their coconuts being stolen.

The cricket bat was not enough. They needed iron. So while Pestonji continued to grip the tribal's neck, Noshir Irani went to the tool shed and came back with a parai.

It was pure iron. They would send a reminder, a lesson deep into this tribal's body, a lesson his entire being would resonate with. They turned him around and shoved the parai inside him.

If a scream came from the tribal, no one heard it.

And even if someone did hear it, it must have been so full of agony, it had to have been unreal.

Or perhaps the tribal did not scream because he was dead.

When they removed the parai from him, he was silent. When they turned him around, he was even more silent. Now the landlords were heaving and panting.

A wedding had made them do this.

They looked at each other. Yes, it was the country liquor at the wedding.

They needed to hide the body. But their heads were still spinning, their judgment so disabled that they took the tribal to a heap of cow dung, a ten-foot mound to be used as fertilizer, and buried him in there.

Then Pestonji and Noshir Irani staggered into their own homes, into beds with wives who could not understand why there was blood on their husbands' trousers and cow dung on the sheets.

We've been to a wedding was all their husbands said the next morning.

When the Warlis found the body they decided it was time to retaliate. To see a brother's face deep in cow dung, to see his shorts all the way down to his shins, a parai stained with blood . . . it was enough to drive away the poverty that crippled the Warlis, the malnourishment that weakened them.

A day later, when Pestonji was going to the beach in his horse carriage, a group of men surrounded him. The driver of Pestonji's carriage was a Warli and he had agreed to help. At first, when they surrounded him, Pestonji was enraged. He threatened to have them beaten by the police, and this seemed to work because two men ran away, and there were only three left. But these three men killed his horses right before his eyes. They ripped the beasts apart, tore their strong, black chests with long knives, and watched as Pestonji shivered in fright. "Where's your big voice now?" they asked him. "Why don't you use a parai now?"

Pestonji had no answer.

When he saw his horses slump, his legs jellied. The Warlis kicked him in the head again and again. They did not get a chance to kill him because another carriage approached from behind, the carriage that carried Pestonji's wife and son.

When Shapur Irani heard about this, he was worried that the landowners were going to hit back. The police were going to help the landowners, and the Warlis had just made their lives more difficult.

Shapur Irani was right.

The first thing the landlords did was have the Lady of the Red Flag arrested. She was responsible for the changing face of the Warlis. For months, the police found out, she had been walking from village to village talking to the Warlis, uniting them under the Red Flag. In every village the Warlis gave her tea and ambil, they treated her like a god, they listened to every word she had to say, and then *their* words would start.

They were not words. They were mountains.

So strong, they could not be made up.

When he heard their stories, which the landowners described as fabrications of a communist mind, Shapur Irani had to bow his head in shame. In every story, the landowner was the demon. Only the religion of the demon changed. He was either Hindu, Muslim, or Zoroastrian.

In one village, a few miles from Dahanu, a Muslim landlord named Abdul had buried his servant alive because he had broken a mango from the landlord's tree without permission. At first, Abdul had severely beaten the servant, but because a crowd of Warlis had gathered, Abdul decided that the beating was not enough. Since there was a crowd of Warlis, they needed to be put to work. So he made them dig a hole, and they had no idea why they were digging this hole, but when they finished, Abdul tossed this beaten-up but living servant inside, a middle-aged fellow named Sukhar.

The other Warlis were then asked to cover Sukhar with mud. While they did this, Abdul smoked a cigarette. When they finished, they were told to leave their shovels and digging tools on top of the covered hole. They were to get back to work, and if anyone tried to get Sukhar out, he would be in next, lying by Sukhar's side.

But the incident that pummelled Shapur Irani was not a story of violence. It was a story of separation. A young man and woman in love, the man standing outside the granary of a landlord on his wedding night, his head hanging in shame, while his bride was inside, and a landlord inside the bride, only a door separating the man from his wife, sobbing silently for choosing a wife who was beautiful, whom he had to walk with afterwards listening to the sound of crickets, an open moon pouring whatever light it could on them, finally disappearing behind a cloud.

This was the story that made him retch.

What if he had been the groom? What if he had to stand outside a granary while some beast tore his Banu apart?

It was not the Lady of the Red Flag who was bringing the Warlis together. It was acts such as these that sent such a shock through Warli men and women that it awoke their ancestors, made their ghosts rip through the chickoo trees with the speed and darkness of bats.

But the landowners blamed the Lady for the Warli uprising.

And when they heard rumours that she was about to organize a strike, when they heard that she was talking about "rights" and "fair wages" and "the abolishment of the marriage slave," they knew her morale needed to be broken. So the landlords fed the police handsome sums of money, entertained them at their bungalows, gave them the finest whiskey and cigars, and encouraged them to take as many Warli women as they wanted.

The police of Dahanu had never been inspired in such a way before. They went after the Lady of the Red Flag like hyenas chasing raw meat. The landlords had her locked up because she was a rare and dangerous bird, and a bird like her should never be seen, she needed to be in a cage until she lost her colour.

But it could not end there.

While her colours faded, the Warlis needed to be pushed back a few centuries so that even the notion of a strike would seem like complete insanity, a disease that could only end in a slow death.

As Pestonji himself put it, recovering from his head injuries with the quick healing only the promise of revenge could bring, "Now the dams of hell shall break loose." Warli spines would be cracked so hard, neither the Lady nor her Red Flag would ever be able to make the Warlis stand again.

"The landlords are going to create mayhem," Shapur Irani confided to Banu. "They are going to unleash torture unlike ever before. I cannot let that happen."

"Don't get involved in this," said Banu. "Please."

"I have to."

Ever since Vithal's beating under the tree, he had been unable to sleep. He had a dream in which he saw little Ganpat crawl up to him. Tears were trickling down the child's face, and as soon as Shapur Irani picked him up to comfort him,

Ganpat whispered in Shapur Irani's ear, *Good Thoughts, Good Words, Good Deeds.*

As a Zarathushti, he would not let anyone be tortured. He had done it once, and even though Vithal's wife had stolen the money, the punishment was far greater than the crime, many suns and moons greater. If Shapur Irani had dispensed true justice, he would not be haunted by his actions.

This was a chance to redeem himself.

As Vamog had told his son, "Ahura Mazda's light is always available. It is we who choose to stand in the shade."

But Shapur Irani knew that the landlords were not interested in doing the right thing. He needed to find a way to convince them that *not* torturing the Warlis would be to their advantage, that it would help them gain more power.

He said a silent prayer as he stood outside Gustad Mirza's bungalow, where the landlords had all gathered to discuss the Warli situation. He knew that if he did not intervene, goons would be hired and violence would escalate. Then no one would be safe.

When he showed up, everyone was surprised because Shapur Irani had always remained aloof. In fact, he was known to dislike the Parsis, even though the Parsis and Iranis were both Zoroastrians. He considered them to be cowards who were not men of the soil. He thought of the Iranis as superior, true wrestlers, and the Parsis as men sitting at typewriters in Bombay, licking the arses of the British. He secretly envied the Parsis; he admired the names they had made for themselves under the British, as lawyers, scholars, businessmen, tax officials—some of them had even become members of Parliament in England. But education and influence notwithstanding, some of the Parsis were brutal as landlords. Parsis like Gustad Mirza.

All the landlords sat in the living room of Gustad Mirza's sprawling bungalow. It was much bigger than Shapur Irani's, with fancy white cutlery and paintings, roses at each table, teak cupboards with carved designs of lions and elephants, large oval mirrors, and guns hanging on the wall. Kerosene lamps had been lit and placed all over, especially on the porch, to make the bungalow look like it was wearing jewels.

Twenty of the most powerful landowners of Dahanu, including five Muslim landlords and four Hindu ones, were present. There was whiskey, there was chicken, but Shapur Irani was in no mood to eat or drink. He looked at the overfed Parsi faces around him and wanted to piss on them.

Gustad was short, stocky, and bald, with pimple scars on his face. He got up from his chair and shook Shapur Irani's hand. His thick neck gave him a mean and bullish look.

"What brings you here, Shapur?"

"The same thing that has brought all of us here," Shapur Irani replied.

"What's that?" asked Gustad.

"A Warli woman's smelly cunt."

He forced himself to speak like that. He had to pretend to be one of them, crude and heartless. He had to act as though he shared their opinion of the Warlis, that they were servants without souls.

Gustad laughed. Shapur Irani noticed one gold tooth.

"I am here," Shapur Irani said, "because I have heard that you are all planning an attack on the Warlis."

"Not an attack," said Tafti, an old man with thick eyeglasses. "We are disciplining them."

Gustad sat back in his chair and placed his feet on the glass table. His brown leather shoes looked very expensive.

"The Warlis are now getting coverage in the Bombay press," said Gustad. "These journalists cannot be trusted. They ate our food, drank our booze, and then went back and wrote whatever they wanted."

You mean they wrote the truth.

"And now there is talk of the Warlis going on strike," said Gustad. "They need to be whipped back into shape."

"True, true," said Shapur Irani. "They must be crushed. But if we hurt them, our reputation as educated landowners will go down the drain. Violence is not the answer."

"Perhaps we should write them a letter?" asked Gustad. "In the finest calligraphy?"

"Torturing the Warlis will only make us look bad. And it will strengthen their case. You are all men of learning. Surely men of learning do not resort to violence."

"Shapur, get to the point," snarled Gustad.

"We make a speech. We offer to negotiate. That way the journalists will be on our side. We show that we are willing to listen to their terms."

Anything to avoid carnage.

"A peaceful attempt at negotiation must be made on our part," he continued, pushing harder, but not too hard, lest his motives be found out. "If that fails, then we can talk about discipline."

By then, Shapur Irani figured, the press would be involved much more, and it would be hard for the landlords to inflict torture without being exposed to some degree.

"We are the ones in power," he said. "Kings do not get sympathy. By talking, we will seem reasonable."

Gustad folded his arms and leaned back in his chair. Tafti removed his eyeglasses and bit his lip. The Hindu and Muslim landlords shuffled in their cane chairs and pondered Shapur Irani's words.

"Even if we agreed," said Gustad, "your idea won't work. We cannot go from village to village making speeches. The hamlets are too spread out."

"Then gather all the Warlis together. Make one speech."

"Why would they come?" asked Gustad. "They do not trust us."

It was the only iota of truth that Shapur Irani had heard all night. But he had no idea how to get the Warlis together.

"Forget about it," said Pestonji. "I am a fan of Bhagat Singh, not Gandhi. Bring on the violence."

Such was the madness of Pestonji that he would not spare a single tribal. A small bullet of terror punctured Shapur Irani when the Hindu and Muslim landlords nodded their heads.

"But it will be to our benefit," said Shapur Irani. "If we—"

"I am not interested in benefit," said Pestonji. "That bloody whore from the Red Flag is responsible for my head wounds."

It was this statement that gave Shapur Irani an idea.

"If that whore has caused all the problems," he said, "she will also provide a solution."

"What do you mean?" asked Gustad.

"The Warlis love her. They worship her because for once they feel someone is on their side. She has lived with them, she has eaten with them, and she has heard their stories."

"So?"

"She will help us gather the Warlis in one place. We spread a rumour that the Lady of the Red Flag is dying in prison. She is very sick, she is on her deathbed, and she has asked the Warlis to assemble at Dahanu beach three days from now to fight for her release. We make sure the journalists are there to record the event."

"What makes you think the Warlis will show up?"

If an iron rod was shoved up your arse for stealing coconuts, if you were buried alive for breaking a mango off a tree, and if your bride had been taken in a granary by someone just after your wedding, and suddenly a woman showed up from nowhere and gave you hope, the least you would do is assemble on a beach if you heard she was dying.

But he did not say this. His disgust for them was simple, and so was his answer: "They will come."

Shapur Irani was not pleased that he had perpetrated a lie, but the ruse was necessary. It was either that or the spilling of innocent blood. He did not truly expect a gathering to bring about any progress; the landlords were too pigheaded and ruthless for that. But once the press covered it, they would be obliged to report any future violence, and the landlords would be forced to parade a more benign persona.

"This is bullshit," said Pestonji. "I've had to take twenty stitches on my head."

"Perhaps it is worth a try," said Gustad.

"Let's just shoot the bastards!"

"Pestonji, calm down," said Gustad, raising his hand, the firmness in his voice stilling the room. "There is some merit to what the man says. Let's see what happens."

Shapur Irani could only attribute Gustad's acceptance to the will of Ahura Mazda. It took precedence over everything.

Over the next three days, the rumour was spread. Through the foremen, the transport trucks, the trains, the coconut sellers, the landlords' goons, through every single person who had a mouth. When these rumours reached Warli ears, when they heard that the Lady of the Red Flag was dying and needed their help, they started running, running like mad from village to village. The news spread rapidly, and the Warli heart started thumping.

"Where are you going?" asked Banu.

Shapur Irani had put one banana, one apple, and one quarter of RB whiskey in a small brown bag. Banu was hurt that he had packed the fruit on his own, that he had not asked her to do it.

"What are the fruits for?" she asked.

"I'm going on a picnic."

"What picnic?"

"The Picnic of the Landlords."

"What's that supposed to mean?"

"It means I need you to shut up and do your job."

"And what's my job, Shapur?"

"To look after Khodi."

"Am I doing such a terrible job now?"

"Please, Banu. I don't want to argue today. Not today."

"Then tell me where you're going. I worry about you, Shapur. I worry about our son. I worry about . . ."

"About what?"

"If I tell you, promise me you won't get angry."

"It makes me angry just hearing you say that."

"Then I won't tell you."

"Just tell me, Banu. Please."

"It's . . . when you leave the house, I get scared."

"That's why Ejaz is here. He will protect you. He is a fierce Pathan. If he is near you, no one else will come close."

"But Ejaz himself . . . can he be trusted?"

"You're not his type. He does not like plump women."

"I am not plump."

"Yes, you are."

"I am not plump. This is what happens when children are born. The body changes shape. Why don't you try carrying a child?"

"Now, now, don't get upset just because I called you plump."

She smiled at him, gave him a peck on the cheek.

With his brown bag in hand, he waited outside the gate of his farm for Gustad and the other landlords to fetch him. He did not want any of them to enter his farm. He did not want them to see his house, his wife, and least of all his son. Children are inspired by the men around them, and these were not men.

Soon they were at Dahanu beach, and the landlords were in good spirits because five police jeeps were present. When the police superintendent saw Gustad, he got out of his jeep and shook Gustad's hand. Gustad gave him a packet of money. Then they smoked a cigarette together and waited.

"Why are the police here?" asked Shapur Irani.

"To make it look official," said Gustad. "To give the event some weight. If we have journalists, why not the police?"

But Shapur Irani could not see a single journalist. The landlords should have offered to pick them up; the tongas could take forever to bring the journalists to the beach from the train station.

Three hours passed. There was not a soul on Dahanu beach. The pine trees that lined the beach angled in the wind and sand blew in the landlords' faces.

"Where the hell are the journalists?" asked Shapur Irani.

"They're probably drunk," said Gustad.

He did not like Gustad's attitude. Shapur Irani would have contacted the journalists himself, but he was uneducated. The very idea of dealing with newspapers intimidated him.

"Anyway, your plan looks like it's going to flop," said Gustad. "So there won't be any need for journalists."

"The Warlis will come," said Shapur Irani.

"What if they don't?"

"If Ahura Mazda wills it, they will come."

Soon enough, the Warlis appeared through the pine trees with sticks in their hands. There were at least five hundred of them. They were completely silent. Then more Warli men emerged. Now there were a thousand. Most of them wore loincloths and had their long hair tied in knots. They saw the police vans, they saw the landlords, but did not stop. They kept on marching, and Shapur Irani was pleased that his plan had worked.

"Look at all these men," said Gustad. "The Lady of the Red Flag has a magic cunt."

But Shapur Irani detected fear in Gustad's voice. The sight of three thousand silent Warlis had left all the landlords in awe. All this time, they had raped or tortured a single Warli. When they came in droves, it was another matter.

"What's that in their hands?" asked Gustad.

Each Warli had a stone in his hand, which he dropped to the ground. Within minutes there were three thousand stones.

"It's their way of showing solidarity," said the police superintendent. "They want to show how many Warlis have come. It's perfect for us. To us, the stones are weapons."

"What are you talking about?" asked Shapur Irani.

But no one answered him. Gustad could not look Shapur Irani in the eye.

The police superintendent was sweaty. He wiped his palms on his faded brown trousers.

"Did you even ask the journalists to come?" asked Shapur Irani.

"I did, but they were busy," replied Gustad.

"Doing what?"

"Writing."

Shapur Irani's ears were going hot. If Gustad's support the other night had not been sincere, why were they all here?

Then Shapur Irani saw the Warlis again, sitting on the flat ground that came before the pine trees, fearlessly, so close to the police jeeps, and a sick realization dawned on him.

"Start firing," said Gustad.

"No," said Shapur Irani. "What . . ."

"Men, get on top of your jeeps," said the superintendent.

"No!" said Shapur Irani.

"Shoot the bastards," said Gustad. "Every single one of them."

The superintendent and his men went on the roofs of their jeeps and started firing. The Warlis had no idea what was going on. Suddenly, someone would slump and his chest would have a hole in it. Or the eye would have a bullet. Shapur Irani held the superintendent back, but it made no difference. The firing eventually stopped on its own, on account of the pathetic condition that the guns were in. The Warlis picked up the stones and hurled them at the jeeps. They came with their sticks, and then the second round of firing started. This time it was much shorter. Some of the Warlis started running towards the pine trees while others just stood dumbfounded.

Shapur Irani could see the forlorn look on their faces.

Why did their Lady call them here? Where was she?

"Now let's get out of here," said the superintendent. "I have to make a call to Bombay and tell them about the violence here that we barely escaped. We must all tell the same story. This is what happened: We were given a tip. We came here, not knowing what to expect, under-armed. Three thousand Warlis attacked us with sticks and stones. We had to fire and kill a few, but there were too many of them so we had to retreat."

"And they broke your men's noses," said Gustad.

"Ah yes, good, good," said the superintendent. "You three, come here."

He called three of his men, raised the butt of his gun, and broke their noses. "You were hit by Warlis. Each of you can shoot one Warli."

The men took their guns and went berserk. They shot aimlessly, but luckily by then the Warlis were on the run. Shapur Irani thought they might shoot the superintendent in anger.

But he had them under his control. He then asked his men to batter their own jeeps. "Not too hard. Make it look like the jeeps were attacked with sticks. Break only one headlight," he said. "Not my jeep."

The landlords were pleased. At least some Warlis had been killed. Maybe only a few, but it was something.

"Now they will doubt the intentions of the Red Flag," said Gustad. "They will think their Lady led them to this."

Shapur Irani saw his bag of fruit lying on the floor of Gustad's jeep. He did not feel hungry or thirsty. Gustad had beads of perspiration on his bald pate. He was quiet, but smiling. Shapur Irani curled his hand into a fist, but he had no strength to strike Gustad. All he could think of were the bodies that lay on Dahanu beach, bodies that he was responsible for. He started to shake.

He could not believe that goodness could lead to shaking.

This was not the only betrayal on the landlords' part. Gustad, Tafti, Pestonji—and the Hindu and Muslim landlords—had hatched another plan of their own. Like snakes laying eggs, they must have hatched it the minute Shapur Irani left Gustad's bungalow the night of the meeting.

It was Ejaz the Pathan who told Shapur Irani about it as soon as he got home.

In order to avenge the killing of Pestonji's horses and the beating that ensued, Gustad asked his foreman, a hefty bhaiyya named Sitaram, to recruit all the foremen of the neighbouring farms and hire some goons.

They had found out which hamlet the men who had attacked Pestonji lived in. It was close to Shapur Irani's farm. In the early hours of the morning, when the Warli men were to leave for Dahanu beach, Gustad handed the money to Sitaram and told him, "Take this money and get drunk. Drink like you have never drunk before. Then go destroy the huts, do what you want. I am giving you a chance to be king for a day."

So while the women were preparing ambil in the morning, removing lice from their children's hair, pouring water into the fowl pits for the goats and chickens, Sitaram and company's assault began. Their fury had the stench of liquor and their appetite was massive.

One of the men who had killed Pestonji's horses, the leader of that group, was a well-known witch doctor. His hut was the first casualty. After the goons left, his wife came running to Shapur Irani's farm. She had been looking after little Ganpat and his mother that day. The goons had caused the death of Ganpat's baby sister.

There was more.

But Shapur Irani did not want to hear any of it. This was enough.

He realized Gustad and his lot were even worse than he thought. And to think that they had tried to recruit Ejaz the Pathan as well for this job.

"Why did you not go?" he asked Ejaz.

He could not believe how shrill his voice sounded, how lacerated his throat was.

"I am here to protect your wife and child," said Ejaz. "You would do the same for me."

"Where is Banu?" asked Shapur Irani.

"She is in the house."

"Where is Banu?" he asked again. Ejaz's words hardly reached him.

"Seth, she is in the house. No outsider will come on this farm as long as I am alive. That is my promise to you."

Shapur Irani started to walk towards his bungalow. His head was spinning.

With each step he took, he was losing his balance. He could not afford to stumble in front of Ejaz. Shapur Irani wanted to run. To his home, his wife, he wanted to run anywhere. But he could not do it in Ejaz's presence.

"Seth, I want to talk to you about my son," said Ejaz.

"My son is fine," said Shapur Irani. "He's fine."

The wind was drumming against his ears.

"No, seth," said Ejaz. "*My* son."

There were bodies lying on the beach. Their eyes had bullet holes in them which would soon be covered by sand.

"Seth," said Ejaz.

The wind was so harsh, and yet not a single leaf moved.

"Seth . . ." Ejaz lightly touched the tip of Shapur Irani's elbow.

Shapur Irani whirled around.

"How dare you touch me," he said. "You . . ."

"Seth, I—"

"You are a servant. Know your place."

The day was a mess. All laws were being broken, crushed like bones under cars.

When Shapur Irani reached his bungalow, the door was open. He had told Banu not to keep the door open a hundred bloody times, but she never listened.

No one was in the living room. He went past the living room into the first bedroom, then into the second where they slept, but the bed was empty. Then into the kitchen, but there was no sign of his wife and son. He rushed back to the living room and saw Banu standing at the door with Khodi in her arms. He went to her, he wanted to put his arms around her, but could not. He had sand in his chappals. He took his chappals off, went to the window, and slapped them against each other to shake the sand off.

Then he went to the bedroom and started undressing.

"How was it?" she asked.

The question deafened him. It would take him years to answer that question. He begged Ahura Mazda not to let any tears form.

"Why are you silent, Shapur?" asked Banu. "What happened?"

"Nothing . . ."

Speaking was crippling. But he mustered up the strength to say more, otherwise Banu would panic.

"Either the Warlis will get violent, or they will be frightened into submission."

She was relieved to hear him speak. He could tell from the way her eyes relaxed.

"You know why I am plump?" she asked.

"No."

"Because I am pregnant, you big fool."

He sat the edge of the bed, sand between his toes. He needed to wash it off as quickly as possible.

"Say something," said Banu. "Why are you silent?"

"Because I am happy," he replied.

For the next few days, Shapur Irani stayed in bed.

He lived there as though it was his own country, a continent on which he could make no mistakes. All he could do was rest his head on a pillow and cover his eyes with his arm. These were simple actions that could not lead to bloodshed or anything else unpleasant. Nothing he did on this bed could cause anyone to die. It was safe, a womb in which he could float for as long as he liked.

He would have stayed there if it were not for Banu.

She walked through the house lighting divas, staring at the small flame, begging the light to absorb all the sadness that had entered her husband, sadness that had been brought by bad spirits, and she had faith that the divas would take the darkness away, cleanse his aura, so he could rise again and be the man she loved so much.

He could not let her down. And so, when he saw the falling leaves outside his window, Shapur Irani rose, ate eggs and meat, drank milk, and polished off a quarter of whiskey in an hour.

Once he went outside the house, he realized that he was mistaken about the falling leaves. Those were not leaves. They were his beloved chickoos that had fallen to the ground in thousands.

"Look at that," he told Banu. "A whole carpet of chickoos."

"The Warlis will eventually come for work," said Banu. "They need to eat too. They also need to survive."

He did not blame his workers for not showing up. They were no doubt still reeling from the attack on the beach.

"What am I to do? Who will gather fruit? All this maal falling to the ground . . ."

"Come, sleep next to me," said Banu. "Talk to your son."

"Khodi's sleeping."

"Not this son. Talk to the one in my stomach. We will call him Sohrab."

"Why are you so sure he is a boy?"

Shapur Irani lay next to his wife, but he was far from comforted.

A carpet of chickoos covered the ground and not a single worker to pick them up. In a way, he was glad. Gustad and the other landlords would feel the pinch. They had much more land than he did, thousands of trees, and he hoped they would see the chickoos rotting on the ground and think about what they had done.

At night, Warlis travelled in groups and started hacking down chickoo trees.

They spat on the chickoo and swore never to eat it again, even if they were dying of hunger, even if they became so thin that their ribs ripped through their skin and plunged into the chests of their own wives when they embraced.

It did not surprise Shapur Irani. He would have done the same.

Perhaps it was only natural that the chickoo had led to so much pain. It had been brought to India by the Portuguese. A tree transplanted by plunderers could only lead to more illness.

The only good thing that came of it was the attack on Gustad Mirza's bungalow.

Even though his granary was full of grain and eggs, the Warlis set fire to it all. Consuming his food would be like taking nourishment from the very thing that their children had bled for. But he had enough goons to drive the Warlis away. While he reclined on his sofa, rested his arm on the carved back of a lion or elephant, his men ensured his safety.

Some Warlis went after Ejaz the Pathan.

By the time Shapur Irani got to Ejaz's shack, the bleeding Pathan was standing with the wooden club by his side, his body heaving up and down like a panther's.

Nothing could kill him.

After three nights of hitting back, the Warlis went home and told their wives and children to run to the jungles and hide so that no one could touch them.

The hamlets were empty. Only faint smoke rose from burning leaves.

Now Gustad Mirza made sure that he got in touch with the journalists from Bombay. Encouraged by a deft bribe or two, the papers spoke of the cruel heart of the Warlis, and how they had hacked down chickoo trees and destroyed the landlords' homes without the slightest regard for their wives and children who slept inside.

The police were employed and men were picked up at random, thrown into jail, and severely beaten. Anyone who spoke of the Red Flag was considered a conspirator, so no one spoke of the Lal Bauta again.

But in prison, the Lady of the Red Flag knew the true course of events. She called the policewalas "motherless sons." Anyone who had a mother would not raise a hand on innocents, she screamed. But her words made no difference to the superintendent. He told her to look outside the window of her cage, at his jeeps. Then he brought policemen in front of her, men with broken noses. "See their noses," he said. "You cannot help animals, O Lady of the Red Flag."

Even though her anger could break dams, she did not call for violent action.

She called for an indefinite strike. The landlords had no hearts, but they had pockets.

Each year, the rice season provided a vast amount of money for the landlords. If the chickoo trees and rice fields were not harvested in time, they would incur a loss of thousands of rupees. When the landlords realized what was happening, they tried to use force again. But this time the men did not mind dying. They refused to pluck chickoos or harvest rice.

Even though Shapur Irani was losing money too, he secretly admired the resilience of the Warlis. Every man had a gladiator in him. No matter how feeble, how poor, how scared.

"Why not give in to their demands?" asked Banu. "What do the tribals want?"

"They want higher wages. They want all their debts to be cancelled. They want the torture to stop."

"Then do it," she said.

"The landlords are afraid that any change could take away their life of luxury."

"Shapur, you call this luxury? Living here, alone, on this farm? You know they attacked Ejaz who lives so close by. They could have attacked us."

Suddenly there was acid in her voice. It had shot out, left a few droplets on his cheek.

"I will never let anything happen to you or the children, I promise," he said.

He got up from the bed and went to the cupboard. It was a teak cupboard with the words "There is nothing like love" engraved on it. Shapur Irani liked the double meaning of this line. He had bought this cupboard from an old Iranian who was broke and had only his furniture left to sell. Perhaps the words "There is nothing like love" were bitter words to the old Iranian, but to Shapur Irani the line was true. He loved his wife and child so much that there was terror in his love. He opened the cupboard and enjoyed the creaking sound it made. When the door of the cupboard was fully open, he moved aside and said to Banu, "Look at this." It was a shotgun, a long one, with a thick handle and a shiny barrel.

"Where did you get that?" she asked.

"You know I don't like guns," he said.

"Then why is this in the house?"

"I am a strong man, but if twenty Warlis break into this house, I can't protect you unless I shoot them."

"Then let us go away from this place."

"What?"

"Just for a short while. Let's stay with my mother in Bombay. Once everything settles down, we can come back."

"I will *never* leave Dahanu. Do you understand? Don't ever ask me to leave."

"But, Shapur . . ."

"Do you even know what I have been through in Iran? My father was once beaten. The Arabs treated us like servants. We had to walk with our heads down in their presence."

"I'm just saying it for the protection of our son. And with another one on the way . . ."

"I will protect him!"

Banu knew now was the time to keep quiet.

His temper was like gasoline. If she spoke even a word more, then she would provide the match and he would hurt himself. She knew he would never hurt her, but her husband was dangerous to himself. He once banged his head against the wall in anger and she had no idea why.

He walked about the room holding his gun. "You don't understand what it's like. I've found a home here. This is *my* land. I was driven out of Iran. When I left Iran, I left a home. Don't ask me to do it again!"

He started loading the gun in front of her.

She wanted to say something to him, but she held her son's hand in the hope that it would calm her. Once the gun was loaded, Shapur Irani stormed out of the main door and started firing in the air.

The strike kept on going. Like a black train on a long, unending journey.

With each passing day, the carpet of chickoos grew thicker.

Not being able to watch his fruit die, Shapur Irani spent his time at the train station, drinking tea, chatting with the station master, catching a glimpse of passengers through the iron grilles of their windows. But no matter where he went, his mind was on the carpet that awaited him at the farm. Light brown at first, then dark, wet with rottenness.

It was futile to pack a few baskets himself. Some Warlis were willing to work for five times the daily wage, but Shapur Irani refused to employ them because by breaking the strike they were letting their own people down. A few even got jobs as foremen, making deals with landlords, ensuring that their debts were fully cancelled, in exchange for which they would force their own tribesmen to work on the farm.

Nothing was clean.

When the train came in from Bombay, the complaint was the same.

The shortage of rice was hitting Bombay hard.

Bombay. That was all anyone cared about. The city produced nothing but consumed everything, and farmers like him were supposed to be grateful for it.

Just as he was about to leave the train station, he saw the superintendent. He was strolling about the platform, sipping coconut water with the buoyancy of a tourist. All he needed was a straw hat to make his vulgarity complete. Shapur Irani wanted to give him a set of binoculars to help him focus on the bullets he had let fly, on the shards of bone, on the droplets of darkened blood that lay on the ground. He could not bear to be near the superintendent. Even the sight of him made Shapur Irani feel that the superintendent was an extension of himself, a limb that had lost its way.

But he stayed and listened because the superintendent had news.

"The Lady of the Red Flag has been released from jail," he said. "It's those bastard journalists. They took photographs of the dead bodies and were about to print them in the papers."

It burned Shapur Irani to see the superintendent pulling his pants up, looking around with an air of lazy authority.

"When the politicians in Bombay got wind of this," he continued, "they decided it would not be wise to print the photos.

The British are still here. We cannot show a divided India. So they reached a compromise. The Lady has been released from prison."

That was not all. Some of her demands had been met.

A law was passed that all previous debts were to be cancelled. There would be no bonded labour from that day on, no marriage slaves. A uniform, fixed daily wage was decided.

The Lady of the Red Flag had asked for one more law to be passed, that no landlord could buy land from the tribals. During the famine that had hit the state of Maharashtra hard, the landlords had bought Warli land for a pittance. An empty belly and a weakness for liquor had caused many Warlis to senselessly leave their thumb impressions on stamp paper.

Nothing could be done about it now, but this could be prevented in the future. However, this law was not passed.

Still, victory had been hers. The faith the tribals had shown in her had made her transform from Lady to tigress.

The landlords had given in at her roar.

From a prison cell, she had fought the likes of Gustad and Pestonji. She had dug her fingernails deep into the backs of all the Hindu and Muslim landlords who had mocked her.

She might not have ripped their backs, but she had left a mark.

When Shapur Irani got to his farm, he stood outside Vithal's hut.

Place and events did not always match. Here he was, standing under the shade of a coconut tree, nightingales above him, his shoulders warmed by the shy rays of evening light, while Vithal and his wife mourned the death of their baby girl, a loss that would never have any meaning.

Nothing could heal the hearts in that hut.

No one would be able to warm their core, which had turned hollow. They would never be able to straighten their necks again, so bent with sorrow their shape resembled that of a scythe.

Nothing could heal Shapur Irani either.

He would have been better off if he had not cared.

From now on, he would make sure that he distanced himself from the Warlis completely. He would think of them as phantoms just passing through, letting out sounds of pain, as perhaps nature itself had intended, just as the nightingales above him let out sounds of love.

He could do nothing for them. Maybe he was never meant to.

The Warlis had found their champion in the Lady of the Red Flag. He could feel her walking through the villages again, listening to stories of loss.

SEVEN

2000

SLEEP CAME AND WENT in great swoops as Zairos saw red flags swaying in the wind—on the roofs of Warli huts, in the shrivelled hands of old men, tied around the horns of bullocks, draped across the faces of children, or caught in trees like kites that had been cut loose.

He was relieved to finally wake up.

Downstairs, Aspi Irani was reading *The Times of India*. He was grouchy because the barn next door had been recently converted into a Pentecostal church. It did not resemble a church at all, for it had no steeple, stained glass, or prayer books, but there emerged from it the sound of wailing, and this irritated Aspi Irani to no end.

To distract himself from the passionate cries of the churchgoers, he glanced through the obituaries to see whether anyone he knew had died. This was a pastime of his, and when he did discover a dead acquaintance, he let out a tsk-tsk to show his regret and said something pleasant or derogatory about the deceased depending on his view of them.

"There's no one today," he said. "Looks like people are taking their vitamins."

Mithoo was at the stove cooking mutton pulav and fish. She had a cream scarf around her head to prevent the smell of cooking from entering her hair. The gold bangle on her wrist hit the rim of the large steel container as she stirred the brown rice with wide eyes and an even wider smile.

"I'm glad you've had a bath," she told Zairos. "It's Nouruz today."

"In exactly five minutes," said Aspi Irani, who had worn new blue jeans and sudreh, and had a red prayer cap on his head. He rose from his chair and loosened his kusti around his waist. He had tied the sacred thread too tight.

Zairos had forgotten that it was Nouruz. The Zoroastrian New Year was celebrated on the twenty-first of March at the exact moment the sun crossed the equator, making day and night of equal duration. That was when Zoroastrian families from India to Azerbaijan ushered in the light of spring together, then called their loved ones around the world and yelled into the phone, "Nouruz Mubarak!"

Aspi Irani always made it a point to call people at the wrong time. Last year, he woke his friend Nari in Melbourne at three in the morning and screamed, "Happy Nouruz!" Nari, a neurosurgeon who truly relished his sleep, stumbled for words because Aspi Irani chided him for miscalculating the vernal equinox. "Those brain operations have made you lose touch with your roots," he said with a chuckle.

Mithoo had prepared the traditional Nouruz table in a corner of the living room. On a green cloth that had been embroidered by her mother lay a copy of the sacred Avesta, along with the Haft-Sin, seven items beginning with the Farsi letter S. Amongst these, Zairos knew the significance of only four— the seb, or apple, was for health and beauty; sabzeh, or wheat sprouts, represented rebirth; serke, or vinegar, warded off any bitterness that life might bring; and sekke, or coins, symbolized prosperity.

Mithoo lit three candles to signify the goodness of thought, word, and deed.

She kept looking at the wall clock every minute or so. She did not want to miss the exact moment. "The sun is approaching the equator," Aspi Irani started, gaining momentum like the commentator of a horse race, "it's coming round the bend and passing Kazakhstan, and now it's zooming ahead of Kyrgyzstan, then Afghanistan, it's taking a left turn towards Pakistan, and now it's crossed Kashmir, and oh, it's only a furlong short of the equator, dear Mithoo, only a furlong short."

Zairos stood with his parents at the table and watched a goldfish in a bowl—the goldfish was part of the ceremonial setting as well. There were sweets, dried fruit, naan, a slice of watermelon, a glass of wine, and a large mirror with its face up, a hard-boiled egg placed in the middle of it.

Mithoo held the mirror in her hand and made Zairos look into it.

"Smile, my son," she said, "so you'll be smiling all year round."

Zairos did as he was told, but apparently it was not enough.

"What kind of smile is that?" she asked. "Show me some teeth."

Then Mithoo took a thin silver bottle the shape of a minaret and sprinkled rosewater over her son's head and face. After kissing him on both cheeks, she said, "Now get married to a sweet Zoroastrian girl."

"No thanks," said Zairos. "I'm suffering enough."

"Look at this idiot. Not at all concerned about his future," she said to her husband. "Won't he need someone to look after him in his old age?"

"True," said Aspi Irani. "But what if his wife gets a stroke? Then Zairos will have to wipe *her* bum for the rest of his life."

"Aspi, please," said Mithoo. "It's Nouruz. Say something auspicious. You bring the whole ceremony to a depressing halt."

"My dear, if Alexander the Great and the Taliban could not prevent Zoroastrians from celebrating Nouruz, what chance do I have?"

"Give me one more kiss," Mithoo said to Zairos. "Now please get me some grandchildren. I'm preparing for my Montessori exam. I need someone to practise on."

The three of them stood around the table again, as Mithoo lit an oil lamp and closed her eyes in prayer, and Aspi Irani walked through the house with an afarganyu, spreading smoky incense that had the most delectable smell. When they were done, Zairos hugged his parents.

"Now eat something sweet," said Mithoo. "And may you carry that sweetness with you for the rest of the year."

When Zairos reached out to eat a raisin from the table, he caught a glimpse of himself in the mirror again. His reflection was a reminder that he was fortunate to have a life like this. But there had to be a reason for good fortune. Good fortune, if it was not shared, would soon turn to dust. Like a daily wage, it had to be earned. If blessings were showered upon a man, it was to inspire him to take a risk.

There was a reason his grandfather had told him about the War of the Warlis the night before Nouruz. The word *no-ruz* meant "new day." It was a sign that Zairos needed to take up the gauntlet. The sumac on the table before him, he now remembered, symbolized a new dawn.

He was careful not to step on the designs of red and blue chalk that his mother had made on the threshold, along with the words "Nouruz Mubarak" written in white. He walked through the front door, caressing the garland of fresh jasmine and red roses that hung above him.

He needed to meet Kusum.

Spring had come. It was a time for change.

The smell of cow dung greeted Zairos at his grandfather's bungalow. Manure had been emptied from the back of a large transport truck until it formed a huge mound.

Reminders were truly everywhere.

Pestonji and Noshir Irani had hidden the body of the Warli man who stole their coconuts in cow dung. It had made the anger of the tribals reach its zenith. Zairos wondered what would happen to him if he saw someone he loved, someone like Bumble, lying there with his Ray-Bans shattered, or Hosi with his Colt's racing form, his hand sticking out in a dying grasp for help.

It made him shudder.

He distracted himself by watching Damu, who was standing on top of the mound, his feet pressed into the dung as though he were crushing grapes in a tub. The dung was to be distributed among the trees as fertilizer. Damu wore an "I ♥ NY" T-shirt. As soon as Aspi Irani had returned from his most recent holiday, rats had crocheted their way into the fabric and rendered the T-shirt fit for Warli use. Damu, of course, had no clue what NY was, but it surprised Zairos that Damu did not know what the ♥ represented either.

Zairos walked over to the bathtubs.

But instead of Kusum, he spotted a dead bat hanging upside down. In daylight, the bat looked unreal, a soft toy, something that would make a sound when squeezed. It was the farm workers' catch, lunch that would be claimed soon. The workers tied nylon strings horizontally between two trees, and at night bats would fly right through them, cut a wing and fall, and get caught on a hook that was suspended just below.

Kusum soon appeared, a long bamboo stick strung across her shoulders. Two steel buckets filled to the brim with chickoos hung at each end of the bamboo stick. The load was heavy, but she did not falter.

She had a white flower in her hair. Zairos could not remember its name.

"I want to talk to you," said Zairos.

"Yes, seth . . ."

She put the buckets down, let the bamboo stick fall to the ground.

"I want you to come with me," he said.

She looked down at her ankles. They were wet and her feet were covered with mud.

"There's no need to be afraid," he said. "Walk with me."

She followed him, making sure she was never in the same line as him. When they got to his red Maruti, he opened the door for her and said, "Sit."

"Where are we going?" she asked as she got in the car. "The workers will ask for me."

"Do you feel uncomfortable with me?" he asked. "Are you scared?"

"No," she replied.

When Zairos drove past Aspi Villa, he waved out to his mother, who was swaying on the swing with the abandon of a schoolgirl. She would assume he was taking a worker to the doctor. He did that from time to time.

Near the station, matkas were on sale, the owner of the earthen pots asleep on a chair, his body limp like spinning clay that had suddenly been abandoned. A woman who owned a sugar-cane stall was sweeping the floor, clearing wafer packets, newspapers, and plastic bags.

Along the beach, young girls in colourful cholis collected water from old wells.

Barbed-wire fence bordered the sandy beach. When Zairos was little, there were no fences, the sea just lay there, open and welcoming, and its froth gave them hope. During low tide, jellyfish sparkled in the sun, mini spaceships that had landed flat on their faces.

The fishing village sent its odour to everyone while leather-faced fishermen slept under straw roofs. Where the village ended, the shoreline expanded, the boulders with smooth wet surfaces, licked by waves, salt burning under the sun. Once they passed the animal hospital and the white windmill, the wired fences stopped, leaving only trees and bullock carts. The land was free, and only the occasional coconut grove broke the monotony of the blue.

Zairos stopped the car at the edge of a small stream, a spot he had found years ago by accident, where the land sloped upwards at first, then dropped suddenly. He turned the car off and everything was quiet. An eagle soared high above them, circled the car.

The way light fell on her face and arms, through the windshield, it made Zairos feel that her beauty was an accident, and she carried it in the manner one carried an extra growth, like a horn or claw. It weighed her down, made her existence more painful. Kusum's beauty elevated her far beyond the ordinary. It was the gods laughing at her.

"Seth, I know what you want," she said. "But I am married."

Her voice sounded unusual in the car. Zairos had only heard her speak amidst trees and water, birds and soil. All along she had been supported by nature, or perhaps fooled into thinking that she had a voice to begin with.

"It's not like that," said Zairos.

"I can see it in your eyes, seth."

"What is your husband's name?"

"Laxman."

They stayed there and watched a buffalo enter the stream— the rip of its black muscles, its horns capable of piercing a bird in the stomach and yanking out the innards.

Zairos had driven so far only to be told her husband's name. She kept rubbing her right ankle with the sole of her left foot, the dirt falling onto the black rubber mat.

There was nothing to do except put the car into gear. The buffalo turned towards them, disturbed by the gnashing of wheels against the earth. The sudden movement of the car startled Kusum as well, but she said nothing.

When Zairos got close to home, a train pulled up at the station, and young boys sold mineral water from the train tracks. Someone threw a newspaper out of the train window. Passengers were packed close together, one collective mass of sweat, inhaling-exhaling at the same time. The sight was suffocating. The roof of the train was the only spot that offered solace.

When the car stopped outside his grandfather's bungalow, Kusum got out without saying a word. Zairos felt deflated. Once again, he had been impulsive, weakened by the scent of Nouruz roses and jasmine. Kusum shut the door but did not walk away. She bent down and looked at Zairos through the open window.

"Seth," she said. "Meet me here in the night."

She walked away from him, the sweat on her exposed back making her skin glimmer, helping Zairos realize that his hunger for her was obvious. She saw it, she called it, and the muscles of her back were strong and inviting. And then slowly whip marks started to appear, one by one, and he felt ashamed that he wanted to lick that same back, because he would be licking her wounds, wounds that his own people had inflicted, and for now all he could do was wait for night.

If Anna's chai stall catered to the stomach, the Big Boss Hair Salon catered to the head. The belly taken care of by Anna's vada-pavs, nothing could help Zairos more right now, as he waited for evening to turn into night, than a head massage.

DAHANU ROAD

Big Boss was a unisex hair salon, but Zairos had never seen a single woman there. It was a small shop in Katy Nagar, one of the first apartment complexes to go up in Dahanu, in the early eighties. The salon had yellow walls—the pale yellow of teeth—that gave off a smell like morning breath. A poster on the wall displayed photos of male and female hair models along with a list of the different types of haircuts and beauty treatments available. There was the Clean Shave, the Semi-Shave, the After-Perm, the Face Mask, the Peel Off, the Body Massage, the Face Massage, the Bob Cut, and the Diana Cut.

Hosi sat in a blue swivel chair outside the salon. Sponge oozed out of its seat in abundance. Bumble, his curly hair rendered rock hard by the high speeds on his BMW, was getting a haircut from Sharmaji, the owner of the salon, with eyeglasses so large they could be magnifying glasses. Sharmaji was using a blade to shave the back of Bumble's neck. Bumble's friend Murtaza was present too. He was angry with his wife because she had failed to tell him that she had been wearing coloured contact lenses throughout their courtship. Upon discovering on his wedding night only two days ago that his wife's eyes were not blue, the gangly Murtaza had wandered around looking shell-shocked.

Sharmaji's son, a teenaged boy named Paresh with one earring and torn jeans, first spread a thick layer of Parachute coconut oil on his hands and then rubbed it into Zairos' scalp. "Your scalp is too dry," he said. Zairos knew the boy was right because he could feel his head sucking up all the coconut oil and thirsting for more. Then Paresh started his magic. He turned his fingers into claws and massaged Zairos' head with the speed of a whirring fan. His massage was gentle at first, he was telling

121

the muscles in Zairos' head to wake up from their slumber, and once they were up he was the conductor of an opera, powerful and glorious. Zairos' head sang and sang, images came and went. Then his body went into a slump, and he kept slumping in his chair and Paresh kept pulling his neck up without ever disturbing that feeling of lazy magnificence.

In the tranquility of the massage, he heard Kusum's voice, "Meet me here in the night," and it excited him.

"What are you dreaming about?" asked Bumble.

"Nothing," said Zairos.

"Why don't you get a haircut? It's too long. Not manly, boss."

"I like it long."

"You like looking like a woman?" asked Hosi. "Sharmaji, give him the Diana Cut."

Hosi dug his finger into a hole in the seat of the chair and came out with sponge. Bumble looked in the mirror and dusted the white powder off the back of his neck. Murtaza stared in the mirror too, but he was talking to himself, perhaps questioning his decision to marry a woman who had not revealed the true colour of her eyes.

"I'm selling my farm," said Hosi. "I'm done with farming. I've had it."

"With what?" asked Zairos.

"It's the end, boss. That chimney is killing our farms."

He was talking about the thermal power plant that supplied electricity to Bombay, its chimney looming over the heads of all farm owners like a 900-foot curse. The chickoo, which used to be an all-season fruit, had become moody. On some winter mornings, instead of fresh dew, leaves were covered with black ash. The fruit vendors in Bombay were complaining that the chickoos had pin-sized holes in them and no one wanted to buy fruit that had already been feasted upon by worms.

"I'm barely breaking even," said Hosi. "I'd prefer to put the money in a bank. It's a safer bet."

"You mean horses are safer," said Bumble.

"Either the trees will kill me or the horses will kill me," said Hosi. "Rather be killed by something I love."

At the mention of love, high up in a tree, egrets nuzzled their beaks into the soft white of their skin, cleaning their feathers, preparing themselves for breeding. They glowed like evening moons trapped among the leaves. When the egrets started chattering, no other sound could be heard, such was their ardour.

Slowly, dusk began to cast its veil on the Dahanu sky. The lights of Hotel Sagar came on, a gaudy necklace of green and red on crumbling walls. Housewives stepped out of Video King with rentals in their hands, not satisfied with the soap operas of their own lives. A young boy delivered chai in small steel cups to the shop owners in Katy Nagar, and a cyclist made his way up the bridge with a bagful of leather slippers on the carrier. A vendor approached the salon, his whole shop slung around his body—combs, brushes, hand mirrors, bindis, mousetraps, matches, and rubber balloons—combinations that made no sense at all. Resigned to fate, he carried whatever his body could support.

Zairos felt frozen in a similar manner. Dusk was the worst time to be alive in Dahanu. He could not understand his fear of dusk. The air became cooler and lights came on in two-storeyed apartment buildings, a sudden snap, a reminder that the sun had left.

Zairos could sense a sound rising above the celebration of the egrets, a heavy growl, a meanness, and he felt it was the thermal power plant breathing, eating coal and throwing up smoke, its ash covering the chickoo trees like a cloth placed over a corpse.

As fog filled the sky and smothered the date palm trees, Kusum tended to a sick cow. It had not been eating for three days, and when she opened its mouth, it was full of sores. Molasses was all the cow could eat until the sores healed.

Inside her hut, a small bulb spread its light apologetically.

Her husband had hooked a piece of tar around the wire of a nearby electric pole and had attached the other end to the bulb. A neighbour of hers ran a black-and-white television in this manner, but it came at a cost. One of her sons had been electrocuted while trying to steal a connection.

She saw Laxman approach, and was glad that the food was ready.

He had white dust all over his face from the hours spent digging up roads and carrying stones in a metal container on his head. On some days, he walked with the swagger of a foreman, while on others he trudged along in search of better days. On some days, he was a decent man. He had the straightforward eyes of a man who had a wife and a hut, a cow, some utensils, a clothesline, a watch, shorts, long pants, sandals, vests, and two green shirts.

He even made her laugh by telling her folk tales that always included rain, a python, and a baby. Sometimes he stood up and enacted the whole thing for her. He would become the rain, the python, the baby, the trees, the soil, the sky, everything, and that is what she thought a man should be, everything.

It was her father who had chosen Laxman for her.

He came home one day and said to her, "You will be married soon."

She was only twelve. She was about to ask why, but her father provided the answer: "He is giving us two goats."

She looked at her mother, but all her mother said was, "It is time."

At her first meeting with Laxman, she had clung to her mother's leg. She held on to that leg with all her might and begged her mother to take her home. Slowly, the boy came towards her and angled his head this way and that way to take a look at her face.

That very day, the boy took her home.

He looked at her closely, followed her every move, as though she was something valuable. Kusum kept hoping her father would come and fetch her. This boy had torn her away from her mother's leg, and her mother had allowed him to.

It was unlike the pain she had felt when she fell down, or the time she had banged her head against the earthen pot.

So when the boy was not looking, she ran.

She found a bush and hid there all night. From now on, she would never cling to her mother's leg again. All she heard that night, apart from the insects and creatures whose bush it was, were her father's words, "He is giving us two goats."

In the morning, she came out of the bush. She had to—she was pulled out by the boy himself. He slapped her hard, his hand hit her ear, and there was a deep ringing, like once when she had stood outside a landlord's house with her father and a steel vessel had fallen to the floor.

He took her home and stared at her again.

This time he did not let her out of his sight. He was older and stronger than her; he was not a boy, he was a man.

He told her to stop shaking. So she remained very still.

He was breathing like a boar in the wild, the ones her father had taught her to be so careful of.

After he was done, he pushed himself off her.

She had started crying by then and he did not know how to calm her down, so he gave her a green comb. Then another one, black. Finally, an orange comb. One by one, he put three combs in her hand. When her tears still did not stop, he took one comb from her hand, the orange one, and started to comb her hair.

That was many years ago.

Laxman had never combed her hair since then.

Now, as he approached the hut, she saw the strength in his limbs. Although thin, they were sinewy, like a jungle cat's, and energetic veins lined his biceps.

"I heard you spoke to the council chairman," he said to her. "Again."

When he was drunk, he lost his sense of distance. He came too close to her, his lips touched her ear when he spoke.

"Yes," she said.

It was always better to answer him. The thing that made Laxman livid was no answer.

"The village council is *my* friend," he said. "They will not grant you a divorce, do you understand?"

She knew it was a mistake to go to the sarpanch. It was his job to settle relationship disputes, but the chairman was not going to support her, even though she had just lost her father. It was like asking an old weak man to carry a fort on his back.

But she did it for another reason.

She did it to humiliate Laxman. Even though they were married for so many years, there was no child. She felt there had been a child once, but it disappeared because he used to box her in the gut so often.

"Did you tell the sarpanch that you pay more attention to the cow than your own husband?"

Now was the time to not answer.

Now was the time to clean. As the evening light all but disappeared, she picked up a straw broom that she had made from the leaves of the date palm. She started sweeping the floor, a flat mixture of brown mud and cow dung. She focused on the floor of the hut, swept it clean of ants and dead mosquitoes.

"I can get any woman I want," he said.

He swayed a bit, but regained his balance.

She would rather not know when the first blow would come. The anticipation troubled her. This was better, cleaning was better.

"I can get any woman I want," he repeated.

She wished she had paid attention to what Kami had told her about the leaves of a special tree. If placed in one's mouth, stuffed to the brim so that the leaves stuck out like feathers, a person's enemy would lose the ability to speak. At the moment, the name of that special tree escaped her.

How did it come to this?

There had been happy days too. On Divali, the festival of lights, the entire hamlet was covered in lamps, and they flickered outside the huts, and somewhere firecrackers burst, which the wind carried as though the sound were its own child, and finally the tarpa was heard, the Warli pipe large as the winding trunk of an elephant, a call to the young couples of the village to hold hands and dance in a ring, a promise of almost-eternity, at least that is what she felt that night.

But the good days were rare. They came in between beatings, gasps of air that were allowed if one were forced to stay underwater for too long.

The first blow came.

The broom fell to the ground.

Somehow she did not feel the pain so much. Maybe it was because she had called out to Vaghai, the Tiger God of the Warlis, for strength. If her husband had the sinewy arms of a jungle cat, only the Tiger God could counter that.

As she crouched on the floor to protect herself, she looked at the walls of her hut, made of karvi leaves, bamboo, and cow dung, and coughed out of pain, but smiled as well, because if the walls of her home were held together by cow dung, a shit life was all she would get.

She had accepted the blacks and blues on her skin with fortitude so far, but now, after her father's death, something needed to be done. And she would not have expected a landlord to come to her aid had it not been for that blue cycle and the white lily on her head.

Zairos waited for Kusum for over two hours.

The cigarettes he smoked did not help him understand what he was supposed to do. He inhaled deeply, making sure his lungs were awake, but the smoke gave him no direction.

After more time passed, he felt she was not going to show up. Maybe she was scared and had changed her mind. Or after a long day's work, she was just too tired to walk. The worn, leather-thick soles of her feet were so cracked and cheated of youth, unlike the rest of her body.

But her legs had not given way.

Kusum appeared from the darkness, from near a barren patch of land where once red roses had been planted. She mounted the motorcycle like a man. The silver silencer burned her leg and she let out a hiss. She was not used to machines. She did not place her hands around his waist like he wanted her to. Instead she held on to the metal carrier at the back.

The headlight of his motorcycle illuminated the bumps in the road and once they reached the beach, took the pine trees by surprise. The sea brought in a comforting breeze that nursed Zairos' forehead. The stars were out in clusters, but one star stood on its own, confident of its light.

He needed a quiet spot, one where no one could be seen for a mile. He slowed down when he approached the fishing village. The moon made parts of the water turn silver, and fishing trawlers rested on the shore, their blue and green lights blinking like magical insects.

The headlight kept on capturing dust until he finally reached a wasteland where stunted shrubs and cacti sprouted from the ground. A baby snake crossed the road in the light of the moon. He stared at the date palm trees, so jagged their trunks.

Zairos looked up at the sky. Its vastness did not comfort him at all. She was at ease in the wilderness. She needed no protection, and it made him feel weak.

Her power was deserved, but his felt unearned.

"Seth," she said. "I need your help."

"With what?" he asked.

"I want to leave my husband."

"So leave him."

"It's not that easy, seth. I have to pay my husband whatever he gave my father on my wedding," she said. "Money, grains, beans, two goats."

She stopped at goats, at an animal that was designed for slaughter.

"I will give you the money," he said.

"He will still not let me go. He is a mad man. Even the village elders do nothing. They are afraid of him. Only you can help me."

"Where is he now?"

"At home. He beat me tonight. But he is unconscious now. Drunk . . ."

Zairos looked up at the sky. This was not something he wanted to be involved in.

"Will you help me?" she asked.

"Why me?"

"Because you are not like the rest of them."

He was exactly like the rest of them.

All he wanted to do was lick every inch of her skin, and he did not know if it was a hunger that a man has for a woman, or a master for a slave, but he did not care. He was exactly like them.

"I will see what I can do," he said.

He did not know if she wanted him to kiss her.

A kiss, at the moment, would be like a handshake, an agreement to move forward. He wanted to kiss her so that his mouth would be unable to make any more promises, ones that he might not be able to keep, and he was about to back out, he was about to offer her money again, when his own name rushed into him like a bull.

Zairos the Great.

Great men did not offer money. They offered protection.

After dropping Kusum a short distance from her hamlet, Zairos bumped into Lucky Lips outside Alan's petrol pump. His lips eaten up by years of tobacco use, he communicated in grunts and moans, which the Iranis of Dahanu had learned to decipher. Tonight, however, the sounds took a back seat and made way for mime: his uncle Gustad had passed away a few hours ago. Why, then, Lucky Lips was chewing tobacco in the middle of the road on an Atlas cycle was an enigma.

When Zairos reached his grandfather's bungalow, he switched off his motorcycle before the headlights came too close to Shapur Irani. Shapur Irani sat in his chair, his white chest hair sprouting out leisurely from over the throat of his sudreh. He was letting the mosquitoes suck his blood. He was giving them his memories. The mosquitoes were the fools, the ones being outfoxed.

"Pa," said Zairos. "Gustad Mirza is dead."

His grandfather's black eyes acquired a mad flavour. Dozens of birds were furiously flapping their wings somewhere, and their image was being caught in his eyes.

"How did he die?" asked Shapur Irani.

"In his sleep," replied Zairos.

"Too gentle a death for that bastard."

After learning about Gustad's role in the War of the Warlis, Zairos could finally understand his grandfather's boiling hatred for this man. But it was a hatred he never cared to explain. Perhaps Shapur Irani believed that by speaking about it, it might lessen, and that was not what he wanted at all. He wanted to keep his hatred alive, a small animal that had to be fed every single day, drop by drop.

"I saw him only a few days ago in the bazaar," said Zairos. "He was so thin . . . carrying a cane."

"Even the devil carries a walking stick."

EIGHT

1946

SHAPUR IRANI STOOD by the window and looked at the chickoo trees, their branches heavy with fruit. It was a sight that always made him happy. But lately, no matter how many baskets of chickoos were packed, he was not satisfied. He had been up all night, walking around the house.

Banu was rubbing her elbows because it was winter and the house was chilly. Khodi, more than three now, was a strong child, big in size for his age, snuggled in a grey blanket.

"Look at how deep his sleep is," she said. "He must be talking to angels right now."

"Forget angels."

"What's bothering you, Shapur? You've been behaving so strange lately."

The night before, she had caught him standing at the stove, deep in thought, staring at the chai bubbling out of its container. Instead of switching the stove off, he did nothing. Even his face had changed. He had become sterner, more rigid.

"Come, Shapur," she said. "Lie down next to me."

Instead of going to the bed, he went to his cupboard and took out his shotgun. He lay in bed with the shotgun by his side.

"Shapur, what are you doing?"

"Sleeping."

"With the gun?"

"Yes."

She lay next to him, the shotgun between them. He reached out for her and touched her cheek. She held his hand while his other hand held on to his gun.

"Shapur, what are you afraid of? The Warlis will not attack us. The attacks have stopped. Everything is back to normal again."

"It's not the Warlis I am scared of."

"Then what?"

"I don't know."

It was her. It was her that he was scared of losing.

She had told him about their second child on the worst possible day—soon after the landlords' disgraceful act on Dahanu beach. It was the unborn child who had made her speak on that very day, to let its father know that it too had witnessed the bloodshed.

The child was here on a mission. To take its mother away from men like Shapur Irani.

He closed his eyes and held on to his gun.

"The mind plays tricks," Vamog used to tell his son. "Ahriman enters through the mind and makes you doubt things, especially the gifts Ahura Mazda has given you."

These were the words Shapur Irani woke up with. He would not let Ahriman win.

Jeroo was in the kitchen, sipping her morning tea in a pink sweater. Her silver hair was so stern. Military hair, not a strand out of line. A complete contrast to her fingers—her knuckles curled inwards more and more with each passing day.

"Come, my football," said Shapur Irani to Banu. "Let's go for a walk."

Banu smiled. At least he was joking again. "I can't walk. What if the water bursts?"

"So let it burst. I will carry you back here in a minute."

Banu put on a white sweater over her housecoat. She asked Jeroo to look after Khodi. Banu enjoyed having Jeroo around. The house was less lonely. Jeroo's big hips always ensured that she bumped into the edge of a table or the back of a chair, and Banu liked the floral dresses Jeroo wore—she was some kind of walking garden inside the house. Even Khodi was comfortable with her. The two did not interact much; they were more like two old people sitting on a park bench, not having anything to say, but still cherishing each other's company.

"Look how soft the sun is," said Banu.

"Soft?" asked Shapur Irani. "What do you mean, 'soft'?"

"My grandmother used to say that there are different suns. In the morning, the baby sun shines. Then, in the afternoon, the mother sun comes, strong and powerful."

"When does the father sun come?"

"There is no father sun. Najamai used to say that the sun is God's female creation."

"So God is a man, hah?" he said as he puffed his chest.

"That's what Najamai used to say."

"She was a wise woman."

"Shapur, where are you taking me? I don't want to walk too much. It's so cold."

"I want to show you something."

He took her through the trees, and she had to bend a little to avoid being hit in the head by low branches. Motes of dust were illuminated by the morning sun—angel breath.

Soon they reached a clearing and Banu removed her slippers. She wanted to feel the morning dew on the grass. She curled her toes and felt every bit of moisture on her soles. She thought of Najamai again, who had an explanation for all of nature's beauty. "Dew is the jewellery of grass," she had once said. "Just as the sky has stars to decorate it, the grass has dew to make it sparkle. Even nature likes to dress up and go out, my dear."

"Look at this," said Shapur Irani. "This is what I wanted to show you."

"This big hole?" asked Banu.

"Do you like it?"

It was more than forty feet deep, and to Banu it looked like an open sore.

"It's . . . it's really lovely," she said.

"Are you teasing me?"

"Darling, what else do you want me to say?"

She moved away from the edge of the hole, but her husband did not let her go too far.

"This is my new well," he said. "When it's done, it will be the deepest well in Dahanu."

"Why do we need another well? The one we have is quite deep, no?"

"What if the monsoons fail? Our lives depend on nature. We cannot take too much for granted. That's why I want one more well, so deep it can store enough water for us."

"Have you found water as yet?"

"No, not yet. But the Warlis are sure this is a good spot. There were holes in the ground, holes made by crabs . . . there was wet mud around those holes. The crabs have gone inside the earth and have come out with wet mud. It means there is water underneath."

"Don't worry, Shapur. In a couple of days, you will get water in this well."

"Oh? And how do you know?"

"When my water bursts, I will empty it in this well."

Shapur Irani roared with laughter, and Banu was thrilled to hear that sound again.

Things were going to be okay. There was fruit on the trees and dew on the grass, and the baby sun was shining, happy in its softness, and as Najamai used to say, the grass had worn jewellery because it too wanted to celebrate the birth of a child.

A week later, Sohrab was born. The minute Jeroo told Shapur Irani that Banu was fine, he went to the teak cupboard. He had stuck a picture of Zarathushtra on the inside of the door. He folded his hands in prayer, bowed his head to the prophet, and whispered a thank-you.

Jeroo was in a good mood. She even spoke with Shapur Irani quite cheerfully. Of course, ever since the day of Vithal's beating, she had been cold with him. Shapur Irani had wanted to explain that his actions were necessary, but the look on Jeroo's face told him that he did not stand a chance. She had formed an opinion of him, one that he deserved. However, he appreciated that she had not mentioned a word to Banu, as it would have surely upset her.

"Now you have two healthy sons," said Jeroo. "May they grow up to become strong men."

"They will be men of the soil," said Shapur Irani. "I shall teach them all I know."

"What about me?" asked Banu. "No one is congratulating me?"

"Yes, my football," said Shapur Irani. "Let me congratulate you."

Jeroo slipped out of the room. Shapur Irani sat beside the bed. The baby was at Banu's breasts. "That's *my* job," he said. "You little rascal, that's my job."

"Chee, Shapur. How dirty."

"Whenever you use the word 'dirty' you know what happens to me. I have to show you how dirty I am."

"Shapur, not now. I'm feeding the baby."

"Feed me also. How am I supposed to celebrate the birth of my son?"

"I don't know. Go out and pick some fruit."

"I want to pick *your* fruit."

"Shapur, Jeroo is in the other room. She can hear us."

Shapur Irani laughed again. This was the second time this week he had laughed from the heart.

Banu had a feeling that Sohrab's birth would change everything. Happiness was theirs now. In a few days, after Jeroo would leave, Banu's mother would come and look after her.

Maybe Shapur Irani would allow Banu to go to Bombay for a while. She knew he did not like her going anywhere without him. She would bring it up later, perhaps. Right now, she was content to feel his hard skin against her cheek, his cold nose nuzzling against her neck. Later, he put his shotgun away. He agreed with Banu that he was being unreasonable, and with two sons now, a gun had no place in their bed.

Even though it was past dawn, the windows were still closed because it was unusually cold. Banu had two sweaters on, and even Shapur Irani, for the first time, was feeling an extreme chill.

"Come here," said Banu. "Let me warm you up."

He went close to her and kissed her hard. He took one sweater off, and then tried to take the next one off, but it got entangled with the first and she giggled. Just then, there was a loud thud. Shapur Irani froze. He listened. One more thud. Then something hit the window and there was a large crack in it. Jeroo came running into the room with the baby. Khodi was awake too. "Mama," he said.

"Stay in here and don't open the door," said Shapur Irani.

He opened the cupboard and took out his shotgun. The Warlis were stoning his house. But why now? The violence had ended throughout Dahanu. Where was Ejaz? He needed to go out and shoot a couple of Warlis. It was only a matter of time before they broke the door and came in.

He slowly opened the main door. He could see no one. Yet there was another loud thud on the wall of the house. He fired one shot in the air. There was no point in going out and exposing himself unless he could spot one of them. Then he closed the door. It was too risky. If they rushed in, he would not be able to fight them indoors. He cursed the Warlis under his breath. "I'll kill them all," he kept saying to himself. "I'll kill them all."

He bolted the door and went to a window. He broke the glass with the butt of his gun, put the nozzle out, and fired. There was complete silence. He watched through the hole he had made. He could see only chickoo trees. Then he saw a rock hit the bark of a chickoo tree. He could not believe it. This was not coming from the Warlis. This was coming from the heavens. He opened the window and saw pieces of ice falling from the sky. They hit the walls of his home, they hit the bark of his trees with great force and he flinched every time it happened.

No, not my trees. Please, not the trees.

A few of the workers were running for shelter. Shapur Irani opened the door and stood under the roof of the porch. His trees were being hacked and there was nothing he could do to stop the slaughter.

Shapur Irani believed that the ice was a punishment for the shooting on Dahanu beach. Now, even though the violence had abated, the violence within Shapur Irani's heart was alive. Perhaps it was not violence but fear, and he recognized that something was amiss, that his heart was not as strong as it used to be, but he told himself that the birth of a child could soften up any man.

Three months after the hailstorm, they left the farm in the morning in a new horse carriage that Shapur Irani had acquired. Banu was not comfortable with the idea of horses carrying so much weight. Still, she sat in the carriage with the newborn Sohrab in her arms. Shapur Irani made Khodi sit beside him.

"Khodi," he said, "don't sit with your back hunched. Sit like a man of authority. Sit like you own these horses."

"Shapur," Banu whispered, "he's only three. Calm down."

But Shapur Irani wanted to treat his son like a man. There would be no room for weakness in that heart of his.

"Let's give these horses names," said Banu.

"No," said Shapur Irani. "No names. They are not pets. They are workers."

"See?" said Banu. "Even Sohrab is crying. Even he wants the horses to be named."

"Ejaz!" called Shapur Irani. "Let's go."

Banu did not like Ejaz the Pathan. He was too bulky and powerful, and that black beard of his had so many knots in it, a sign that he was crooked. Even her husband was just as mighty as Ejaz was, but her husband was not crooked. She hated the wooden club Ejaz carried with him everywhere. Just a few hours ago, she awoke to the sound of glass breaking. When she opened the front door, she saw her husband and Ejaz smashing empty bottles on the porch. When she asked what they were doing, Ejaz replied, "We are using the glass for my club." Banu did not like the fact that Ejaz answered when she had asked the question to her husband. But the club Ejaz had made fascinated Shapur Irani and he painstakingly inserted glass shrapnel into the end of the club himself.

"Does he have to carry that club with him?" she asked, as Ejaz took the reins in his hand.

"Yes," said Shapur Irani. "It's for safety."

"But it's such a beautiful day. Why spoil such a beautiful day?"

"Terrible things can happen on beautiful days."

They set off for the bazaar where a mela was taking place. Khodi had never been to a fair, and even Banu wanted to eat candy floss. The first time she had tasted it as a child, her mother had told her that it was just like eating clouds, and then she said, "But in truth it is an old man's beard. You are eating the beard of a dead old man!" And Banu shrieked in fright but ate the candy floss anyway. If an old man's beard tasted so delicious, she did not care.

On the way to the fair, she marvelled at how pristine the air was. She took in deep breaths, and Sohrab puckered his lips, and even though she knew it was time for his feeding, she did not want to do it in front of Ejaz. She also did not like how Khodi was staring at Ejaz's club. He seemed to have the same fondness for it that his father did. This was a time for toys, for colours and fairy tales—not clubs. To distract herself, she closed her eyes and listened to the clip-clop of the horses. When she was a little girl, she would wake up in the middle of the night and rush to the balcony whenever she heard a horse carriage. There was something about those empty Bombay streets and two majestic horses . . .

A cry from Khodi brought her out of her reverie. He had cut his finger on the shards of Ejaz's club. Instead of shouting at his son, Shapur Irani took the finger and put it in Khodi's mouth. "Suck the blood off," he told his son. "It's good. Now you know what blood tastes like."

"Don't do that," said Banu. "What are you—?"

But a deadly look from her husband silenced her. To placate her, he sucked Khodi's finger himself and made bird sounds to distract the child. By the time Khodi was quiet, Banu's fear and anger had gone in and found a resting place somewhere inside her.

Once they got to the fair, Banu said she wanted to eat the old man's beard. "Here, take him," she said to Shapur Irani, and she handed Sohrab to him. She made Khodi walk with her, and he tumbled along, hanging on to his mother with one hand and rubbing his nose with the other.

"Why didn't you bring Jeroo?" Shapur Irani grumbled. "What is a midwife for?"

"*You* didn't want her, Shapur."

She giggled at the sight of him, this giant of a man standing in a fair, holding a newborn in his arms. He looked just as ridiculous with Sohrab as she herself would look holding Ejaz's club. She immediately regretted that thought.

"Have some candy floss," she said, offering her husband some.

But Shapur Irani had to refuse. Sweets of any kind triggered a painful memory, that of Aflatoon of Esfahan. Perhaps the celebrated confectioner's heart was not as pure as his father had thought it to be. Why else would disaster strike with such force? It was a day when his father's tongue should have tasted cream and butter, not his own blood.

Or maybe Aflatoon's heart was noble. Perhaps he sat there at the counter of his shop, his head hanging in shame, and said a prayer, sweet as the fillings in his delicacies, for young Shapur. That was why in India, another confectioner, Daryoush the baker, provided what Aflatoon of Esfahan could not. And for that reason, Daryoush was the greater artist.

"Shapur," said Banu, "where have you gone?"

"Nowhere," he said, the bittersweet tang in his voice betraying him. "Some of the old man's beard is stuck on your nose."

She put the pink beard to his face, rubbed it on his chin.

"Now you also have a pink face."

"Not fair, Banu," he said with a lilt. "I'm holding Sohrab. I can't fight back."

Shapur Irani's smile suddenly vanished. Banu followed his gaze to a man and woman approaching them. The manner in which the man was dressed suggested that he was a landowner, a rich one. He was short and bald, and had pimple scars on his face.

"Shapur," said the man. "How are you?"

Her husband stiffened up.

"I had no idea you had become a nurse," taunted the man. "A big strong man like you holding a baby, while your wife . . . She is your wife, I hope?" Then he winked at Shapur Irani.

Banu threw the candy floss to the ground and took Sohrab from his father's arms. Khodi was by her side, clinging to her.

"My name is Gustad Mirza," said the man to Banu. "And this is my wife, Coomi."

Coomi smiled at Shapur Irani and Banu. She had too much powder on her face and her eyes were too big, as if she were perpetually in a state of shock. Even her hair was too curly. Her curls had a life of their own, a madness almost.

"So you have come to the fair for some enjoyment?" asked Gustad.

He wiped his bald head with a white handkerchief, and Banu wondered why he was sweating when it was not hot.

When Shapur Irani did not respond to Gustad's question, Coomi stepped in.

"Would you like to see that stall over there?" she asked Banu. "They are selling shawls from Kashmir. We should leave the men alone and buy some shawls."

Banu looked at her husband, and when he nodded his head she took Khodi and Sohrab and went to have a look at the shawls from Kashmir.

Glad that his wife was out of the way, Shapur Irani finally spoke.

"Gustad, I have nothing to say to you. You are a snake. The worst type of snake . . . what you and the other landlords did . . ."

"Did what?" asked Gustad. "We protected our own interests. Anyway, it was your idea to get them together."

"To negotiate," said Shapur Irani.

He was going hot, then cold, then hot again. The fire would not lie low.

"Did you really think we would make a *speech*?" said Gustad. "We are landlords. We do not negotiate."

Shapur Irani suddenly doubted himself. Had he, at some level, known that a betrayal would take place?

No, he did not. That was Ahriman talking again, getting under his skin, making him believe there was something wrong from the inside.

"People died that day," he said.

"Only five died, Shapur. Only *five*. It happens when there is a revolt. Anyway, it's in the past. Why don't we talk about pleasant things? Your wife seems nice. She is quite pretty."

"I don't want to talk about my wife. And I don't want you anywhere near my wife."

Standing in front of Gustad was proving to be too much for Shapur Irani.

Something was rising within him, and he could not make out if it was Ahura Mazda's strength or Ahriman's poison. Either way, it could not be contained. He needed to walk away.

"Where are you going?" asked Gustad. "You think you're too good for us? Is your wife special? Is she made of gold?"

Keep walking. Keep walking.

"I understand," said Gustad. "I'll stay away from your wife. But will she?"

Shapur Irani's hand was shaking now, and once his hand shook, he knew what it meant. It was time for the earth to shake.

"What are you talking about?" he asked.

"There are rumours about your wife . . . that while she was in Bombay her mother used to rent her out to the British."

Shapur Irani elbowed Gustad in the nose and Gustad was on the ground. That was for his wife.

"This is from the Warlis," he said.

Then he kicked Gustad hard in the stomach. Gustad doubled over, wheezing.

One more kick. It did not matter that Shapur Irani had worn kolhapuri chappals. His foot was a hot, furious brick.

Gustad was trying to get up, crawling on all fours. Shapur Irani kicked him on his back with his heel. He unbuckled Gustad's leather belt from his trousers. A crowd was watching. Some of the men worked for Gustad, but when they came to his rescue, Ejaz the Pathan stood there with his wooden club and said, "It is between two men. No one will interfere."

Shapur Irani started belting Gustad with his own expensive leather belt. It was not as thick as Shapur Irani wanted it to be.

"This is what it feels like to be whipped, you bastard," he said.

But Gustad was not making a sound. That scared Shapur Irani. This short, bald man was tough. He did not have the physical strength to fight Shapur Irani, but he could take a beating, and this angered Shapur Irani even more, and he resumed the whipping with renewed vigour.

Still, not a sound from Gustad.

Banu had Sohrab in her arms, Khodi by her side, and Gustad's wife next to her, shrieking. She saw Ejaz standing, a mountain, so that no one could reach her husband. She finally walked towards Shapur Irani, and Ejaz moved to block her way, but her eyes must have shot poison because he let her pass, and only when she screamed "Stop!" right in his ear did he stop beating Gustad. Shapur Irani was breathing extra hard.

Gustad raised his head and, through a mouthful of blood, gave him a red smile.

"You will pay for this, my friend," said Gustad. "One day, you will pay for this."

Shapur Irani dropped Gustad's belt to the ground and made his way back to the horse carriage. Khodi started to cry, and Shapur Irani told his son to shut up and be a man. By the time they got to the carriage, Khodi was bawling beyond measure, and Shapur Irani asked Ejaz, "Your son is the same age as mine. Does your son cry too? Does your son cry like this?"

"No," said Ejaz. "My son does not cry."

"That's what I thought."

"My son does not cry because my son is dead," said Ejaz. "He died in Bombay a few days ago."

NINE

2000

A FEW DAYS AFTER Gustad Mirza's death, Zairos saw a group of Irani men, all dressed in white, pass Anna's on their motorcycles. They were on their way to the fire temple to attend prayers that were being offered for Gustad. Gustad's body had already been taken to the Tower of Silence in Bombay, where, according to the Zoroastrian practice of Dokhmenashini, his body would have been eaten by vultures.

"It is sad that the good deeds of the past are seldom remembered," Shapur Irani had told Zairos. "And history is created by a few rotten apples."

Zairos thought of the many Irani landlords who had refused to take part in the butchery on Dahanu beach. They stayed at home, tended to their gardens, and held on to their prayer beads, hoping that the waves of violence would subside.

But Zairos did not wish that his grandfather had been one of those men.

The man had tried to save the Warlis. He had intervened in

the name of goodness, and even though he failed, his music was more powerful than that of those who did not try. Unfortunately, his grandfather did not view things that way. Failure had created a mesh of wires that had clung to his neck and left him choking.

Seated on Anna's green bench, Zairos experienced a similar smothering.

He was hoping that Anna's would revive him, and thanks to the men on their way to Gustad's prayers, Aspi Irani started talking about the way the Zoroastrians disposed of their dead and the problems the community faced.

Lately, there had been a drastic decrease in the vulture population in Bombay. However, there was no dearth of dead bodies in the Tower of Silence. So the vultures, spoiled by the veritable feast before them, were not doing their job. After eating their fill, they were dropping off bits of flesh on the windowsills of nearby posh high-rise apartments.

"Just imagine," said Aspi Irani, chewing on an unlit Marlboro. "On Monday, a man dies. On Tuesday, he shows up at your house again."

"I don't think that's possible," said Keki the Italian. "Bombay vultures belong to a species known as *Gyps*. They can't hold flesh in their beaks for too long. So it would be hard to fly to any buildings."

"And who told you that—Camus?" asked Aspi Irani.

"No, said Keki. The pallbearer at the Tower of Silence. I got to know him when my father died."

"You flirted with a pallbearer at your father's funeral?" asked Aspi Irani.

"I think each of us should adopt a vulture," said Merwan Mota, munching on glucose biscuits with Pinky the orphan by his side. "I'm sick of those rich fools in Bombay walking around with their stupid little Pomeranians."

"That's a great idea," said Aspi Irani. "I'd rather be eaten by a vulture who *knows* me. Not by some ungrateful stranger. In fact, I'd like to import mine from France. I'll tie an embroidered napkin round his neck, and he can sip red wine and dip fancy cutlery into my flesh."

"Yes," said Merwan Mota, boosted by the support. "We could keep him in a cage, like a cockatoo. We'll call him Pierre."

"And my wife speaks French. The two could converse."

"On second thought," said Merwan, "*we* should eat the bastards for a change."

"Barbarians," said Keki the Italian.

"At least I didn't sleep with a pallbearer at my father's funeral."

Hosi did not seem interested in the "Adopt a Vulture" program. He sat in a corner holding the sides of his paunch in utter disgust, blaming Anna's oily potatoes for his weight gain. He looked at the picture of Bruce Lee that he had pasted onto the wall. He longed to have a body like that.

But instead of muscles, only his beard was growing. It was thicker than ever, there were now *seventeen* strands of white hair on his chest, and, of late, he had been leaving his fly open wherever he went, which he was convinced was the first sign of Alzheimer's. He had read about it in *Reader's Digest*.

"I'm off to prison," he said, looking at his watch.

That was how he passed his time in Dahanu. He would find out from the prison authorities when an inmate was being released, and he would stand outside the prison to see the look of freedom on the man's face.

"I will never know what that's like," he once said.

Bumble, on the other hand, spent his afternoons fast asleep in a bedroom rendered igloo-cold by air conditioning. But today, even though it was time for his siesta, Bumble was smoking, looking glum. His curly hair was more dishevelled than usual and he had dark circles under his eyes.

"What's wrong?" asked Zairos.

"Nothing," said Bumble, sucking the cigarette to the bitter end. "My dad's upset because I haven't been to the farm for three days."

"Why's that?"

Bumble grimaced, took his Ray-Bans off, cleaned them with the bottom of his red T-shirt, and put them back on again. "It's nothing," he said. He put his forefinger on the rim of his aviators and pushed them back. "I caught one of the workers stealing cement poles from the farm. I was about to scream at him, but I had barely said a word and . . . I saw a stream of urine trickle down his leg. I just walked away. I don't feel like going to the farm now. It's just . . ."

Zairos understood what Bumble meant. It was shameful that one man wielded so much power over another. A few cement poles made no difference to Bumble, but if he did nothing, he would be considered weak.

At the end of it all, perhaps there was not much they could do besides let Anna's chai soothe them. It was pompous of Zairos to think that landlords needed soothing, but he felt it was true. Just because they had money did not mean nothing affected them. And as his grandfather pointed out, they were paying for the mistakes made by only a few men.

But that was history.

No matter how beautiful the roses on the path, men only noticed the dead cubs along the way, lying on their backs, their small paws now limp, a reminder that the ones who had survived could not be trusted.

Like a piece of meat stuck between his teeth, uneasiness was stuck in Zairos' rib cage.

On most occasions, Anna's chai stall was a sanctuary where that uneasiness dissolved. At Anna's, a congregation of men assembled for an hour or two, shared their stories, and tried to find togetherness without losing their machismo. Anna's was a source of relief, but at the moment it seemed false, a yellow bulb trying to pass as sunlight.

It was because Zairos had done nothing about Kusum's husband.

After their last meeting, he had exchanged glances with her at the farm and paid her daily wage. But he had ignored her plea for help. It was time to do something.

He went to the counter, where peppermints were kept in glass jars, where small plastic bottles of Hunny drinking water were lined up, and Anna's small book of accounts, with a sketch of Lord Krishna playing the flute, was lying next to the black telephone.

Zairos made a call.

It was ringing, and once the voice on the other line answered, there was no turning back.

The next afternoon, Zairos sat in the blue swivel chair outside the Big Boss Hair Salon, awaiting the arrival of an important guest. The guest was not a member of Parliament or a religious man. The man Zairos was waiting for was a bona fide bandit from Bihar, the most lawless state in the country.

The dacoit's name was Chambal—not a very original name, since most dacoits had terrorized the Chambal Valley. Zairos had met him a year before through Santosh, the unofficial singer-poet of Dahanu. Santosh was a wholesaler of chickoos who, while weighing his fruit, sang old Hindi songs and recited his own poetry.

Santosh's cousin was a part-time prostitute. Chambal, apart from being a former dacoit—he was now in retirement— was a truck driver. He passed through Dahanu on his way to Bombay and slept with Santosh's cousin. When Zairos first met Chambal, he had parked his truck outside Santosh's wholesale shed. About six foot three, with a handlebar moustache so typical of his ilk, each half twirled to perfection, the tips pinpointed to enter the smallest hole, Chambal wore a dhoti and a white shirt, and was talking with great pride about how ruthless he was. "But after retirement, I have slowed down," he said. "After retirement, I have done only two murders. One with my sword and one with my gun." The long-haired Santosh continued weighing his chickoos on a large scale and recited a poem under his breath. Chambal did not seem to mind that Santosh was not paying attention. He was more interested in having Zairos as an audience. "This man in my village," continued Chambal, "he courted my sister, slept with her, and did not marry her, so I killed him. That was the honour killing with the sword. I cut his head off in front of his brother. The other killing I did as a contract. A landlord paid me to get rid of a man who refused to sell his land. So I shot him and then his wife had to sell the land. Apart from these two murders, I have done a few more but they were during my days as a dacoit and I do not want to talk about that."

Then Chambal climbed into his truck and got his shotgun. The truck was at a height, so he towered above Zairos. All of a sudden, he aimed the gun at Zairos. Santosh stopped reciting his poem. "I could kill you just now and feel *nothing*," said Chambal. Santosh stepped out from under his shed. "Chambal, my friend," he said. "You should wear some underwear." Zairos could not believe his ears. Was this a poem? Was it symbolic of his death, of his getting shot?

"What are you talking about?" asked Chambal.

"This truck is very high," said Santosh. "I can see your spare parts beneath your dhoti. You should wear underwear."

Chambal roared with laughter. He jumped off his truck and thumped Santosh on the back. That night, the three of them had drinks together. Chambal was a lovable killer. He was a killer in love. He told Zairos how much he wanted to keep Santosh's cousin for himself. He told her he would marry her, but she was too fiery a woman to tame, and when she rejected him it excited him even more, and she was heartless because when Chambal said he would kill her other clients she said that it was a horrible thing to do—it would hurt her income.

Zairos thought of that first meeting as he waited at the Big Boss Hair Salon for this killer in love to appear. He told Sharmaji to treat Chambal to the most expensive body massage, and while he was getting massaged, Zairos planned to talk to Chambal about Kusum. Hosi and Bumble warned him that he was getting too involved.

"No woman is worth fighting for," said Hosi. "Unless she's a horse."

Outside the Big Boss Hair Salon, a madman walked up and down the road. He looked like a Rastafarian and his face had seen some tough sun. He had a strange routine. He walked three steps, then touched his right toe and opened his mouth wide, stretched it as far as his jaw would allow.

Soon, an auto rickshaw pulled up, and Zairos saw Chambal's great hand holding on to the roof of the rickshaw. He paid the driver and greeted Zairos with a salute. Zairos liked Chambal's shoes. They were black leather mojris, and the tips curled exactly like the tips of his handlebar moustache. Zairos led Chambal to Sharmaji's inner sanctum, where a bed awaited, along with Sharmaji's oils, his own concoctions, which had been passed on to Sharmaji by his father, an expert in Ayurveda.

Sharmaji did not even wait for an introduction. He opened the cap of one of his small bottles, poured some oil into one palm, and started rubbing his hands together. He indicated for Zairos to start the blue table fan that was in a corner of the small room. Particles of black dirt hung off the blades of the fan, some of which would soon blow all over Chambal's body and into everyone's noses. Chambal took off his white shirt and hung it on a hook on the wall.

Sharmaji slapped his hands onto Chambal's back. There were two patches of coarse black hair. The oil flattened the hair and made it stick to his body. Chambal had his head to one side and his eyes were closed. Sharmaji became inconspicuous almost immediately, which was his gift, a sign of a true masseur.

"I was glad to get your phone call yesterday," said Chambal. "It's always good to hear from an old friend."

Zairos was hardly an old friend. But who in his right mind would argue with a dacoit?

"After hearing your problem, I can tell that you are a passionate man," said Chambal. "I have a good feeling about you. I am sure you would be able to do a couple of murders."

"Thank you," said Zairos.

"So you want to help this woman whose husband beats her."

"Both her parents are dead and she has no one."

"Is she your woman?"

"I just want to help," said Zairos. "Is this something that can be solved?"

"A gun can solve anything."

"No, no," said Zairos. "I don't want you to kill him."

"But that's the simplest thing to do," said Chambal. "Aaah . . ." Sharmaji was forcing his knuckles deep inside Chambal's lower back.

"I just want you to scare him," said Zairos. "To make sure he leaves Kusum alone."

"Kusum? That's her name?"

"Yes."

"My woman's name is Rekha. You know Santosh's cousin . . ."

"Of course," said Zairos.

"I have killed men, but this woman kills *me* every time I meet her. What can I tell you about women? They are so deadly. Your problem will be solved. We will do it tonight. But let me tell you that you are making a big mistake by not killing the husband. A wounded man is a dangerous man. But your wish."

"How much would you charge for this kind of work?"

"Nothing," said Chambal. "If I was killing him, I'd charge ten thousand, but for wounding a wife beater, I'll do it for free. I'll do it for love. I'll do it on the condition that you tell Santosh about my kindness so that he can tell Rekha and then she will ask me about it."

"It's a deal."

"We'll get him tonight," said Chambal. "But you will have to come with me. I don't want to wound the wrong man."

Zairos did not tell Kusum that they were coming. He did not want to warn her in any way because her nervousness would tip Laxman off. When a man was prepared for a fight, he had time to transform—into an animal, into something ferocious. But when a man was home alone with his wife, he was vulnerable.

"Let her see what we do to him," Chambal said. "Let her realize the extent you have gone to protect her."

But there was one problem. Chambal refused to sit in Zairos' car or Bumble's because one was red and the other was white. "Not good colours for me" was what Chambal said.

That meant Hosi would have to drive his car. It was black, perfect for Chambal, but it was the worst getaway vehicle ever. It ran on cooking gas. The front seat had been removed and a gas cylinder installed in its place. It was Hosi's way of fighting rising fuel prices. He did not care about decor: "As long as the car is functional, what I save on petrol, I can spend on horses." Each time Zairos sat in the car, it brought a smile to his face. Hosi's Maruti had been manufactured in Japan, and if the Japanese could see Hosi with the gas cylinder sitting by his side like an old lady, they would, despite their culture, be forced to show some emotion.

Chambal put his shotgun in the hutch of the car and they took off.

As he drove, Hosi kept looking at the gas cylinder, worried that she might hit her head on the dashboard. The metal fittings that secured the cylinder in place had come loose. Chambal was most amused with the gas cylinder. He kept tapping it and chuckling. In response to that chuckle, Hosi lit a cigarette. "Just imagine what would happen," he said, looking straight ahead as he drove, "if this car overturns and there is a gas leak." Then he looked back at Chambal. "I'm not a fan of suicide. I find pills and rope hangings very stale. But this . . . a sudden, unexpected explosion . . . there's something visionary about it."

The car grunted along the dirt road, crept closer to its target with the stealth of a tank. "There's no moon tonight," said Chambal. "It has gone to warn Laxman."

Midway through the journey, Chambal asked Hosi to stop. He got out of the car and started collecting large stones. Five in all, round and heavy. Then he took the long white cloth that hung around his neck and laid it flat on the ground. One by one, he neatly placed the stones in the centre of the cloth and wrapped the cloth around the stones, securing them with a knot. He swung the weapon over his head a few times to test it. "I call it my hathoda," he said. "A hammer that leaves no marks. My father taught me this. He was also a dacoit," he said, almost sounding nostalgic. "The gun is for bigger jobs. Tonight, the gun is just for safety."

They stopped a short distance from Kusum's hamlet. Hosi lit another cigarette, but Chambal told him to put it out. "The light will tell Laxman we are coming."

The hut was ideal for attacking—the other huts were not too close. As they moved forward, Zairos could feel the blood swirl around his heart.

There was a glow in the hut that came from a cooking fire.

Chambal was the first to go in. Laxman was on his haunches fanning the flames of the cooking fire with one hand, smoking a beedi with the other.

As he tried to stand, Chambal struck him with the hathoda in the ribs.

That was surely going to leave a mark.

Zairos tried to get Kusum out of the hut, but she stood her ground. Laxman was bent over in pain.

"We just want to talk to you," said Chambal. Then he bludgeoned Laxman again, in exactly the same spot. "We just want to talk to you," repeated Chambal, softly.

He was a master at this, cool and calm; this was his meditation.

"Now listen carefully," said Chambal. "From this day on, Kusum is no longer your wife. You will not speak to her, you will not follow her, and you will not touch her ever again."

Laxman looked at Chambal and Zairos. Then at Kusum, the look of a betrayed man, the foolishness of being outwitted. He started uttering gibberish.

Chambal slapped him hard across the face. It was an extra touch that was not required. Chambal was used to feeding men bullets. Laxman was still alive, and that in itself was something Chambal could not deal with.

"This woman is no longer your wife," said Chambal. "You do not know her. You do not know where she lives even though she is going to stay in her father's house from now on. If you even look at her, I will come back and kill you. My name is Chambal and I have killed many men. Remember my name. Remember that I have killed many men."

Then Chambal looked at Zairos to signal that his work was done.

Zairos reached into his pocket and took out a bundle of notes, three thousand rupees in all, and placed the bundle on the floor.

"That is much more than what you spent on the wedding," he said. "Now she is free."

Laxman tried to lift his head, but it was useless.

The cooking fire had lost its glow, the paper fan still by Laxman's side.

Kusum looked at her husband's hut one last time. Her face revealed no emotion.

Zairos admired her courage, how unshaken she had remained throughout the car journey to her father's hut. He asked Hosi to wait in the car with Chambal, about two hundred yards away from Ganpat's hamlet. The sound of a car at this time of night would arouse the curiosity of neighbours.

Not a single tremor, not a trace of remorse.

She was pure steel, but he wondered what she was like on the inside.

Neither of them spoke.

They walked in the darkness, and this time Zairos was the one who followed Kusum because his eyes were unaccustomed to the dark. She knew the path the way a mongoose knew it. Her feet made no sound, but his sneakers crushed the pebbles and he kept flicking his hair off his face, but it made no difference to the quality of his vision. His blue jeans got caught in a thorny bush, and she did not wait for him to disentangle himself.

Only a few feet away from her hut, a man lay on the ground.

Liquor had knocked him out. During the festival season, especially during and after Holi, the tribals drank themselves to sheer death. There was a day called Gutter Ammas, when tribals were found collapsed in gutters in the darkness of Ammas, a night of no moon.

They walked past the man, not checking if he was breathing. If he was dead, nothing could be done. At dawn he would be spotted, or he would wake up himself and go off to work. Kusum continued to walk in front of Zairos, and the only time she acknowledged him was when she once looked over her shoulder, just slightly, to see if he was still with her.

Then, when she reached the opening of her hut, she finally faced him.

She was breathing heavily and Zairos could hear every gasp.

Things were clear to him now. It was up to him to keep her alive. From now on, she would depend on him for breath. Her lungs would be his, her heart's pounding in his hands. He walked to a car two hundred yards away, where Chambal the dacoit was emptying the round stones from his white cloth onto the ground and Hosi had fallen asleep with his head on the gas cylinder.

~⚬~

Rami's snoring could be heard from inside the hut, an old woman's music.

Kusum could not go inside. Not yet.

She sat on the ground and looked around at the huts. No one in sight, except for a goat tied to a peg, and the shaking of trees.

Her mind was on Laxman. He was alive and impotent, a creature who had been left twitching on the floor of his own hut. She was responsible for that, not the dacoit with the gun, not the man walking away from her, running his fingers through his hair.

What would her father think of all this? His little girl, who once came up to his knee, then his waist, then his chest.

She had done what her father could not do. She had struck back the only way she knew how. Her father, a mortal, could not fight. Vaghai the Tiger God did nothing either. So she had no choice but to turn to a landlord, a being who was neither man nor god.

By taking his own life, her father had done something too. She was not going to let his death be wasted. His breath was wasted, it had no effect on anything around him, but his death was worth something.

And even if it was not, she was making it count.

That was what daughters did. They loved their fathers, and made their failures into trees. Or if not trees, shrubs. And if not shrubs, then one small blade of grass.

A blade of grass had a function too. It sheltered worms. It let worms snuggle together, and that had to mean something. Her mother had told her that.

Everything in nature had worth. Except the Warlis.

The folk tales tried to convince her that the Warlis were the last beings created by the gods. They were like unwanted seeds that were thrown from the sky. Being unwanted, no one offered them protection. No one encouraged them to grow.

She would do something. Walk a better road, a brave road that the wolves of the past would never be able to touch.

She was sitting on her haunches right now, in exactly the same way her mother Kamla used to sit. Her mother was named after a river. Some of her people were named after rivers. It felt like a cruel thing to do.

We hardly move, she said to herself. We wait. Have you ever seen a river wait?

But she had done something. She had chosen to move.

After dropping Chambal off, Zairos knew he had to see his grandfather.

It was a day of mourning for Shapur Irani, the death anniversary of his eldest son, Khodi. Shapur Irani preferred to be alone on this day, but Zairos felt no man should be left alone on such a day. Even cobras sobbed under the quiet shade of a tree once in a while.

Shapur Irani, custodian of the family's memories, custodian of everything past, from the birth of insects to the beatings administered on his land, was in his chair holding his son's photograph in his hand. It was too late for him to hide the photograph, too late for him to prevent Zairos from knowing that he had sat there for hours, certain of the fact that the heart attack that killed his son was meant for him instead. But the gods, cruel in the way children were cruel, changed fates, assigned him a rocking chair instead of an electric one so that his punishment would be slow, meticulous, the only perfect thing in this imperfect world.

He remembered how he screamed for joy the day Khodi was born, a scream so loud he felt after all these years his voice was still travelling. That is why he was silent in his chair right now. He was trying to listen for that cry of joy he had let out years ago.

"When a father outlives his son, it's a curse," he said. "In some ways, Khodi was not my son. He was Banu's son. Very gentle, very caring."

"That photograph," said Zairos. "My father has it too. Is it true that it was taken on the day Khodi kaka died?"

"Yes, it was your father who took the picture. Khodi's last cup of tea. Taken here . . . at that table."

Shapur Irani slowly pointed to an empty space on the porch. The table he was referring to was inside the house, but it did not matter. His eyes were closed and he could be any-where by thought.

"Aspi, Sohrab, Khodi, and myself used to have tea together every Sunday morning without fail. Once Khodi died, we stopped."

Zairos already understood why his grandfather did not touch tea. It was for the same reason that Hosi never came to visit Shapur Irani. Nor did he ever speak about his own father. For Hosi, Khodi Irani never existed. One body gone, one heart silenced, and the living were scrambling for cover, terrified of the landslide that followed.

Shapur Irani ran his forefinger along the edges of the black-and-white photograph, perhaps hoping to make a cut in his own skin so that he could feel his son again.

Khodi was the only one in the family who'd had a moustache. Zairos was surprised to see a soft smile on his grandfather's lips. Maybe it was not a smile, just his skin playing tricks.

But Shapur Irani was smiling. It was not the kind farmers smiled when they saw the first sign of rain, but it was something. He was having a playful moment with his dead son. On the photograph, he was twirling the ends of Khodi's moustache to see if he would make a sound. He knew that the dead did not speak to the living, but they might speak with the ones in between, men such as himself.

"It is also your father's birthday today," said Shapur Irani.

"I know," said Zairos.

"Death and Time are like two clowns. They play pranks only they find funny."

Shapur Irani's eyes were still on the photograph.

"Your father does not celebrate his birthday," he continued. "He does it out of respect for his brother, and for me. On this one day, the garrulous Aspi Irani retreats into the shadows. But he thinks he does it by choice."

"What do you mean, Pa?"

"Right from the start, your father was a child of shadows."

TEN

1947

BANU SAT IN HER rocking chair and traced shadows on the wall.

Shapur Irani pretended not to notice her. He continued doing his push-ups, his temples swelling red.

"Look," said Banu. "Look at that one."

She fanned herself with a white paper fan. It had a blue hummingbird on it.

"See how fast they move," she said.

Khodi joined in, pointing at the wall. He had his father's strong limbs, but in their movement one could catch Banu's grace.

"That one looks like a bull," said Khodi, now staring at the grandfather clock. "A bull with wings."

Shapur Irani was relieved that his son did not realize something was wrong. Khodi thought Banu was playing a game, doing it all for him.

"He's so imaginative," said Banu. "He'll become an actor or writer."

"Be quiet," said Shapur Irani. "My sons are landowners. Landowners command respect. They do not act or write."

It was all those books she was reading.

Each time he took Banu to Bombay to meet her mother and sisters, she would come back with novels by Charles Dickens and other English writers that Shapur Irani did not care about. On the train, he sat with a pile of books in his lap and watched his wife read, the wonder on her face something he knew he could never create.

To him, stories were a waste of time. They were too thin and invisible. He preferred the solidity of land.

After she got home, she left those books all over the house, in small piles, like stacks of bricks here and there, and she would not let him touch any of them. If he picked a few of them up to get them out of the way, she would, in the kindest tone, request him to put them back in exactly the same spot he had found them.

She made him feel he was not good enough to hold her books.

"This one is so large, Shapur," she said about a shadow again. "It's playing with me. Up and down, up and down . . ."

Khodi was watching his mother, but the wonder had disappeared from his face. Maybe he could feel the heat of his mother's intense belief in those shadows.

Shapur Irani certainly could. "Banu," he said. "Let the shadows be."

With the clockwork movement of a puppet, she bent to one side and picked up a book from the stone floor.

"Aren't you from Iran?" she asked her husband.

She was talking to someone she had recognized after years, after oceans of separation.

"This poet was from Iran too. Do you know Hafez?"

She folded the white paper fan and placed it in her lap.

"This poem is my favourite. It's about selfless love. How the sun never asks the Earth for anything in return for providing light."

Shapur Irani remained unmoved. He could hardly read English, and each time his wife held a book under the light, something in him dimmed.

"I'm going outside," he said to Banu.

He took his shotgun and fired in the air. It was to let the Warlis know that he had a gun and he knew how to use it. That is what he would tell his wife in case she asked.

But he knew the truth.

Each time he fired, he was shooting himself, punishing himself for not being learned, or he was shooting the books that she read, but at least the books took her mind off the shadows, and of the two, he would rather that the books remained.

By the time he got back in, Khodi was trying to console his mother, who was crying. She was staring at the paper fan, opening it, then snapping it shut, then opening it again, caressing the jagged edges of the blue hummingbird.

Shapur Irani knelt beside Banu and rubbed her thigh.

"Banu, what's wrong?"

"It's so sad," she said. "I've crushed the hummingbird's wings."

Something happened, Banu wrote to her mother, *but I wish I could remember what it was.*

That was all she wrote. She stared at the letter while Sohrab slept in her lap. She folded the letter and put it inside the book she was reading. She needed *Oliver Twist*, a novel thick enough to make the days at the farm seem bearable.

Her husband was in the living room doing push-ups again, this time with Khodi on his back. She was glad that Khodi loved his father—his thick neck, his biceps, the way he opened a soda bottle with his teeth, how he suddenly stripped down to his undershorts and slapped his thighs like a wrestler, sending a resounding echo throughout the room.

Banu dreamt of sending both the boys to private school in Bombay, but she knew her husband would never allow it. So she bought books, lots of them. Fairy tales by the Brothers Grimm and Hans Christian Anderson, Aesop's fables, children's books on ancient Indian history, even cookbooks for herself to pass the time, but Shapur Irani would never appreciate the English food she made, the shepherd's pie, for instance. He could not live without his dal and potatoes dipped in red masala, so spicy that their eyes would water, their noses would run, and they would sweat as though they were toiling in the fields.

She wished he could read. Then he might be perceptive enough to notice the shadows on the wall. On some days they were so large and obvious, it almost made her giggle that he could not see them. And they were not the shadows that the lantern cast on the wall. She knew the difference between those shadows and the ones that were following her, strangling her, creeping up on her like thieves—only they had taken everything she had, and now there was nothing left.

The shadows had a terrible smell. There was one in front of her right now.

It was near the grandfather clock, moving with the chimes. A shadow thick and heavy as a drunken man's black winter coat, it had the stickiness of a leech, and the closer it came, the worse the stench got. It was even making Sohrab wail.

She rubbed her belly, hoping to comfort her child. There was one more on the way. It had come sooner than she had wanted it to, but she would find a way to protect it from these shadows.

"Banu," said Shapur Irani.

Even he was panting, trying to catch the thieving shadows.

"Sohrab has dirtied himself," he said. "He has been crying for a long time."

The shadows were clever. She would have to find ways of trapping them. She needed a camera. Perhaps she could hire a photographer.

"Banu," said Shapur Irani firmly. "You need to wash Sohrab."

"Yes," she said to her husband. "We need a photographer. A good one."

For the first time, Shapur Irani wished Jeroo were with them. But she was in Bombay, helping deliver another child, and it would still be a month before she could come to Dahanu.

He went to the station master's office and placed a trunk call to the home Jeroo was in. She was tending to the wife of a Parsi barrister, a man rich enough to enjoy the privileges of having his own telephone.

The crackle on the line was ominous, but she assured him that everything would be fine. She gave him instances of women who experienced similar delusions before or after the birth of a child.

A young girl from Bombay, she said, only seventeen years old, had been forced to marry a much older man, a wealthy Parsi shipbuilder with bucked teeth. When she gave birth to a daughter, she asked Jeroo why the child had bucked teeth. When Jeroo explained to her that newborns do not have teeth, the girl flew into a rage and broke dishes and anything else she could get her hands on.

"What I mean to say is that it's normal," said Jeroo over the telephone. "Her behaviour will pass in the way floods or famines pass."

On his way home, Shapur Irani wondered if he should have told Jeroo that Banu had stopped bathing. It had been more than a week, and she kept blaming the smell on the shadows, and he did not have the heart to tell her that she was the one sending out an odour.

When he got home, both Khodi and Sohrab were asleep. Banu was standing at the stove, boiling water for tea. For a moment she looked exactly the way she did the time he first met her, when she was sixteen. He remembered her blue frilled blouse and the long earrings she used to wear, at the ends of which were pearls, ivory raindrops hanging six inches below her ears.

"Is that for my bath?" he asked, knowing full well she was preparing tea. "I need to have a bath."

She nodded, her pale cheeks showing a few red blood vessels.

He replaced the small container with a larger one. When the water was hot enough, he used a thick white towel to protect his hands while he carried the copper container to the bathroom. He emptied the water into a green bucket.

He did not ask her permission. Slowly, carefully, he removed the strap of her pink nightgown, and was pleased when she stepped out of it herself. Her belly was white and large, and there was a child in there, and if there was anyone who could help Banu, it was this child. Someone from the inside.

She let him bathe her, but all throughout tears ran down her face along with the soapy hot water. She kept staring at the lantern, flinching each time it flickered. The dark stone walls of the bathroom were not helping her.

When he was done, he dried her with a towel and made her sit on a bath stool. He then went to her dressing table to fetch her hairbrush from the drawer. Her back was hunched by the time he returned, one leg placed ahead of the other, as though her body was trying to go somewhere but had suddenly forgotten how.

He propped her up and brushed her hair, felt long wet strands against his palm, let them slide off, then caught them again, and stood behind her, wordless.

Perhaps he needed to take her to Bombay for a few days.

Here, she was so close to slipping away into a fearsome solitude that even the single tick of a clock could provide that final push.

Against his will, he went.

Against his better judgment, he passed by the very building in which Daryoush the baker used to have his small shop.

Many Irani cafés had sprung up in the city now, the Yazdani Bakery and Kyani & Co. being the two most reputed. Most of the Iranis who had left Iran were creating a new kind of eatery in Bombay—the chaikhana. The moustachioed owners proudly walked on black-and-white-diamond-tiled floors, ensuring that their white marble tables were spotless, their wooden chairs had adequate nails hammered into them to hold customers of all shapes and sizes, while they dipped crusty brun bread, with a layer of butter thick as snakeskin, into hot chai. Apart from the buttered bread, pudding, and biscuits, they sold cigars, medicine, rosewater, soaps, anything one needed. One store, the K. R. Sassanian, was gaining fanfare for its three-tiered wedding cakes.

But no matter how successful these Irani restaurants got, for Shapur Irani there was one store that towered above the rest. It did not have a name, for it had no tables and chairs, just a large wood-fired oven and a glass showcase, and it supplied bread to the other Irani cafés—and anyone else—quietly, peacefully, as though that were its humble mission.

Someday, Shapur Irani would tell his sons about Daryoush.

He would tell them that the baker's profession was just a camouflage.

To him, Daryoush was one of the Amesha Spentas, the holy immortals. The heat of his oven provided the warmth a young boy needed to forget his dead father. Or if not forget, to remember without collapsing.

His dough was, and would remain, a reminder of the simple goodness human beings were capable of. It was worth more than the treasury of Cyrus the Great, and was more powerful than the armies of Alexander.

In Bombay, the Iranis had gathered a reputation as honest, dedicated bakers and café owners because they had put all the gratefulness that came with survival into their tea and cakes. All the warmth that a new land had offered them was offered back to the inhabitants of that land. But while the owners sat at their counters and collected money, and their wives spread aromatic incense around pictures of Zarathushtra, their minds were in Iran, the sweetness of their pastries dissolving when they thought of the ones they had to leave behind.

To lose land, to be driven away from it, was like losing a loved one. No wonder it was called the motherland.

Shapur Irani knew what it was like to lose both—land and his mother. It was strange, but what he remembered most about his mother was not the taste of her saffron rice, the smell of her hair, or the way his heart found a rhythm so impossibly peaceful when he was in her embrace. What he remembered most about his mother was a sound.

A door knock.

Even though his parents' home was made of modest mud bricks, the door was something to be proud of. "It's so wide," Vamog would say, "that even the warrior Rostam does not have to shrink his broad shoulders to enter."

But the door had two door knockers.

The knocker on the left was used by women, and the one on the right by men. When men knocked, the sound had weight, and Shapur Irani loved to imagine all the things it could possibly contain: the batter of a mace, the slap of a thousand droplets of sweat, the power of a heavy forearm and thick fingers that circled around the knocker.

And when women knocked, it had a lilt, the secret strength that allowed man to exist in the first place, allowed him to have weight, inspired him to shed a thousand droplets of sweat. When little Shapur heard that sound, it meant that his mother's friends had come to visit and suddenly the small house with a low roof transformed into a haven where laughter skipped across the room and songs through the air.

After his mother's death, it was not Vamog's subdued wails that made Shapur Irani truly understand that his mother was no more. Nor was it the cold food, or the heaviness of the low roof, or the dark circles under Vamog's eyes as though Ahriman himself was darkening them with his charcoal spit.

It was only when the door knocks of women stopped that Shapur Irani knew his mother was truly gone. No women came to visit, the softness had vanished, and only the gloom of the weighty knocks of men remained, and neither son nor father wanted to answer those.

Shapur Irani knew what it was like to lose his land, to lose his mother, and now he was losing his wife. He held Banu's hand, squeezed it hard to let her know that he was with her. After leaving Khodi and Sohrab at Banu's mother's house, Shapur Irani and Banu went to a movie at the Excelsior. It was a Chaplin film.

"Look at what he is doing," Shapur Irani said to Banu. "That little man is fighting the rich, the ugly, the bullies of this world."

He smiled as he watched Chaplin outwit the police. Shapur Irani loved the fact that people of authority were stupid giants and Chaplin got the better of them without really trying.

But there was no response from Banu. Not a smile, not even a crease of a smile.

At that moment, he wished he could read. If only he could read those thick books with hard, unyielding backs, he would be able to discuss stories with his wife, he would be worthy of being her husband. As of now, he was a man with land and a shotgun, and perhaps she regretted her decision to marry him. Maybe he was the problem.

Unlike the Parsis, who pondered over important papers under the glow of electric lamps, whose signatures meant something, whose voices could be heard on acting stages, who were sons of rich cotton traders, Shapur Irani sometimes felt like a heathen. That was why he hated Bombay. The city made him feel inadequate. At least on the farm, the trees depended on him. Each step on his farm was the equivalent of an ink signature on an important document.

In his heart he knew that maybe Banu was right, that the boys needed to read books. They might develop into mathematicians or accountants, but there was another part of him that told him his boys would be exactly like him, men of the soil. He had no education, but he had guts.

That was all one needed in the world. The courage to start.

He left his homeland on a donkey, but then he started his liquor stall and understood that land was gold, and now he was a landowner. If he were an accountant or a mathematician, what would he leave his sons? His knack for numbers, an explanation of the laws of the universe? Those were not things a man could bequeath. Those were things that evaporated, that were eaten up along with a man's flesh.

He looked at his wife's face again.

She was paying for his sins.

So much pain had unfolded before his chickoo trees and yet they continued to give fruit. It was the same with his wife. She continued to bear him children and he feared that she was now paying the price.

She was not even talking to him anymore. His wife's mind was a place to which he no longer had entry. He envied those writers. She welcomed them in. But the books were almost capturing her, they were spreading all over the floor, contaminating it, some overturned, some pages fluttering in the breeze when the main door was open, Khodi glancing through them, Sohrab eating the edges of the lighter ones, Banu stepping over them, not allowing any of them to be moved.

When Banu was asleep Shapur Irani would hold a book in his hand and beg Ahura Mazda to help him read, and an hour or two after he had failed, all he could do was smell the pages and hope that their yellowed wisdom would somehow stay with him, help him heal his wife, make him understand, how, why, something had come over her.

She had stopped speaking about the shadows now, but something else had entered her world. Stillness.

He had never seen a living being go so still. After walking over her books, she would sit in one position for hours, with not even the slightest movement such as a flick of the wrist. At the most her nostrils would flare, or he would notice a twitch in her neck, and he would have to draw assurance from that.

He looked her way again, in the darkness, wondering what he had done to her.

Just then the audience in the theatre had a hearty laugh. His wife got up from her seat.

"I'm going to the toilet," she said.

Shapur Irani got up as well. She was too pregnant to go on her own.

"No," she said. "I want to go alone."

Not knowing what the right thing was, he sat down again.

She walked past him, apologizing for stepping on his foot. She went down the aisle, but did not walk towards the exit. Pushing the hair off her face, she walked towards the screen. She kept on walking with her arms outstretched until she was close enough to touch it. Shapur Irani went after her, shamed by the silhouette of her waving arms in front of all those people, and even Chaplin, that timeless troublemaker, stopped for moment, a look of sadness in his eyes.

After the episode in the theatre, she stopped speaking completely.

Weeks later, when her son was born, the labour pains had a muffled quality. It was not the sound of release. In stifling her screams, she was trying to stifle her son. She did not look at him until Jeroo made her hold him.

But she could hardly care for her child.

She refused to bathe, she did not cook or clean, she just lay in bed and stared at the cracks in the wall.

And then one day she snapped out of it all, like a limp neck that suddenly finds all the correct joints and sockets.

She had a shower, she cooked beans and potatoes, and Shapur Irani was glad. She even placed Aspi between the two of them, kissed him on the forehead, and rubbed her nose against his. She smiled. He had forgotten what her smile was like, those full lips coming alive, her face relaxing once more, eyelids opening and closing as they were meant to, unlike the cold stares of the past months that brought desolate whiteness to everything.

He ran his finger along her arm. It had been ages since he had touched her. Even she reached out to him and held his hand. He longed to make love to her again, but it was too soon.

"I have to go to the bathroom," she said, sliding out from under the grey blanket.

She was back soon, fanning herself with the paper fan that had a hummingbird on it. She opened the fan as wide as she could, tried to carefully flatten out the creases.

"Please don't ever close this fan," she said to Shapur Irani. "The bird cries when we do that."

ELEVEN

2000

AT THE FARM the workers stood in line for their daily wages. It was the men who were always first, who would spend their wages in a flash as though if they held on to their money for a while, or even thought of saving, some terrible misfortune might strike them. Once the men collected, the women stepped forward, and Zairos put a tick next to their names in a ledger.

Sukhar, Navsia, Kasia . . . Laxmi, Sevanti, Saku . . .

After collecting their money, they started to leave. Zairos noticed an oddness in their manner. They had the gait of men and women who had never known freedom. There was a permanent stutter in their walk, sometimes fast, sometimes slow, and they always went in single file, as if fearful that if they moved naturally, the dream of a better life would vanish and a new set of monarchs would take charge.

But Kusum's walk was different from theirs.

Her day had been spent fixing a wire net around the ends of long wooden sticks, so they could be used to scoop chickoos from the higher branches.

"Seth, he will come for me again," said Kusum.

"Who?" asked Zairos.

"Laxman. He will not stay quiet."

The minute Zairos had woken up that morning, he had questioned his attack on Laxman. It had been a bold, impulsive move, the aftermath unpredictable. But perhaps that was its appeal. There was no remorse from Zairos. That meant he had done nothing wrong. Otherwise he would have felt something in his chest, the way the first hit of nicotine tingled the brain when he smoked after a long time.

He would have to see it through to the end. To some extent, he wished there was a man other than himself to whom Kusum could turn to for protection.

"Does your father have any brothers?" he asked her.

"No," she said.

After listening to his grandfather the night before, Zairos wondered if the protection that he offered Kusum could make any difference in the first place. Banumai had all the cover a woman could hope for, such was the ferocity of her husband's love, and yet her descent into sadness was so rapid that love was not enough.

"Laxman won't come," said Zairos. "Not after a beating like that."

"We are used to beatings," she said.

She stood in front of him like a child. Both her parents gone, she was out in the open, with only a yellow blouse to cover her. It occurred to him that this was the same blouse she had worn the night before. When she had left Laxman's hut, she had to leave all her belongings behind.

Like someone whose house had been burned down. All she had was the knowledge that she was still breathing. At the moment, she needed objects. A few blouses, a hair net or two, who knew what else.

"Come with me," he said.

He sat in the car and started the engine. She fiddled with the doorknob before figuring it out. When he passed Aspi Villa, he waved out to his mother, who was on the swing, listening to French dialogue on her headphones. It always amused Zairos how Zoroastrians butchered the French language. His favourite skewering was of *eau de cologne*, which old ladies affectionately referred to as colon water.

"That's my mother," he said to Kusum.

But Kusum did not look. She stared at her ankles and at the black rubber mat that slept on the floor of the car like night.

When they reached the Big Boss Hair Salon, they turned right towards the bazaar, a mutant being where shops of every kind sprouted from thin air. A man sold old hammers, another repaired seats for two-wheelers, an old woman weighed magazines and newspapers on a scale to sell as scraps, and an "optician" displayed fake Ray-Bans. These were the mobile stores, one-man operations that found homes depending on the tiredness of their owners' legs.

Then came the main entrance to Dahanu station with auto rickshaws buzzing, going round and round in frenzied circles, sometimes without passengers. Once they passed the station, the bazaar ended and a long street began, the most famous, populated street in Dahanu, known as Irani Road.

Irani Road got its name because the majority of land was once owned by a man named H. K. Irani. Each and every kind of Irani could be spotted here—men with handlebar moustaches walked with their chests out, old-timers with walking sticks waved out to people at random, and white-haired women in their housecoats talked to themselves because their husbands were no longer alive, women who carried an air of resignation and asked the printed flowers on their housecoats where the old days had gone.

Zairos found a parking spot outside Santosh's wholesale shed. He got out, but Kusum remained in the car. There were too many people not of her kind. The sun was too bright. Sometimes light did a disservice, did not know when to back off.

"Why are we here, seth?" she asked.

She could not bear the zooming of scooters and motorcycles, the Hindi music blaring from the first floor of an apartment, the rubber tires piled in a heap outside the tire shop. She looked at Zairos, at how white his shirt was, and she was afraid to get out. He wanted to tell her that there were a few Warlis walking around as well, but she could see that herself, and they were working—either carrying twigs on their heads or washing cars. Here she was *in* a car . . .

"You'll have to come out," he said.

He said it firmly. Now it was an order, not a choice, something she could easily follow. She cleaned the edges of her feet on the rubber mat and stepped out, and it made Zairos smile because she was trying not to dirty the road.

She walked behind Zairos.

"Walk with me," he said.

But she continued to follow. He noticed how she moved away from the paved road, which was too hot and would burn the soles of her feet.

"Do not follow me, Kusum."

Once again, she nodded her head. Once again, she walked behind him with her head down.

"This is the dairy where I used to drink falooda with my father," he said, doubting that she had ever tasted the drink, a deliciously sweet mixture of cold milk, tukhmari seeds, a generous dose of rosewater, and a chunk of vanilla ice cream. "Do you want to try some?" he asked.

Without looking up at him, she shook her head. Zairos felt he should not have told her the name of the street. It did not matter to the many Gujaratis, Marwaris, Muslims, Jains, and Hindus living here as well, but Kusum was different from them. With every step, her head was dropping lower and lower.

When they passed a clothing boutique, she looked up, darted glances to the mannequin in the window. Up she looked, and then away, as if afraid that at any moment the plastic woman in jeans would move and speak to her.

He stopped by a coconut stall and asked for two coconuts. Kusum gulped the water down, and some of it fell on her blouse just as one of Zairos' distant relatives, a young woman named Roxanne, stood in front of them.

"On a date?" asked Roxanne. Roxanne was also known as TG, the Town Gossip.

"No," said Zairos. "She's my English professor."

"Really," said Roxanne, adjusting her cream T-shirt and taking off her sunglasses to take a better look, her pink skin flushed by the sun. "She's got a hot body."

"You could learn something from her then."

It was not the politest thing to say, especially considering that Roxanne was plump and at one point wanted to marry Zairos. But the woman could not be encouraged. No matter what he told her, by the end of the day she would have her own version anyway, more complete than any Encyclopedia Britannica.

Away they walked from TG's teeth and her pink cheeks, to a roadside stall that sold all the knick-knacks that the Warlis needed. All the goods had been placed on the ground on a white sheet.

"Pick what you need," Zairos said.

Kusum just stood, next to a tall man in a brown shirt and shorts. She hid behind the man, but he bent down to have a look at a bracelet, and that was the end of her cover.

Zairos knew he would have to start.

The first item he picked was a pink mirror with a large frame. He held it towards Kusum, encouraging her to look at herself. Next, he chose two black combs, one with the teeth far apart and one with the teeth very fine.

Seeing that his hands were full with a pink mirror and two combs, Kusum bent down slowly and took three cloths, all dull grey, to cover her below the waist. She glanced towards Zairos to see if that was okay, and it was, so he took a red basket that was for sale and placed the mirror and combs in it, and she put the grey cloths in as well. She added hair bands, kajal, and some bindis, and the woman who owned the stall sat cross-legged and waited, the bored expression on her face suggesting that she would rather be on the high seas battling waves and snaring fish than selling makeup and blouses on Irani Road.

When they got back to the car, Zairos put the red basket in the hutch. Once they passed the showroom that sold Mitsubishi tractors, the air became much cleaner. Zairos noticed that as the car picked up speed, Kusum held on to the seat with both hands, and when he took a sharp bend, she swerved away from the door.

"Don't be scared," he told her.

"I'm not scared."

"You were fine the last time. Why are you afraid now?"

"I like to walk, seth. I am used to walking."

"We are travelling a great distance. If we were to walk from the farm to Irani Road, it would take too long."

"Maybe we are not meant to go that far," she said.

Zairos went off the main road, over the roots of an old tree, the trunk of which had yellow paste on it, which signified that it was holy or that some ceremony had taken place. A bullock cart wobbled towards them, the wizened man at the helm looking just as tired and whipped as his bullocks.

It was time to stop the car. It was time to face her.

He would have to show her his face without wearing a master's sheen, let her know that she was free to do or say as she pleased.

Maybe Zairos did not need to speak. He needed to touch.

With one hand still on the steering wheel, he slowly took his other hand towards her, towards her cheek, and she closed her eyes, she was clearly nervous, and so was he, but he let his hand remain there, and his fingertips touched her ear, and he could feel her breath from her nose on his forearm, or maybe it was from her mouth.

"I knew it," he heard a voice say.

It was TG, penguin plump on her scooter, the round sunglasses on her nose ready to slide off in disgust.

"Don't you have any shame?" she said to Kusum in Marathi.

"I think you should be asking me that question," said Zairos. "And the answer is no."

He wondered if there was a Marathi word for "penguin."

It should have been expected. TG derived pleasure from this sort of thing. She loved scandal. And if it did not exist, she manufactured it.

Zairos looked at Kusum, hoping that she was not cowering.

But she was. She had tightened up and her hands were clasped together in unconscious prayer.

He thought of driving off, but that would only give TG pleasure.

Then he realized that this was not about TG or himself.

Kusum needed to know that he was with her. That would give her the strength to become visible again.

"Her name is Kusum," he said to TG.

His voice did not have the tone of a rebuttal. It was tender; he was introducing someone he knew. This woman is tougher than all of you, he seemed to be saying. And more beautiful.

"It's okay, Kusum," he said. "Don't worry."

Now there was no need for him to leave.

He turned the car engine off. With only the stutter of her scooter remaining, TG had no choice but to waddle away.

That evening, Zairos was at the beach shielding his eyes from the sand. He had dropped Kusum off, and they were in different worlds again. She in a hut without windows, and he facing the vast unconquerable sea.

He had done his duty.

He had bought her combs, a mirror, and three grey cloths— enough protection against Laxman.

In any case, he was at the beach now, where the salty breeze healed the day's tiredness, and people in countries on the other side of the Arabian Sea experienced a similar healing. Even the weary heads of prisoners as they rested against stone walls were touched by the sea breeze, and women in burkhas lifted their veils just an inch to let it sneak in. Sand and wind worked magic in ways even God never intended.

The beach was an Irani ritual. After the men had finished their afternoon siestas and made obligatory rounds of the farms, all Iranis went to the beach. It was their outing for the evening. Decades ago, they clip-clopped to the beach in their tongas; now the horses had been replaced by cars, but certain things never changed, like the straw mats and whiskey bottles.

Aspi Irani sat on a straw mat with Mithoo, an ice bucket between them. Mithoo was studying for her Montessori exam, and Aspi Irani was studying ice cubes, deciding which ones to put in his whiskey glass. When he spotted one to his liking, he put his hand in the ice bucket and plucked it out. "Use the tongs, Aspi," said Mithoo. So Aspi Irani took the tongs and used them to scratch his feet. He took his first sip of whiskey and then pointed the tongs towards an abandoned boat on the shore. "These tongs are useful," he told his wife.

A few feet away from him, women, mostly unmarried, huddled together on one mat. They all had dreams of escaping from Dahanu Road and having lives in France or Switzerland, or at least Bombay, and some of their friends had escaped, but sadly not to Paris or Geneva but to Halifax or New Jersey, only to freeze and yearn for the warmth of Dahanu Road again. Some were naturally beautiful, with names such as Navaz and Farzeen; others were dolled up, red lipstick so loud they could pass as mob molls.

"Je suis un homme!" Aspi Irani shouted out to them.

"Very good, dear," said Mithoo. That was all the French he knew.

While the women dreamt of flying to far-off countries, high above their heads Xerxes the dentist soared over the pine trees in his blue and red glider. Years ago, when people saw him at the beach constructing his airplane using the modified engine of a Java motorcycle, they thought him insane. But up he went one day, no doors to enclose him, just vast sky on either side, a mad dentist gritting his teeth, red helmet stuck to his head like a velvet prayer cap, offering rides to anyone who dared make the journey.

As Xerxes clipped the tops of pine trees, below, whiskey filled the bellies of Iranis, and Zairos heard a cry from a ten-year-old boy whose father, Tehmuras the Lame, had slapped him in full view of everyone.

"This dumb bastard keeps failing in his exams," fumed Tehmuras.

Frenny, a silver-haired schoolteacher, got up from her mat and said, "Tehmuras, I've told you, your son is dyslexic. He has a learning disability. Show some compassion."

"Iranis are not known for their compassion," said a gleeful Aspi Irani. "We would make great Nazis. Except that were are too lazy to kill, and we have such a low intelligence quotient that instead of gassing the Jews, we would gas *ourselves* to death."

As if on cue, Marzi Psycho appeared in his jeep with his pale skin and shifty eyes. Each evening, he would bolt the main door of his house with a heavy Godrej lock, which in itself was unusual, but what took the cake, the pudding, the entire bakery in fact, was that his wife was still inside. She was not allowed to step out of the house in the evenings.

"Marzi!" shouted Aspi Irani. "The Taliban called. They got your résumé and are sending you a work permit!"

One by one, the beach was filled with these obscene marvels, men without aim or purpose, men who allowed themselves to be ravaged by time. They were at the beach every single evening.

The women on the straw mat suddenly turned around and looked at Zairos. The young ones giggled and the older ones showed some sort of disdain. Zairos knew why. TG was among them. All he had done was comfort Kusum by giving her the warmth of his palm, but TG's fondness for poison would turn it into something more salable. Soon his name would be on the lips of all Irani women, how vile he was, how demeaning, how this, how that.

Somehow, he wanted this. He wanted people to know.

Zairos stared at the abandoned boat on the shore. The way it slanted was almost pitiful, in dire need of human touch. The drone of Xerxes' airplane softened, he was as far away as he could be from gums and root canals, and Zairos wanted to be far away too, far away from it all, and he felt neither happy nor unhappy, neither at peace nor at conflict, just a person who was afraid to look at the beasts around him because that was exactly what he was destined to turn into.

TWELVE

ZAIROS SAT BY his grandfather's side late into the night. He had just watched a petty human drama unfold. When he had gone to his grandfather's house a couple of hours before, the rocking chair was empty. The main door was open, and when Zairos entered, his grandfather was on the floor. Shapur Irani was trying to get up. He was on his way to the bathroom. He had soiled himself.

Get out of here. That was Zairos' first thought.

Shapur Irani, the proud general that he was, would never allow anyone close to him when he was sick. Only his servant Lakhu was allowed to help him, but Lakhu had gone to a wedding. Zairos wanted to flee, but when he saw his grandfather on all fours, trying to get up again, he just picked the man up and helped him to the bathroom. Neither of them said a word.

Shit stains. The slow degradation that comes with old age.

Shapur Irani now sat in his easy chair an ashamed, exhausted skeleton. This once upon a time tall man, this once upon a time muscular man, was panting. He was running in his mind. His skin was waiting to leave his skeleton, but was not getting permission because the degradation was not complete.

"Banu," he said.

Zairos wished he had a clear picture of what his grandmother looked like, but there were no photographs of her once she met Shapur Irani. The man did not take any, not even on their wedding. "When you live with someone for so many years, you don't need to," he had told Zairos. A photograph was such a cheap imitation anyway, looking at the truth from one side only. Banu still moved in his mind, danced in and out of his life. But when he uttered her name, Zairos could not tell what emotion was behind it.

"I want to go," said Shapur Irani.

Zairos reached out, placed his hands under his grandfather's armpits to lift him up.

"No," said Shapur Irani. "Not to the bathroom."

Zairos understood.

"The more I want to go, the more my body keeps me here. Remember that, Zairos. The man who is eager to die shall live the longest."

Zairos fetched his grandfather a glass of water. He did not know what else to do. It had been the same glass for years, with a pink plastic plate that covered the mouth to prevent flies from falling in. When Shapur Irani drank the water, he did so hesitatingly, knowing that by drinking water he was giving life to himself, and that was the last thing he wanted.

"I did not understand Banu," he said. "I should have understood her dreams."

This was one of the things his grandfather said uncon-sciously and it would have been wrong for Zairos to pursue it. One night, after he fell asleep in his rocking chair, just as Zairos was about to leave, his grandfather said, "Don't drink from that cup. It was Khodi's last cup of tea. I have put a label on the bottom."

Shapur Irani held his stomach and grimaced.

"Should I call the doctor?" asked Zairos.

"You go home, Zairos. Go to sleep."

"I'll sleep here today, Pa."

"Go home. I'm fine."

"I want to talk to you about something. Will you listen?"

Shapur Irani nodded his head slowly, the white bristles of his eyebrows pointing upwards. Zairos told his grandfather about Kusum and about what he had done to Laxman.

Shapur Irani did not say a word. He listened.

At the end of it all, there was heaviness in the air like the silence that came after cannons had blasted.

For a second night in a row, Shapur Irani was being taught humility by his bowels. He was in a trance again, that death-like state that birds are in when they lose a wing.

"From the time I found out her name, I knew she had to be mine," said Shapur Irani. "She was truly my Banu-Pars, my Lady of Persia."

His love was one deep wound, bullet after bullet. It was the price a man paid for giving himself to one woman with such abandon.

"I was unable to talk to my Banu," said Shapur Irani. "But Dickens, he was able to reach her. Dickens, he understood Banu better than I did, and she felt he cared about her. But I promise you no one loved your grandmother more than I did. No man has loved a woman so . . . so . . . what's the word, give me a good word, my son."

If only he could transfer that feeling he had to his grandson. If only he could take one of those thick black pipes that ran through the farm, attach one end of it to his heart and let it all flow through, towards Zairos, there would be an outpouring so strong, a rumble so loud, it would cause the chimney of the thermal power plant to shake.

"I loved her but I did not understand her," he said. "And Dickens was giving her a chance to escape."

"From what?" asked Zairos.

"I wish I knew."

"Then maybe it's not about escape."

"How would you know?" said Shapur Irani.

There was anger in his voice. It was not directed at Zairos. It was put out there, in the air, and it had enough poison in it to kill an insect.

"Do you even know what I did? Let me tell you what I did. You must know."

Zairos had never heard his grandfather speak like that. Confession was universes away from the nature of this man. Confession was a failure, an act of cowardice, something leprous. But his bowels had temporarily destabilized him.

"One night, when she was reading, I said to her, 'Banu, come to bed.' She did not answer me. The boys were asleep. I said again, 'Banu, please, I am not well.' She replied, 'I am coming in a minute. I am at the end of this book.' The book's cover was blue. She said to me, 'This book is very interesting, Shapur. There's this man, and his wife has committed suicide, and he is in so much grief that he is unable to speak. Then at night he dreams of her and asks her why she killed herself. She tells him that she left because he did not understand her. It was *he* who had killed her because of his lack of understanding. It is the most beautiful thing I have ever read, Shapur. You should read it.' I don't know what happened to me, but when she said, 'You should read it,' I went into a rage. I got up and gathered all her books from the floor and threw them in a heap outside the house. She started shouting at me and I had never heard Banu shout before, so I got even more scared. I felt the books were evil because they were making her mad, so I hurried even more. Then I went to the kitchen, took some cooking oil and a box of matches and went outside. When she saw the box of matches, she started screaming even more. I put my hand over her mouth to shut her up, and just then Khodi came into the room. I went out and bolted the door. I poured oil all over Dickens and the fairy tales and started praying. I prayed and prayed and poured oil and set the books on fire. It was a burning, mangled train of books. And I continued to pray and Banu watched through the window and after a while she stopped screaming. I will live very long, Zairos. Very long."

THIRTEEN

IN THE SUMMER AFTERNOONS, Dahanu was a pot of boiling water. So hot that flesh melted, slid off arms and legs like loose clothes falling to the floor. In the olden days, before ceiling fans, the Iranis ate watermelons and placed the over-turned shells on their heads to cool down. That was what Zairos felt like doing as he saw his sweat drip to the floor at Anna's.

Running from the same heat, a white stray dog had housed itself in an overturned auto rickshaw. The rickshaw was miss-ing its tires. Five other strays, all brown, ate crushed glucose biscuits that Zairos was feeding them as they strolled about the place or lay like queens in their mud holes. The clashing of metal could be heard from Manu's mechanic shop. Sparks flew from his welding gun as workers at the adjoining petrol pump walked about in brown uniforms with grease on their faces.

Once the regulars arrived with their sagging chins, per-spiring foreheads, handlebar moustaches, and silver reading glasses, Merwan Mota opened his little blue diabetes pouch and lifted his white shirt until the pink balloon of his stomach rested on Anna's table. Then he injected himself in the stomach with a needle and let the needle remain there for a while. "Look," he said. "No hands."

Aspi Irani kept glaring at the book Keki the Italian was reading. Camus had been replaced by Hamsun, and when Aspi Irani read the title, *Hunger*, he pointed to Merwan Mota, who had gobbled up twelve lychees by then, and said, "Merwan can write that book better. He has first-hand experience."

But soon Aspi Irani was cocooned inside the Mobile Casino with his brother and other devoted gamblers. The car was running and the AC was on. There had been complaints about the Mobile Casino from the residents of the apartments above Anna's, as well as from the nursing home, and in response to the complaints Aspi Irani had installed a "buffalo horn" inside the Mobile Casino. With the precision of Big Ben he pressed the horn every hour, the loud grunt of a buffalo a reminder to the residents that the Mobile Casino would not budge. If anything, it had found a voice.

Zairos was playing carrom with Behrooz, who was scratching his back with a screwdriver from his spare-parts shop next door. The blue ivory striker slid across the board, delicately cut the Queen, and she fell, gently, into the pocket. Each time Behrooz missed a shot, which was often, he spat out an abuse in Farsi, a language so sweet even curse words sounded like blessings.

An old black Fiat pulled up at Anna's. Manu, who had been resting against the overturned auto rickshaw, quickly got up. He assumed the car was in need of repair. A woman in a green salwar kameez got out of the car and walked straight up to the carrom board.

"Who is Zairos?" she asked.

Zairos was sure she knew who he was. They had never spoken, but in Dahanu everyone knew each other. Havovi was from Bangalore, and she had married a promising lawyer from Bombay. They had come to Dahanu on their honeymoon, and by the time the honeymoon had ended, she had filed for divorce. The owner of the Pearl Line Resort had said that she had caught her husband with a tribal. After that, she stayed in Dahanu, the very place that had destroyed her marriage even before it had begun.

"Who is Zairos?" she asked again.

"That's me."

"My name is Havovi," she said, wiping the perspiration from her upper lip.

"I know who you are."

"Good. Then you know that I belong to an organization for Warli rights."

"Yes," said Zairos. "You're famous."

Havovi must have been an attractive woman at one time, but now she had too many veins on her neck and forehead, the result of the anger she must have felt when she saw a tribal woman coiled around her husband.

"A case is being filed against you," she said. "By a man named Laxman. Do you know him?"

"I know him."

"He said that you and some others attacked him in his hut at night. You beat him and then took his wife away."

Behrooz looked at Zairos, puzzled. He took his screwdriver and scratched his neck with it.

"Well, did you assault him?" asked Havovi.

"I don't need to answer you," said Zairos.

"A police case is being registered. I am taking Laxman with me to the police station. Now do you have anything to say?"

The man was a wife beater and it was time someone thrashed him to a pulp. This was not a matter for the courts to settle because it was not about Warli rights. It was about preventing a woman from turning black and blue.

But Zairos kept silent.

Merwan Mota, however, had something to say.

It came in the form of a strange sound, of him sucking on a one-litre bottle of Pepsi. He sucked with much love and craving as though the bottle contained oxygen. After finishing it, he crushed the bottle and threw it on the floor.

Then Bumble changed the angle of his Ray-Bans and placed his hands on his hips, a pose he had been trying to perfect since he was eleven. He blew cigarette smoke all over the carrom board. He was constipated and had smoked ten cigarettes in two hours in the hope that it would ease his condition.

"Havovi," he said. "Do the Warlis have a remedy for constipation?"

"You think this is a joke," she said.

"No," said Zairos. "I am on the same side as you. You are protecting the man. I am protecting the woman."

But then he checked himself.

This was not a matter of sides, of right and wrong. This woman could create trouble for him. He welcomed it. Sometimes the Bedouin in the desert longed for the sand to blind him.

The next day at Anna's, as flies pushed their way through cigarette smoke like fighter planes through clouds, Zairos waited
for the police to show up. He would rather they found him at
Anna's than Aspi Villa, as it would surely disturb his mother.
So he stayed at Anna's for as long as he could.

The stray dogs that made their home at Anna's were nowhere
in sight. Their sudden disappearance meant one thing—the
circus was in town. Lions and tigers had to be fed, and at night
the stray dogs were kidnapped by locals who freelanced as
meat suppliers.

Keki the Italian brandished a copy of a new book, Nietzsche's
Thus Spake Zarathustra. "It has nothing to do with our prophet,"
he said. But the title got everyone excited, especially Aspi Irani,
who read a few pages, drove off in his car, and returned with a
Sony two-in-one. He pressed Play, and as Anna fried vadas in a
sea of oil, classical music was heard for the first time within
those walls. "It's by a composer named Strauss," he said. "It's
called 'Also Sprach Zarathustra,' and even *this* has nothing to do
with our prophet."

Then another song followed, a rock number by Queen,
whose lead singer, Freddie Mercury aka Farrokh Bulsara,
was Parsi. "Now this man sings the truth," said Aspi Irani as
he joined his fellow Zoroastrian in singing "Fat Bottomed
Girls."

But the mention of bottoms had no effect on Anna, who
was not his usual self. The Clark Gable smile had disappeared
because his wife had gone back to Udipi to nurse her dying
mother. When Anna poured tea for Zairos from his tall steel
jug, it was without zest. Even the tea tasted different; it had
absorbed his longing.

At the day's end, Zairos had to go back to the farm to dispense the wages. He was disappointed that the police had not shown up. The wait was troubling, like a mosquito trapped in his ear.

When he saw Kusum missing from the line, Zairos left the money and ledger with Damu and went to her hut. Old Rami was on her haunches, smoking a beedi. When her lips closed, one diabolical tooth jutted out. A straw broom lay against the wall of the hut, its weak bristles unable to support its own weight.

"Where is Kusum?" he asked.

"At work," said Rami.

"I just came from the farm. Why are you lying to me?"

"Seth, you have done enough for us."

"Has something happened to her?"

Rami sucked on the beedi for a very long time. Then she pulled the beedi away from her, examined it at length. She wiped her brow with the palm of her hand. Her movements were slow and deliberate.

"She's inside, isn't she?" asked Zairos.

"Seth, you did not do a wise thing by beating up Laxman. Kusum is young and in time she will learn that what she asked you to do was wrong."

"Did Laxman do something to her?"

Zairos should have listened to Kusum. She had warned him that Laxman would come for her and all he had done was buy her combs and clothes.

Two women from a neighbouring hut were staring at Zairos. Zairos could not tell if it was the setting sun that made them frown or his presence. They stood very still.

"Kusum," he called out.

There was no reply. A dog panted its way towards Zairos, its tongue hanging out of its mouth with heaviness. An old man with powder hair ambled by, chewing on something.

"Did he touch her?" asked Zairos.

He had taken things too lightly. Now his negligence was churning inside him, bolting like a mad steed.

"What did you think he would do?" asked Rami. "Just sit and let you take his wife away? Just because you are a seth does not mean you are a god. You are not a god. Even the gods are not gods anymore."

"Call her out now or I'm going in."

But Zairos did not need to. Kusum stepped out of the hut.

There was a bald patch on the side of her head, red, the size of a large orange. The bastard had pulled out her hair.

Kusum slowly walked towards Zairos but stopped a few feet away.

Zairos could not bring himself to circle his arms around her. Rami was watching. The old man who chewed on something was watching. The two women from the neighbouring hut who did not move were watching.

For over an hour, Zairos waited among the bushes for Laxman to appear.

He understood how Ganpat must have felt. Laxman was painting his daughter's body with his fists and there was nothing Ganpat could do. That is why he had droopy shoulders. They carried the shame of his daughter's beatings.

At the other end of the hamlet, men sat in a circle and passed a pipe around. Laxman might be among them. It was hard to tell. But even if Zairos did spot Laxman, there was nothing Zairos could do. The fact that he was here was demeaning.

Laxman had an Irani seth hiding in the bushes.

If Zairos' grandfather saw him now, he would get off that rocking chair and roar. He would set fire to the entire hamlet the way he did his wife's books.

Maybe Chambal the dacoit was right. Wounding a man only added to the dragon breath, increased the fury tenfold. Zairos had not considered talking to Laxman. But it would have made no difference. With every strand of hair that Laxman pulled out, he was clutching in his hand the constellation of his own sickness, and if he could not see it, if he could not see the damage he had done when proof of it lay in his own fist, then no words could reach him, not even if they were distilled into the very liquor that he loved so much.

Even the wrath of the gods was something the Warlis did not seem to care about anymore. Zairos did not blame them. Just a few days ago, he had seen Damu walking through the farm with some sort of painted idol in his hand. Damu wanted to perform a religious ceremony in his hut, and had borrowed the idol from a neighbour.

It was as if the gods were scarce. There were not enough of them to go around, no one to keep count of misdeeds.

Finally, Laxman walked out of his hut. He was in a daze, so inebriated that he was unable to stand properly. Zairos was greeted by a foolish intoxication. He knew that it was beneath him to fight a Warli. It was unheard of.

In any case, violence had failed.

All he could do for now was hold Kusum's body under the light of the moon and watch her bruises fade, like one season slowly moving into another.

That night Zairos did not feel like a seth. He was just another man with a whiskey glass in his hand, an impotent pawn. As he sat on his porch, the Rajdhani Express tore past Dahanu Road, a shrieking, piercing reptile. Fifty years ago, Zairos could have ordered Laxman to jump in front of the train and it would have been done. If there had been the slightest resistance, he would have been pushed and the matter settled. Today, Zairos might as well be the corpse, a well-dressed one, trying to pass as a landlord.

All he could think of was Laxman pulling out Kusum's hair.

Zairos was unable to sleep. There were no dreams to haunt him. Everything was in front of him already, forcing him to lay in bed, wide-eyed with helplessness.

In the morning when he walked to his grandfather's bungalow, his anger continued to rise, erupting like a land mine no matter where he placed his feet. His tea went cold, faster than usual, the cardamom and ginger failing to do anything as he waited for Kusum to show. He paced about the farm, the softness of the morning light unable to calm the trembling in his bones.

The moment she came, he went to her. He did not care who was watching.

He wanted to get away from the farm, from its bathtubs and black pipes, to a place without Iranis, where no one would recognize him or her.

The drive was muted and sober, Kusum sitting next to him with a defeated stare. It was pure acceptance of the fact that pain was inevitable, a hacking cough from which she would get no release. By the time they reached Dahanu Village, every single thing that Zairos could have done to prevent Kusum from getting hurt had sizzled in his brain.

It was early morning but Dhenu Gaam had already woken up long ago. The Portuguese and the British had galloped through its streets through the centuries, but the only lasting mark was the Fort of the Marathas, which now served as the town prison.

The streets were extremely narrow, with houses on each side. Marwari moneylenders, small-time lawyers, Jain priests, and government officials lived here, exchanging pleasantries from their verandas, lying on their cots, Gujarati newspapers on their undulating stomachs, snoring like a hundred babies in a fairy tale, their wisps of hair flying in the breeze of table fans, while their servants ran errands on Hero cycles and cooks inhaled the tanginess of their rivals' dishes, mixed with the smell of snuff, attacking their mucous membranes, as their masters' bellies rose higher, a mountain of pride, until they finally awoke from their slumber with the smiles of men who had wiped, cleaned, and fed.

As at Anna's, languages bashed into each other, on some days a train wreck, on others a tasty mix bouncing into temple bells, sinking into yellow laddoos and other sweetmeats, the Jains trying not to let any of the languages defile them, the Marwaris

welcoming the defiling and murder of words, the sulphur diox-
ide from the thermal power plant coating the languages, giving
them an acidic smell.

A smell that was making Zairos anxious.

"Why are you silent?" asked Kusum. "Don't you want to
know what he did to me?"

"No," he answered.

"Laxman got into the hut at night and started kicking me.
He dug his heel into my stomach. Then he pulled me by the
hair and I started screaming. By the time the men came from
the nearby huts, he was gone. In the morning I saw some of
my own hair on the ground."

Zairos held on to the steering wheel. It had black leather
covering on it which absorbed his sweat.

"I don't know what to do," he said. "We have given your
husband money and we have given him a beating. Your husband has lodged a police case against me."

"Seth, you will pay the police some money and the matter
will disappear."

Zairos looked at her lips when she said this. When a person
spoke the truth, the lips took on a strange form, of one possessed. He had seen it happen when his grandfather spoke of
burning his wife's books.

Ahead, a goat chewed an old newspaper. Women sat in
their nightgowns under the arches of small cement homes
and they reminded Zairos of courtesans in an ancient kingdom. A man energetically swept the courtyard of his tailor's
shop. His feet were swollen. Everywhere Zairos looked, young
women were asleep on cots on their verandas. These young
women were a little better off than Kusum. They were free

for the moment, but at some point they would marry an old moneylender or the tailor with swollen feet, and they would lead unfulfilled lives, and their husbands would know it, the women would know it, the grass would know it, and yet nothing would change.

They approached the fairground next. At night, the lights of the giant wheel drew the Warlis here, and some of them dared to buy a ticket while others stayed on the ground considering it unwise to share the skies with the gods.

He drove the car to the edge of the village, to where the fishing boats stood on the shore with orange and green flags lazing in the morning light. Far away, a man sat on a stone and read a newspaper. That man was the only one around.

Zairos ran his fingers along the bald patch on Kusum's scalp. She flinched a little. He blew on it and she smiled.

"The hair will grow back," he said.

"I don't care."

"You should. You're still young."

He looked at her face. There was not a single line on it and it could not be touched by sun or grief. He put his palm against her cheek, the way he had some time ago.

But this time he would not stop there.

She needed more than comfort, more than just a palm.

He needed something too, he needed it all.

She was breathing softly, her mouth admitting what her body already knew, and it sent a surge of power up his spine, as his mouth moved closer to hers.

He raised her chin slightly, but she did not look into his eyes. She watched her own hand as it went inside his shirt. She traced her own fingers as they ran across his hairy chest.

Her hands were rough, they had been roughed up on the soil of his own farm, and they were now tending to his skin.

Slowly, he lowered his lips on hers.

Never before had she felt the touch of an Irani seth. She pushed herself against him, and he kissed her hard, tasted her in ways only lions could, licked her neck and shoulders, coating her, protecting her for life. That was when she pulled him back, and now she tasted him, and they lost track of who was master and who was slave, it did not matter anymore, and Zairos challenged the god of breath, if there was such a god, to distinguish which breath was which because they were both just as proud, just as scared, and just as angry.

In order to save Kusum from her world, Zairos needed to bring her into his. At first, he dismissed the thought. But he realized he could not just drop her off at the farm. Their love-making had left him electric.

Anna's was his world, but he could not take her there. To be honest, he could not take anyone there. *A crazy place for a crazy race* was what Hosi had scribbled onto one of Anna's walls, and it was true. No matter how strong, wise, handsome, beautiful, spiritual, crippled, deformed, deaf, dumb, deaf *and* dumb, or close to genius a person was, if they were not born into it, the environment at Anna's could easily set them back an eon or two.

If Anna's was completely, utterly crazy, the Crazy Crab, an outdoor restaurant by the sea, was only borderline demented. It would be perfect for their first outing together. But he would have to wait for lunchtime. So after leaving the fishing boats, they walked around the village, where they shared an ice cream cone. He saw her smile for the first time and wondered how her teeth were so white while his were pitted with cavities. He wanted to let down her hair and see her in all her glory, but it was not the right moment.

When they got in the car again, she decided to take him somewhere, to her haven. They sat on the steps of the lake outside the Shree Kevda Devi Mandir. Pink lotuses floated on the still, green water, and coconut trees lined the shore on the other side. Like the farm, it gave Zairos the feeling of being alive a century ago. So did the way the pujari rang the temple bells from time to time. It was a gentle reminder of devotion— there was no hysteria, it was playful, like cherubs revealing secrets to each other.

"Seth," she said. "This used to be the village of the untouchables."

He looked around, at the life surrounding the temple. A boy, no more than three, was alone in a green tub pouring water on his head with a mug, occasionally opening his mouth and swallowing some of it. Women walked around with small branches in their arms. There were the usual goats as well, but they were serene, there was no fear of them being slaughtered, and an old lady was washing clothes, beating orange and green robes with a soft mallet.

They did not enter the temple. Neither of them felt like it. The bells, the lotuses, the sun setting soft fire to the coconut trees was enough for them. When she walked to the car, he made sure he stayed behind her. He wanted to follow the way her hips moved; her hips were like something that had been calibrated, just the right amount of swing, enough to titillate, to drive wild. And she had the strongest back he had ever seen on a woman. Beneath the brown flesh shining with sweat, the muscle was alive, trained to hold any amount of weight. But the flesh itself was so soft and smooth—he was only a lick away from ecstasy.

In the car, by the sea, with the tires sinking slowly into the wet sand, he had her again. The back seat did not give them much space, but they relished it, turning this way and that, coiling, winding, stopping, exhaling, and when they were done, they leaned against the seat and let the salty wind hit them. Another couple were farther away, on a Vespa, the man shirtless and in trousers, the woman in a green sari, kissing each other.

"Jairos," said Kusum.

He laughed when she said his name. He laughed because she could not say it, and he rejoiced because she had said it in the first place. For the first time she had not called him "seth."

"Z . . . Z . . ." he said.

If only his English teacher Mrs. Costa could see what he was using his pronunciation for.

"Try and say my name correctly," he said.

She put her head on his chest and said it again, "Jairos."

"Z . . ." he said again.

Zairos wanted to know this woman. He wanted to know everything her lips could reveal, the howls her ears had heard, the weight her arms had lifted, the cracks in the soles of her feet which stuck out like the marks left by a razor blade.

When Kusum saw the Crazy Crab, its tables with maroon cloths, the white plastic chairs, the large fans standing like sentries on the side, she did not want to go. But when he said, "Look at the wall, they are straw walls just like your hut, and even the roof is just a shelter. It's like putting tables and chairs in your hut," she squinted at him, the tiptoe of her nose the pointe of a ballerina, and finally got out of the car.

When Zairos walked with her, it gave him a feeling of power and purpose. The Crazy Crab was one of the spots that the Iranis frequented, but it was a nighttime haunt. It was amusing for the tourists staying at the Pearl Line Resort to suddenly see an army of tall, strong men in jeans and goatees and five o'clock shadows walking in, young men, rich men in expensive shoes and belts who gave off the smell of family inheritance and told jokes and smoked Marlboros.

The restaurant was fairly empty. An old man sat at a corner table reading a newspaper, enjoying a cold beer and peanuts, and three tables away middle-aged women conspired against their husbands. Gambhir, the manager, was behind a wooden counter, his head buried in yesterday's accounts, his hair prematurely turned white and too thin for a man his age.

A gentle breeze came in from the sea, and Zairos admired the old Parsi mansion that was a short distance away. Even though no one lived in it, and the building was yellow and tattered, it still had some grace, a trace of its former glory. Kusum had her head up, she was trying to be strong, but as soon as the waiter arrived with the menus, she clenched her hand into a fist.

Zairos had no fear of anyone asking Kusum to leave. Even if Gambhir noticed a Warli straight off a farm, he would ignore her. Aspi Irani had given Gambhir a hefty sum of money for his cataract operation, so if Gambhir did see Kusum, Zairos would remind him it was due to his father's generosity that he could see her, or anything, in the first place.

The waiter hovered, bent, and placed the menus on the table like an arched, ugly bird. Kusum looked down again but could not find her feet. She found the surface of the table instead, scanned it as though her life depended on it.

"You can look up now," said Zairos. "The waiter is gone."

"Why did you bring me here?" she asked.

"To eat."

"You got me here to teach me a lesson."

"And what lesson would that be?"

"That I am different from you. You don't need to teach me. I know," she said. "Why do you want people to see us?"

"I don't *want* them to see us, but if they do, it's fine."

"I don't like it here. I want to go."

"Let the food come. Then you'll not want to leave."

"I want to go. Please."

The sea breeze came in, circled around them, confused about what a young Irani man was doing with an even younger Warli woman. The sea breeze had seen such a union before, but in darkness, or behind closed doors, and it was always a one-sided attack, the Iranis sinking their teeth into unwilling Warli skin. But this was something new for the sea breeze, this conversation that took place in a restaurant.

The waiter approached them again with a tray that had two bottles of lemonade and two glasses full of ice. He put the glasses down and poured lemonade into them. At that moment, Zairos reached out and held Kusum's hand. When he did that, he felt her entire body go rigid.

"Why are you doing this?" she whispered the moment the waiter left. "What are you trying to prove?"

"I am not trying to prove anything," he said.

I am just trying to start a dance.

Zairos finally heard from the police the next day. Instead of their showing up personally, he got a phone call at Anna's. But it was not the Dahanu police who got in touch. The call was from Gholvad, the next town.

Havovi was a shrewd tactician. She knew that Shapur Irani would have close connections with the Dahanu police, so she lodged Laxman's complaint with the Gholvad police, stating that her organization had an office in Gholvad as well.

The main cop, a Maharashtrian named Mhatre, asked Zairos to come by at six o'clock. It was an odd telephone conversation—formal, matter-of-fact—and Zairos felt like he was talking to a receptionist at a doctor's office, fixing an appointment for a checkup.

"You've come with an army," said the bald, pigeon-chested Mhatre as he shook Zairos' hand.

Bumble had come along for support, and Hosi insisted on joining them as well because he liked police stations. He had a fondness for prisons, asylums, and hospitals.

"Any place that is more hopeless than I am," he had said.

Mhatre escorted them through brown saloon doors. The wooden chair Mhatre sat on had a rib missing. He rolled a cream hand towel and used it to support his lower back. The faint trace of a beedi was on its way out of the room. The brown cardboard files on Mhatre's desk were piled on top of each other, neatly aligned.

"These power cuts will one day lead to rioting," said Mhatre, looking up at the dead fan. "There will be bloodshed in Maharashtra, you mark my words. You leave people at the mercy of heat, what else can they do but boil?"

He removed a white handkerchief from the pocket of his cream trousers and slapped it on the back of his neck. He dabbed here and there, like a burlesque dancer readying herself for stage. He had the thinnest lips Zairos had seen on a man. When he spoke, his lips converged into a diamond-shaped pout for the briefest of moments.

"As I was saying on the phone," said Mhatre to Zairos, "you have a complaint against you. And let me be very frank, it is the end of the day, so I am not in a mood to *register* this complaint."

"I'm grateful for that," replied Zairos. "Ten thousand times grateful."

Mhatre smiled. He seemed to appreciate Zairos' tact, his manners. A bribe, a generous one, had been offered with the grace of a wedding invitation.

"And a bottle of Scotch," added Bumble. "Black Dog."

"I've never tried it," said Mhatre.

"It will make your insides bark."

Mhatre chuckled. His pigeon chest went inwards even more. He rang the silver bell on his desk three times. Zairos and Bumble waited for a constable to appear with a cup of chai, or dirty tap water, but nothing of the sort happened.

"Oh," said Mhatre, seeing the bewilderment on their faces. "It's a habit. Like a nervous tic."

"Mhatre saab," said Hosi, who spotted something strange. "This notice board is unique."

Hosi was staring at a yellow board with sketches of a bear with a chain around its neck, a snake charmer, a monkey with a pink cap on its head, a dog lying on its back, and other animals. Below the sketches, painted in black ink, were the following points:

1. *You cannot do bear shows.*
2. *No catching snakes. Or charming them.*
3. *No taming monkeys.*
4. *No killing cows. They are holy.*

There were other charismatic lines, but Mhatre interrupted. "This board has been here for many years."

But by then, Hosi had lost interest. He yawned, raised his hand as both apology and goodbye, and walked through the brown swinging doors. The police station had not appealed to him. There were no screams of torture from an inside chamber, no lowlifes begging for mercy.

Bumble got up from his chair, shook Mhatre's hand vigorously, and went to the car for the bottle of Black Dog and the ten thousand rupees. Suddenly, the fan came on. It announced itself with a few *wong-wong-wong*s and then calmed down.

"It's interesting that he mentioned this board," said Mhatre. "It was here during your grandmother's time."

"You mean my grandfather," said Zairos.

"No," said Mhatre, "your grandmother."

Mhatre was mistaking his grandmother for someone else. Zairos had never heard anyone speak about his grandmother, especially a non-Irani like Mhatre. Mhatre was in his fifties, too young to know his grandmother.

"Banu Irani," said Mhatre. "That was her name."

Zairos did not like hearing her name from Mhatre's lips. He was not sure why this made him uneasy. A motorcycle went past the station. Zairos could tell it was an Enfield from the guttural sound the engine made as though it were doing a salt-water gargle.

"How do you know her name?" he asked.

"She came here one day," said Mhatre. "Fifty-two years ago. I was only five years old. I was sitting on the stairs outside with my father. My father was a policeman like me. No, forgive me . . . I am a policeman like him."

Instead of extracting information, which was what cops excelled at, Mhatre was giving Zairos something, and he found it unnerving.

"She came here in a horse carriage all by herself," he said. "Her hair was wild, all over the place. I will never forget that day. Your grandmother was like a fierce huntress. She said something was after her. It terrified me."

This was the first time he had heard someone speak of his grandmother in that way. His idea of her was that she was a gentle woman, a loving woman, so timid that she was haunted by shadows. Mhatre was dipping his thin lips in ink and writing his grandmother's story in the finest calligraphy.

"Why did she come to this police station?" asked Zairos.

"To seek protection," said Mhatre.

"From my grandfather?"

Zairos was shocked at the words that came out of his mouth. The burning of his grandmother's books was fresh in his memory. A carpet was being pulled from under him and he was somersaulting in the air, a novice circus hand, unsure and dizzy.

"Why would it be from your grandfather?" asked Mhatre.

"I . . . What did she want protection from?"

Zairos had come here to offer a bribe. That was all. Information about his grandmother was not what he had bargained for. There was a tingling sensation in his right hand.

Mhatre wiped his face with his handkerchief again. Zairos wanted to do the same. But it was not sweat he wanted to wipe. It was the remark he had made about his grandfather.

"Have a closer look at the board," said Mhatre. "Below the last point."

Zairos got up from his chair and walked to the board. His steps had never been so quiet, so careful. He had the walk of a man who did not want to wake anyone up.

He faced the board, the dizzying caricatures of animals. Cobras, cows, monkeys, donkeys, bears, and dogs vied for his attention. It was too much for him. All those animals hissing, roaring, braying, and barking at the same time.

"Below the last point," Mhatre had to remind him.

Something had been deeply scratched into the wood. Only a hundred claws feverishly working as one could have that effect.

BEWARE OF THE BEARD

"When my father asked Banumai what was after her, she remained quiet," said Mhatre. "She took a long nail that was lying on the ground and started etching this on the board. 'I am a lady,' she said. 'You will not stop me.'"

It was all so illogical. His grandmother had charged into a police station an entire town away in a horse carriage.

"What is the beard?" asked Zairos.

"I don't know," said Mhatre. "To this day her face is before my eyes. Some faces, you see them once, you remember them for life."

Mhatre got up from his chair. Again, he rang the desk bell thrice. This time it was not done with nonchalance. Mhatre was jolting himself out of the past, into the world of the Black Dog Scotch that Bumble now placed on the table with much aplomb.

The only image that floated before Zairos' eyes that night was that of Banumai with her hair loose, flying through the streets on a horse carriage. It made no sense at all.

So when he woke up the next morning to the words "Hundreds have died," he thought he was still in a dream. But it was Aspi Irani being his usual stirring self, examining the mosquitoes that had perished in great numbers on the stairs. He was collecting them in a dustpan, while Mithoo, cream headscarf on, was trying to ignore the mosquitoes because she was cooking.

"I ambushed them," said Aspi Irani. "For a few days, I did not spray the stairs at all. Then . . ." The mosquitoes had indeed been slaughtered. Aspi Irani examined the carnage— this was his Vietnam.

Once he had emptied the dead in the garbage can, he sat at the dinner table. The churchgoers next door had started wailing again, so he put on his wife's thick black headphones and spoke loudly over the French recording.

"Je suis allé au mail acheter des boucles d'oreilles. Je vais aller au mail acheter des boucles d'oreilles."

Then he took the headphones off and asked Mithoo, "What did I just say?"

"You said, 'I went to the mall to buy earrings.'"

"Oh," he said. "How do I say, 'If it were not illegal to kill people, I'd stab those churchgoers, every single one of them'?"

"That sentence is too advanced for me," said Mithoo, placing a cup of tea on the table. "Maybe next year."

Zairos noticed that the large vessel Mithoo was cooking in was brimming with enough beef to feed ten sweaty men.

"Why are you cooking so much?" he asked.

"Our servant has quit," she said. "And I'm cooking more so you can freeze it and eat. We're going to Bombay. For a *wedding*."

"You mean funeral," said Zairos.

"Just see," said Mithoo to her husband. "Not at all concerned about his future. He's going to die old and miserable."

Aspi Irani, however, could not be bothered. When he had his morning tea, nothing could come in the way. He had a funny way of drinking his tea. It was the Irani way—he liked his tea piping hot, so hot that any tongue would sing songs of torture, and he never drank from the cup. He poured the tea into the saucer and drank in loud slurps.

"Do me a favour," said Zairos to his mother. "Enlarge my photograph, a glossy one, and put it on the stage, just behind the couple, so all the guests can see. Then announce on the mike that I am available."

Mithoo shook her head and said, "We'll be gone for a week."

Zairos wanted his parents to leave. He wanted light to leave as well and allow night to descend, swoop down on him with all its hubris, searing enough to lead him to hidden places.

He waited until it was late, until Shapur Irani was an explorer ready to traverse the plains and deserts of his own past.

"Pa," asked Zairos. "What did Banumai mean by the beard?"

"Candy floss," said Shapur Irani.

Lakhu burned a mixture of cow dung, coconut coir, and dry grass a few feet away from Shapur Irani's rocking chair. The strong odour of cow dung kept the mosquitoes at bay. They were always more ferocious at night. After all, they were blood-suckers, miniature vampires.

"When Banu was small she called candy floss the old man's beard."

"That makes no sense, Pa."

Back then, it made no sense to Shapur Irani either. When his wife spoke about the beard, she became a doll with a scary face whose features changed without warning. The madness of a hundred asylums had entered her.

"Why did she go to the police station, Pa?"

Shapur Irani had a bottle of brandy by his side. He poured some brandy in his palm and applied it to the soles of his feet. He had a slight fever and this was his wife's remedy.

"Banu was ill," he said as he wiped his palms on his white pyjama pants. "When she was pregnant with your father, she started getting high fevers. In her delirium, she would talk about a beard. The connection to candy floss was the only connection I could make. Sometimes, the happy memories of our childhood develop fangs and attack us later on in life."

"Do you think it could be something else?"

"No."

His "no" had the surety of a knife.

Shapur Irani's face was covered in sweat. He was shivering, but tried not to show it. Zairos went inside to fetch a shawl. He draped it round his grandfather and bade him goodnight. But by the time Zairos had walked a few steps, Shapur Irani had thrown the shawl to the ground.

Zairos heard the rattle of machine guns. *Rat-tat-tat* fell the rain on the tiled roof of Aspi Villa. He walked to the porch, leaned into the night, and let a spray of water hit him. The first rains of the season had come, and they had come hard. Leaves were being battered, the bark of trees lashed. The ferns in the garden below acquired a darker, wetter green.

"Each time it rains I think of my father," Shapur Irani once told Zairos. "As a child he was afraid of rain. The Arabs used to force the Zoroastrians to stay indoors. If even a drop of rain-water touched a Zoroastrian body and fell on the soil, the land was polluted. So my father used to huddle close to his mother and wait for the rain to end."

For Shapur Irani, everything had meaning.

The past kept interwening, contaminating things.

Zairos closed his eyes and let the rain do as it pleased. He wished he were an octopus, so he could stretch out eight arms instead of two, that reached far into the night and partook in the celebration of the first rains: he would help old-timers by hold-ing silver snuff containers under their noses, enabling them to go into a trance. He would pull a large banana leaf with Pinky the orphan on it and let her float away from Anna's all the way to the sea and continue on and on. And the rest of his tentacles would slide into the circus tent and offer pats of assurance to the performers—clowns, acrobats, a tired old announcer—who wished they had chosen safe jobs, anything to escape the lonely uncertainty of what they were doing right now. Most of all, he wanted eight arms to put around Kusum, wrap her in an embrace so tight and complete, unlike any woman had experienced before, covering her from all sides, so if she were to come under attack again, he would be the only one to get harpooned.

In the morning Zairos raced to Kusum's hut on his motorcycle, the rain striking his chest mercilessly as though it were looking for a confession. The skies had been ripped open and there was water everywhere—trickling, gurgling, angry, and energetic. At the railway station, auto rickshaws swallowed customers. By the time Zairos reached Kusum's hamlet, the sky had gathered the anger of a religious fanatic.

As soon as the Warli children saw the motorcycle, they ran and hid. That was always the case whenever they saw any vehicle. The children played with cycle tires, but a vehicle was too alien for them. Once the children disappeared, Zairos saw a man lying on the ground. It was the same man he had seen the night he had walked with Kusum to her hut, after Laxman's beating. The man had passed out again, and the water hit his face and bare chest.

When Zairos entered Kusum's hut, there were chickens. At least ten of them flapping madly, with Rami in the middle. In the darkness of the hut they had the menace of bats. Zairos quickly walked out. All that clucking, all those wings.

"Why are there chickens in your hut?" he asked.

"It's raining," replied Kusum. "Where can they go? You see that hut opposite? That's where the goats are."

She held him by the hand and took him underneath a large banyan tree. The trunk of the tree had fat veins going up and down, snakes that were either trying to reach the heavens or stick their heads inside the earth. They stood there for a while, and she smiled and watched the rain come down. It made sense not to speak, to listen to the torrent.

The man who had passed out on the ground suddenly woke up. He took a few steps and crashed, nose first, into the ground. A chicken ran out of the hut, darted around as if possessed, and made a futile attempt to take flight. Then it went back into the hut and was greeted by applause—the clucking and the flutter of wings.

Inspired by the chicken and drunken man, Zairos ran out into the rain, but once there, did not know what to do. He quickly got on his motorcycle and started it. He kept revving the engine and realized that this was even more absurd. Fortunately for him Kusum ran too and got on.

When they got to the fishing village, Kusum pointed to a group of children who were creating a commotion. They had surrounded a man who held a large fish in each hand, and his red vest was rolled up to reveal a fat belly, and the rain bounced off his belly while he kept raising the fish higher and higher out of the children's reach. Kusum was learning to enjoy speed, the machine was leaving everything behind—coconut trees, palm trees, barbed wire, telephone poles, old men, fishing nets, bullock carts, transport trucks—*she* was leaving everything behind.

But when they reached Zairos' house, he could feel her body tense up behind him.

"The house is empty," he said to reassure her. "My parents are in Bombay."

When he opened the main door, she stood at the entrance and stared at the brown sofa, the TV, the cane chair, the family photographs, and the calendar on the wall. She had entered homes before, she had seen their clocks and carpets, but it was never as lover. As lover, she was forced to look up and address the walls and the house's trappings.

"Come in," he said. "It's okay."

She scrunched the end of the grey cloth she wore into a ball and wrung out the water. Her feet were muddy and droplets of water hung from her nose. Zairos had to hold her hand and pull her in. She did not welcome his touch. She stood in the centre of the room and did not move.

Then she sat on the floor.

She was not used to the hardness of floors.

"Don't be scared," Zairos told her.

"It means Mahadev, god of the gods, is angry," she replied.

Her voice was heavy. It was the voice of a woman trying to get some invisible weight off her chest.

"What do you mean?" he asked.

"When rain falls with so much anger, it means Mahadev is throwing the water down with his fists, spraying it from between his teeth. Mahadev is angry with me."

"What for?"

"I have abandoned my own people to be with a seth. One of the village elders spat on me last night."

The rain fell on the closed windows even harder, shattered them almost.

"Sit next to me," she told him. "Please."

She now had her knees drawn to her chest and she circled her arms around her shins. It reminded him of the day he first saw her, huddled in the back of the tractor like a frightened chicken. He did not want to see that woman again, a woman in a coma, with her eyes wide open, refusing to recognize anything.

The yellow refrigerator shivered all of a sudden.

Zairos came back from the cabinet beneath the television and sat beside her with a photo album in his hand.

"I want you to meet my family," he said.

He did not know what it would accomplish, but he felt it was better not to touch her at the moment. He opened the purple album, the black-and-white photographs pasted on thick black paper. The tracing paper crackled as he lifted it, and slowly mothers, fathers, uncles, and aunts came to life, some of their smiles ages old, yet ready to provide whatever warmth was needed. She needed to realize that these men and women were just like her, even if they were poles apart. They had tears, they had hearts, smiles, and wounds, oh they had wounds the size of craters in the moon.

He started with his father. "His name is Aspi," he said, pointing to a photograph of his father leaning against a black Standard Herald, with his famous pointy boots that had stepped on his mother's toes in Café Military, proof that boots could lead to marriage. Next, on a large silver chair, their wedding chair, Zairos showed Kusum his mother, Mithoo, whose name meant "Sweet" in Gujarati, and sweet she was with her love for children and stray dogs, sweet she sure looked in a white dress with her hair as long as a princess's in a fairy tale, and he told her how she oiled her hair every night, and when Zairos was little he asked her why she oiled her hair so much and she replied, "So that if anyone climbs up, they will slip and fall and eat brinjal," an answer that amused and enthralled him, and in this manner the journey continued, up and down his family tree Kusum went, like the men who climbed the coconut trees at the farm, and she met the odd ones too, the odd dead ones such as Aderji, his father's distant cousin who placed a piece of plastic shit, bought from a magic shop in Bombay, in the first-class compartment every time he travelled, making sure he sprinkled the right amount of water on the prop in order to make it look fresh from the oven, and, as a final touch, held a handkerchief to his nose with an expression so truthful he managed to ensure he had the whole cabin to himself, and this story and the photograph of Aderji holding the plastic turd brought a faint smile to her face, and it was exactly what Zairos was looking for so on he went, turned more pages, took her up different branches, and then Bumble showed up wearing his father's Ray-Bans at age seven looking like a bug, and suddenly Kusum's eyes lit up, or maybe Zairos imagined it, but she did hold his hand, she had stopped at a photograph of him, when he was maybe eleven or something like that, on a blue cycle, and she squeezed his hand hard, but when he asked her what happened she just asked him, "This is your cycle?" a strange question to which he nodded yes, and Kusum felt a gust of hope blow against her breast because it was that same magic cycle, it was the same boy who had placed a lily on her head, and if he could make her feel like that once, he could do it again.

❧

When Kusum returned home, Rami was waiting for her.

"What do you think you are doing?" she asked. "He is an Irani seth. He will eat every bit of flesh on you."

Kusum could tell that Rami had a headache because she was smoking the bark of a tree to clear her sinuses. Whenever she was upset, her head got heavy.

"Remember who the enemy is," she said.

"What if he is not an enemy?" asked Kusum. "What if he is a friend?"

"He is not our friend. The man you are seeing is the cause of our illness. How can someone who causes illness be a friend?"

Rami coughed hard, the skin above her eyes sagging. Her hand was in a fist, circled around the tree bark, and she inhaled deeply and blew smoke rings, noose after noose, sending them out into the night, hoping they would land around a landlord's neck or two.

"Do not forget your grandfather's thumb," she said.

Kusum could never forget. It was something she had been fed again and again. It was breast milk to her. Her grandfather, Vithal the storyteller, whose voice could boom mountains, whose voice made the orange flags on Mahalakshmi Hill flutter and awaken the goddess Mahalakshmi herself, how could Vithal's thumb be forgotten when the sacred hill shook in remembrance?

"I have not forgotten," said Kusum, deferential, loving.

"You have," said Rami. "Take a moment and remember your ancestors. I can still see my father standing over the fire . . ."

Kusum could see him too, standing tall, the flames rising in a hiss, the villagers huddled around Vithal, holder of their wounds, emitter of their cries.

The night always began with the invocation of one name.

"The Breeteesh," Vithal would say, letting the name hang in the air, over the fire. To the Warlis, the name was full of poison—they could tell from the way Vithal's lips stretched to reveal gleaming teeth.

"The day the white demon came, things started turning black for our people," he said. "The forests, they suddenly decided, belonged to them, the savkar. So the savkar appointed officers to prevent the felling of trees, even for the simple warmth of a fire."

A hush fell upon the villagers. Some of them started swaying, unable to withstand the winds of the past. All of them knew too well how they were viewed by the white demon. Uneducated savages, only a stage more developed than gorillas.

Gorillas could not own land.

So the gorillas' land was taken and given to Hindus, Muslims, and Zoroastrians. And these educated men swooped down on the land with the ravenousness of vultures, but, since they were educated, they gave the Warlis *some* land, land that was theirs to begin with. An inch's worth, no more. But even the fetid scraps came at a cost.

In exchange for a plot of land the size of a fingernail, the Warli had to till the landlord's land, and the Warli was given a scoop of paddy, which he would convert to rice, then to rage, to sorrow, to pity, to hopelessness. Each morning at the sound of a bell, the Warli had to toil in the landlord's fields, his dark tribal back releasing sweat as though it were some dreaded sickness.

At the end of the day only a handful of rice awaited him, and, if he was lucky, a lump of salt.

"Do not cry," Vithal said to his people. "No tears. Our ancestors had fought for salt. It would be wrong of us to waste salt."

His lips were wet with the palm wine he was drinking and the fire played with his face, made it darker, redder, more alive.

"Their long white claws yearned for us all," he said. "So laws were passed. But they were not laws. They were our death sentences. Overnight, they turned the Kings of the Jungle into peasants. How is that possible? Can a tiger be called a goat? Can a lion be called a mouse?"

"No," the villagers replied.

Since the Warlis were peasants, they were forced to buy seeds from the white demon, seeds they could not afford, and Warli land did not like those seeds, it spat them out. Little did the land understand that the Warlis still had to pay taxes. So they had to go to moneylenders, and the taxes went on rising, their loans kept on building, but the land remained silent. And when the land remained silent, the Warlis turned to liquor, but that too had been taken. Their mahua was now made illegal, so even for liquor they turned to the money-lenders, whose rates were high as pine trees.

And in all this, a young liquor store owner named Shapur Irani made a well of liquor available to Vithal on credit, and when Vithal could not pay up, a thumb impression was taken.

Vithal had lost his land.

He had lost his land so he decided to lose his thumb.

He went home drunk, angry, crying like a beaten woman. He hated his thumb. He hated the sight of his thumb's impression on stamp paper, so he used the sickle that hung on the wall of his hut.

A few years after he lost his thumb, he lost his wife as well. She left him for another man, a man who could provide for her. But not once did his father's voice betray any bitterness or longing, so both Ganpat and Rami decided to be the same way. "Our mother has chosen to live somewhere else" is what they told themselves. They made it a matter of geography, not a matter of the heart.

FOURTEEN

KUSUM LAY ON THE FLOOR of Zairos' living room and stared at the burning candle. Above her, the ceiling fan was motionless, the victim of a power cut.

No matter how hard Zairos tried to bring Kusum to the sofa, she refused.

Zairos wanted to touch her, but all he could think of was Vithal's thumb.

He stared at his own thumb, at the concentric circles in the skin, like the lines made by a plough in the soil. To him, it was just a thumb. But to Vithal, it was something that had brought shame, a leprous trickster. And when it was cut off, what remained? A stub as barren as Vithal's remaining days on earth.

Twice Zairos nearly placed his hand on Kusum's naked stomach, but then withdrew. If he was going to touch her, tonight would be different.

So he used only the tips of his fingers, very lightly, on hers.

So light it might as well be imaginary. He did not look at her face, did not check if her eyes opened or not.

Then he let his palm rest on hers, his thumb the last to make contact.

He could now feel their fingers generating a current, a transmission of all their fears, loves, and desires. Even if an Irani man had touched the hands of a Warli woman in this manner before, none of those touches could have exchanged so much, of that he was sure.

The candlelight searched the walls, the photographs of Irani faces lit by the flames. It reminded Zairos that people acquired meaning only if someone shone a light on them. If he blew the candle out, the faces on the wall would disappear.

There was a loud thump against the main door.

The candle almost fell off the table. Kusum sprang up and looked at Zairos. For a few seconds, nothing. Then another thump, even louder, the sound of a body ramming itself into the main door. It could be an animal, but Zairos did not want to take a chance. He took Kusum by the hand and went upstairs. He slowly opened the door to the upstairs porch. He stayed low and peered through the railings. It was no animal. It was a man, a Warli in shorts and vest. Zairos looked around but saw no one else. This man was too conspicuous to be a robber.

Then, in a long drunken yell, the man called out Kusum's name.

It was Laxman.

Chambal the dacoit's words rushed into Zairos' mind, *A wounded man is a dangerous man.* Laxman walked away from the door, then spun around and ran straight into it. He did it again and called out her name. Laxman was shattering bone in the darkness on purpose. He held his face in an attempt to stop the blood. Then he walked a few steps and fell down on the lawn. Then he got up again and ran into a tree. It did not matter if he had mistaken the tree for the main door. He was here to hurt himself, to wake the gods up from their slumber, to leave a trail of Warli blood on the lawn.

His goddess was next to Zairos. She was his now, and Laxman knew it.

By morning, the blood had dried up. Some of it was on the door, and when Kusum saw it, she used her hands to rub it off with the hurry of the shamed. Zairos had to hold her to make her stop.

Kusum said that Laxman's appearance meant Rami had told him where she was. Rami was loyal to tribe, not soul. Zairos, however, looked at Laxman's arrival differently. By attacking Aspi Villa, Laxman had made his own case weaker. Havovi the Benevolent would have a hard time finding sympathy for Laxman after this. A misdemeanour like this one gave flavour to the bribe, made it more moral.

Zairos went indoors and made tea for Kusum. It was Lakhu's tea, the ginger-cardamom combination. She sat on the floor, amused that a seth was making her chai. He gave her toast, which she hated, but there was a look of delight on her face when she tasted ginger marmalade.

"You will come with me to the police station," said Zairos. "If you speak to Mhatre personally about Laxman, it will help."

At the mention of the police, Kusum stopped eating.

"You will not come to the police?" Zairos asked. "Are you scared?"

"Yes," she said. "You would be too if you were named like my people."

"Named?"

"We are named so badly. We are named Patlya and Barkya, we are named Manglya . . . Of what use are such names?"

Patlya and Barkya. Thinny and Smally.

Zairos understood. Names were based mainly on appearance. And what appearance did anyone expect when malnutrition was rampant, when malaria shook mothers during their pregnancy as though they were in the grip of a malevolent storm? And Manglya, the boy born on a Tuesday. It was pathetic. When others named their children Shiva or Vishnu, when others had the names of gods, the Warlis had names even the dogs would refuse.

"Even our folk tales," she said. "A great Warli king is fooled by a Brahmin into giving up all his cattle and kingdom. Why is a child told such a story? So that we realize from birth that we are stupid, that we lost our land."

"I will take you home," he said. "I want to speak with Rami."

The roads were still wet even though the rain had stopped. Everything was fresh, the boulders, the soil, the roofs of temples and huts, the leaves of coconut trees, all had a sheen, a rebirth. Except for Kusum. Zairos thought of her as cobwebbed in her past. As soon as one web broke, another formed, stronger and stickier.

"Seth, you will never know what it's like. First, I am a woman. That is one leg cut off. Then I am a tribal. Now both legs gone."

"I am with you because you are a woman," he said. "I don't

think I could play with Laxman's hair or listen to him talking about folk tales."

"Seth . . ." Her smile waned before it could reach full bloom.

Kusum's hut was still recovering from the heavy rain. Even though the hut was made of reeds that were meant to make the water slide off, the rains had been too formidable an opponent. So was Rami. He could tell from the way her lips crushed the beedi she was smoking.

"I came here to tell you that Kusum will stay at home with me," said Zairos.

He could tell that there were many things she wanted to say to him, but years of subjugation were stopping her, and the beedi bore the brunt.

"She is safe with me," he said. "If she is here, Laxman will harm her. Do you want that?"

"No," said Rami.

"Just for a few days. I will bring her back."

"What exactly will you do with her for a few days?"

"I will look after her."

"Seth, I am a woman. I may live in a hut, but I am a woman."

Kusum was enjoying this. In some small way, her man was fighting for her, and for that reason, she stepped in. She bent down and placed her hand on Rami's head, a simple gesture that meant she was going, but not leaving. When she did that the skin on Rami's forearms sagged even lower.

"I need her help this afternoon," said Rami. "You can collect her in the night."

Kusum had to tell Rami the truth about Zairos. She saw him as a way out, perhaps more than just a chariot on which she could leave, even if it was only temporarily.

But when Rami said, "There is something I need to tell you," Kusum knew that Rami was trying to bash sense into her young brain.

"There is something you must know before you go with this man who will spit you out one day," said Rami. "You say he is not like the others. There is a way to find out."

"How?"

"Tell him a story. A story your father told."

But Ganpat was a dry well, a famine. The moment he was asked to tell a story, his heart thundered out of fear, his shoulders drooped, and he rasped for mercy like a lamb being skinned.

"It was the only story Ganpat ever told in his life, and he discovered its meaning on the morning of his death," said Rami. "But your father took that meaning with him the moment his neck snapped."

"I am willing to listen," said Kusum.

She was also willing to take a chance on Zairos, even if it meant she was exactly like all the stupid peacocks, partridges, and quail that had mistaken that same look in their hunters' eyes for something else.

At night, as Zairos and Kusum lay on the floor, his head on her bosom, she told him what Rami had revealed to her.

"It started seven days before my father's death," said Kusum, "when Laxman had given me one of his worst beatings ever. My father was full of tears."

Ganpat looked to the skies, begged the gods for help, but realized that the gods were just as old and tired as he was. Even their backs were bent. Even their bodies were in pain. So much that they stuffed clouds in their mouths to muffle their moans, to prevent the Warlis from hearing their screams and losing faith.

It was too late. He had lost faith already. Just as his father Vithal had when he lost his land and his thumb.

His father had lost faith in the gods, but not in stories. Ganpat heard his father's voice come to him in a torrent. "Whenever there is pain, it is time to start telling stories."

But Ganpat was not a mountain of a man like his father, who had the courage to sing of the beatings, to sing of the torture, to sing of the malnutrition. Everything that had been lost by the Warlis could be found in Vithal's voice again.

"I feel like all the wild animals of the forest are in my stomach," he said to Rami. "There is this great rumbling, they are all running down a hill, bringing rocks and stones with them, trees and snakes and who knows what, all are coming down the hill, and this is all happening in my stomach."

"You are speaking like our father today," said Rami. "Maybe our father is speaking through you."

If only Ganpat could get enough money to free his daughter.

He needed to go in search of the black moha. The witch doctors swore that whoever found this plant would attract money beyond his dreams. But no one Ganpat knew had ever found the black moha. The black moha was nothing more than a black phantom.

All he had was pain, and it was forcing him to tell a story.

He had no idea what good it would do. He might not be able to make even a tiny leaf flutter. "I must tell a story that has been forgotten," he told Rami. "Father used to say that the greatest stories are the ones that have been forgotten."

For the next few days, he wondered what his father wanted him to tell.

A tale that would empower him, give him the strength to curl his hand into a fist and bang it on the ground so that whoever walked the earth was made to jump and cry out for justice.

But nothing came.

Defeated, he lay on the ground outside his hut and closed his eyes.

The dry grass poked his back and he smiled because the grass was dead and it still had the power to trouble him. He lay completely still on the ground, as ripe for dying as a human fruit could be.

That was when Rami found him.

She had found him in exactly the same position many years ago, when he was only five years old. She felt she had to tell him about that time.

"If I remembered all the things that I made myself forget, I would not be alive today," she said. "By remembering, I have gone back to some terrible times. But maybe some good will come of this, brother. Long ago, I found you in this same position on the ground."

He was just a boy then—small, thin, full of ribs. He had vomited. He was unconscious, ready to depart this world. Rami picked him up, did not know what to do, so she splashed water on his face. His mouth smelled of liquor, but it could not be, for he was only five years old. Some evil spirit must have entered his mouth.

After an hour, he came to the world of the living again. In that half state, in the world of neither the living nor the dead, he told her a story.

"Maybe it is wrong to call it a story," said Rami. "Because all you said was, 'Shapur seth . . . the well . . . Shapur seth . . . the well . . .'"

"That is all?" asked Ganpat. He wondered if his sister was mocking him.

"That is all you said," replied Rami. "But the way you said it made me feel you had seen something. You were shaking the way a goat shakes when it sees the blade."

There was one more thing.

"That day, you held a bottle cork in your fist. I thought that the cork had a spell on it so I kept it with me all these years in the hope that the spell would come on me and kill me instead," she said. "But I am still alive."

Rami reached out towards Ganpat, her thin black arm jingling with red bangles, and placed a bottle cork in his palm.

"You had seen something," she said. "I am sure of it."

Ganpat held that bottle cork for hours, but he had no idea what his sister was talking about. This cork was alien to him. It could be anything. It could be the eye of an injured god. He took it with him everywhere. Down a hill, up a date palm tree, around his hut, he walked backwards, sideways, he rolled on the ground, did everything possible to make the eye talk.

Nothing.

Then, the night before his death, he heard a scream so loud he thought Vaghai the Tiger God was having his teeth pulled out. Ganpat had gone to sleep with the cork in his fist, and now the cork was trying to tell him something. It was helping him remember.

Slowly, images came to him. Shapur seth standing near a well. And Ganpat, five years old, watching through the chickoo trees. The images repeated themselves. Shapur seth near the well, through the tangle of chickoo trees. There was a whiskey bottle in his hand.

When Ganpat woke up the next morning, he remembered everything. He had never felt younger or more powerful in his life. He was a coiled snake ready to strike.

"If it is money Laxman wants, he shall have it," he said to Rami. "They think we are invisible!"

"Who?" asked Rami.

"The landlords! The landlords think we are invisible!"

He held the cork high above his head. "The bottle may have destroyed our people. But today, the bottle shall save us. The bottle shall save my daughter."

He handed the cork back to Rami. "This will give us our life back."

"What do you mean, brother?" asked Rami.

"Rami, you are right," he said. "Many years ago, I saw Shapur seth do something terrible."

But he did not tell her what. There was no time. He had been transformed by night into something wild. He could not afford to waste this wildness. He could not afford to let it cool down.

"They think they can take our land and we will remain silent. They think they can take our women and we will remain silent. They think they can take our forests and we will remain silent. I will hurt them. I will hurt the landlord. I will hurt him just to remind him that I am alive. I am coming for you, Shapur seth. I am coming for you," he chanted.

Then he stormed out of the hut.

"I want to know what this story means," Kusum told Zairos.

She had tried to remain calm in the telling of it, but her voice broke at certain points, and her mouth gave forth the aroma of defeat. They had started off with his head on her bosom, but now it was her head on his chest, her long black hair spreading out like a pool of black water, like something that should not be spreading.

She lifted her head and looked straight at him.

It was hard for her to do. The ropes of labour were tugging at her, reminding her to lower her gaze because she was still a labourer on his farm.

Zairos did not question her intentions. Her intentions were good and solid, but he doubted Rami's. Her teeth were too crooked, there were too many lines on her face, lines that were taking her off the path, leading her astray.

And Shapur Irani would give Zairos the same explanation about the Warli heart—it was impossible to fathom, the tribals were nothing more than a mixture of bitterness and folk tales, and this ludicrous, nonsensical yarn was proof of that.

Zairos did not want to abandon his own people, spin away from them on a romantic whim. He did not want to be a champion to a tribal woman. He did not want to be a champion at all.

There was nothing he could offer her. No answer, no promise.

They slept, close but not touching. The mention of his grandfather's name again had drawn a line between Zairos and Kusum, and he did not want to cross over yet. Her side of the line might have quicksand in it. He wanted to wait.

In the middle of the night, he woke up and went upstairs. He had had enough of the floor. He left her there. He became a landlord in his bed again, a floor above.

Hours later, the light made him notice a crack in the window.

The light was too strange, too harsh for it to be early morning. How had he not woken up with the sound of the Gujarat Express?

He heard noises downstairs. There was more than one person.

As soon as he went down, he was greeted by his father's singing. Aspi Irani was seated at the table, knife and apple in hand, sending out his song, purely in English today, which had the rhyme of "wedding" and "beheading." Mithoo was at the stove telling Kusum to add red masala to the potatoes.

"What are you doing here?" asked Zairos.

"Your father is sick of attending weddings," said Mithoo.

"I prefer funerals," said Aspi Irani. "You can never attend someone's funeral twice."

"You are not happy to see us?" asked Mithoo.

"No . . . no, I'm happy," said Zairos.

"How did you get a servant so fast? She was startled when we entered the house, poor thing. She had the marmalade bottle in her hand. I think she was about to eat it. We'll have to keep an eye on her. No spoiling these people. Train them from day one."

Mithoo went back to the stove and asked Kusum, "How much has my son agreed to pay you? Has he talked about payment?"

Kusum looked at Zairos, who did not know what to say.

He knew what Kusum was thinking. In the jungle, higher does not protect lower. Higher eats lower. He sat at the table and took a slice of apple.

With lowered head, Kusum started cleaning the bathroom.

~⊙~

"Something terrible . . ." said Shapur Irani, ruminating over Ganpat's words. "By that time, Banu's dementia had taken a hold of her completely. I did not have the strength to do anything terrible. I promise you, Zairos, apart from that one incident with Vithal, no Warli has ever been beaten on my land."

It amazed Zairos how even decades later, just the thought of Banumai's illness contorted Shapur Irani's face. At the snap of a finger, pain made him lose his deadpan expression, showing the world that he was perhaps better off numb.

Zairos left his grandfather in his rocking chair, regretting that he had broached the subject.

At the farm, Kusum stood in line for her daily wage.

The chickoo was moodier than ever. It was turning bipolar, happy and giving one minute, dry and withdrawn the next. The chickoo was turning suicidal, throwing itself to the ground without allowing itself to ripen.

With not enough fruit to pick, Zairos gave the workers a half day.

He noticed how Kusum counted her wages twice, then a third time. There was hope in her counting, that magic would occur due to repetition and an extra ten-rupee note would materialize in her hand.

After all the workers had left, she stayed on.

But they had nowhere to go. They walked into the thickness of trees, hoping to be enveloped, made safe, being touched by nothing other than themselves.

They lay on top of one another, their bodies madly singing.

Once they found each other, nothing mattered. Even if snow rose from beneath the ground or the chickoo buds started speaking, it would go unnoticed.

He liked the moments after, her hot breath on his skin.

"Seth," she said. "Is this your god?"

She held the fravashi, the winged guardian spirit that hung from a gold chain around his neck. Each man had a fravashi who encouraged his soul to enter the physical world, gather experience, and choose asha over druj, the truth over the lie.

"Seth . . ."

"Yes," he said. "This is my god. He looks after me. There is another one for my mother, father, and grandfather."

"Is that because you are landlords?" She asked that question seriously.

To the Warlis, even guardian spirits could be bought. He did not blame her for thinking that way. She had been left unprotected. As a Zoroastrian, he had the power of centuries behind him. Zarathushtra was a pioneer, a star whose teachings had inspired an ancient Persian Empire; then, on that same soil, the Arabs called Zoroastrians infidels. When the humiliation got too hard to stomach, it was the magi who reminded the Zoroastrians of their lineage. With their sacred fires and texts, they came to India and the infidels rose once again, became doctors, lawyers, artists, businessmen, and landlords.

But Kusum's magi had no such history. Her magi had let her down.

They were witch doctors she had no faith in. She could not get strength from men who believed in witch hunts, who demanded liquor and chickens in return for the simplest advice, whose only solution seemed to be the practice of black magic.

"Seth," she said, "I feel women are sent to this earth to become men."

He understood what she meant. She was in a duel with her own husband, a man of her own tribe who should have protected and nurtured her.

"It is normally the men who climb coconut trees," she said. "One day, my mother was ill. She needed coconut water. But my father was too drunk to climb. That day I decided to learn to climb a coconut tree."

"You can climb a coconut tree?" he asked.

"Yes," she said. "I'll show you."

She got up and ran to the nearest one. Suddenly she had something she could show him, something he could not do, and the satisfaction on her face was palpable. She had found inspiration from her own past, which was unusual.

Soon she was thirty feet high and without a harness.

This a landlord could never do. For once Kusum was not making footprints on the soil. She was moving as far away as possible from land that had betrayed her, into air that was welcoming and without manacles.

Zairos wished he could be there with her, close to the sky.

He wanted to see through the blue, beyond it even, into space, where his travashi lived. He had questions for his travashi.

By listening to Kusum, was he was being unfaithful to his own people?

Each time he undid Kusum's hair, hundreds of Warlis came cascading down, and he was listening to all their stories. He could see their faces, their long hair, their loincloths, he could hear their screams. After Kusum and he made love, these men and women appeared out of nowhere, from decades ago, and down the torrents of her hair they slid until they rested on his chest. They spoke to him from strange places, like the man who was hanging upside down from a tree, his long hair on fire, and beneath the tree a Muslim landlord was striking more matches . . .

Zairos would tell these Warlis that he was Zoroastrian, not Muslim, not Hindu. He could not take responsibility for the actions of men taken ages ago, men belonging to other religions, and the moment he said that he knew he was wrong, and the Warlis retreated, went into hiding again in the dark night of Kusum's hair.

Now that he had met them all, he was carrying them. He could feel them even when he rode with Kusum on his motorcycle; the engine sounded like it had no power, the strain showing in its voice as it went up the bridge.

What did Zairos' fravashi want him to do?

It was the first time he had spoken to his fravashi. He had carried him around his neck since he was a child, but that was not enough. It was up to Zairos to look up to the skies and ask. And if his soul truly longed for a conversation, only then would the fravashi's wings unfold and with them the wisdom he longed to impart to the man or woman he was in charge of.

When Kusum started coming down the tree, Zairos looked away, afraid that she might fall. But even if she did lose her grip, her own fravashi existed. She had her own set of wings just as soft and loyal as his. If Zarathushtra spoke of One God, then irrespective of religion, one was born with a fravashi, and fravashis did not care about land or status, they believed in ethical value. They would weigh Kusum's thoughts, words, and deeds, and if that were the case then there was every chance that she was just as rich as he was.

So the weeks passed quickly for Zairos, maybe five, maybe more, and the egrets in the tree near the Big Boss Hair Salon continued to clean themselves with their beaks, prepare themselves for aerial lovemaking, while on the ground Zairos and Kusum did the same, chattered like birds when no one was looking, the rosy banks of their lips clashing against each other, but always fitting in.

And late one evening, just after dusk, Kusum became the first female customer of the Big Boss Hair Salon. Much to Sharmaji's credit, he did not say a word about treating a tribal. In fact, the moment he let down Kusum's hair, after much embarrassment and deliberation on her part, Sharmaji's eyes lit up, magnified times ten through his thick eyeglasses, and he took his scissors out. But Zairos stopped him.

"Only a head massage, Sharmaji," said Zairos. "Go slow."

He did not want to change her hairstyle or her clothing. That would be too brash. All he wanted was for her to meet the yellowed walls of the salon, the absurd photographs of bob cuts on the wall, to taste chai in small steel cups that the boy Munna made, a magic potion that could leave its imprint on any heart.

Kusum stared dead ahead at the mirror, afraid to move, unable to relax.

Zairos was enjoying every moment, locking eyes with her in the mirror, while Hosi and Bumble locked eyes with each other, convinced that their cousin had lost his mind. Hosi was seated in his blue swivel chair as usual, the foam inside now completely depleted so the seat was almost as hard as a plank of wood.

"You're worse than Mother Teresa," he said. "A little nun on a motorcycle who will one day hit a speed breaker and lose his halo."

"You've become a fairy," said Bumble. "Get a white dress and a wand so you can fly in Xerxes' glider and sprinkle tinsel all over Dahanu."

But no matter what anyone said, Zairos kept coming closer to Kusum.

Perhaps it was inevitable because the two of them had something in common from the time of their birth. When a Warli child was born, she told him, a few drops of liquor were fed to it as lullabies were sung. And he revealed how his father gave him whiskey when he was a baby. Aspi Irani used to dip his finger into a bottle of Black Label and let Zairos suck on it, so he would be man enough to hold his booze when he grew up. When Mithoo protested, Aspi Irani said, "Black Label is my breast milk."

"What is all this going to achieve?" Hosi asked Zairos. He scratched his beard, let out a few grunts to show his disapproval, swivelled in his blue chair, enjoying the distinct squeaks that it made. "I can understand your attraction to her," said Hosi. "But at the end of the day, it's just simple, lethal cleavage."

What he meant to say was that any contact beyond the physical was unnecessary, perhaps impossible.

And maybe Zairos was showing that it was neither.

Or maybe he was just waiting to hear from his fravashi.

Until then, the woman could have a head massage.

There was nothing wrong with that. There was nothing wrong with waiting. Nothing needed to happen. Nothing needed to be achieved. This was enough.

He looked at her in the mirror again.

With each day that passed, he saw her through the eyes of a sniper. She was all there was. She could take her long black hair, coil it around his neck, and choke him if she wished. She could do anything and he would rejoice in it.

After weeks of searching for a lover's nest, a hideout for two bandits whose only real booty was each other, Zairos had found a spot. An old burnt-down shed outside the Cottage Hospital.

He had been bringing Kusum here lately, not knowing where else to take her. He had bribed the watchman and had placed a small mat on the ground. The watchman would get them wafers and Pepsi and go away, leaving them alone to their sweating.

The year 1954 was embossed on the faded white hospital wall just above the entrance, and Zairos thought of a dying man with his date of birth printed on his forehead. He could see the lone ambulance from a hole in the shed wall, parked under a tree, the glass of the siren cracked, waiting to transport the sick and the dead. The white walls had black streaks on them that gave the place an ashen look, the look so many of its patients had in their last days. The tall dry grass in front of the hospital moved like the feelers of cockroaches, alert, ready for anything.

At first Kusum liked their secret spot. It was a chasm they both fell into, the nuts and bolts of hearts fitting into each other, with dust and spiders, moonlight seeping in through the roof, offering a courteous glow, the mark of flames on the shed walls, and the occasional wildflower, its small yellow petals like laughter in the face of all that rust and mildew. In this shed, even the stories they shared were brighter. Behind the landlords' stubbles and gold chains, she was discovering a whisper, of wanting to reach out, to mend . . . and it was something she discovered in the form of an elderly woman who had showed up at her hamlet a few days before.

Dressed in expensive clothes, yet possessing an earthy humility as she walked towards a hut, her eyes wet with remembrance, possible only if the hut she was walking towards had once sheltered her, kept the rain and wind away, allowed her to rest in her mother's lap.

She was a Warli who once sold key chains at a bus stand as a child, and her life changed when an Irani couple noticed her. Smitten by the curls around her forehead, they bought all the key chains she was selling, which were in the shape of tiny slippers. They asked her if she would come live with them, forever, and so the little girl took the Irani couple to her hut, got her mother's permission to leave, and sat in their car with a small bundle in her hand that contained, among other things, a collection of herbs given by her mother, who was sick herself, a lone parent unable to care for her daughter. The Irani couple then brought her up on their farm along with their two children, sent her to school in Bombay, taught her English, found a husband for her, and she now lived far, far away, in a land whose name Kusum could not pronounce, but

this woman was living proof that some landlords had goodness hidden inside them like secrets.

And as she thought of that elderly woman taking photographs of what once used to be her hut, Kusum hoped for an
ounce of similar luck because throughout the time she had
spent with Zairos, throughout the many suns and moons that
had now come and gone, something else had been forming
besides an alliance between her and a landlord.

Kusum had told her father's story to Zairos. But now there
was another one brewing, another one she wanted to tell, that
was running alongside Ganpat's story like a desperate passen-
ger trying to catch a train blazing along the tracks, screaming
and yelling, begging for someone to notice. There was another
story, and it was not just a story, it was something that was about
to come into this world, alive and screaming, and it could be
his. And it was there in her voice, it was there in the shiver of
her eyes, this seed that was growing, this sapling that would
develop arms and legs and eat and suck, and it was sad that she
could speak of her father's death far more easily than the birth
of her own child.

She had no idea how he would take the news.

She chose not to take the trembling of her body as an answer.
There were other signs, encouraging ones—the fact that they
were outside a hospital, the number of times he had kept her
close to his body, so tight that upon releasing her, he held her
tight again, the way he cut pieces of fruit for her, pears and
apples, in odd clumsy shapes that only heightened their taste.

Those were the moments she would pull from.

Zairos had fallen asleep on the straw mat in the shed. She
shook him awake.

She was very close to him. She had to be.

She did not know what to call him: Seth or Jairos. Did she have to offer the news with respect, or celebrate it with a lover?

Ultimately, she chose neither title nor name. She chose touch.

She pushed Zairos' hair off his face. She did not want anything to obstruct his vision, so he could see that if she was shivering it was not because she was lying. She pressed her body against his but not sexually. It was just a need to not be separate.

She let it out like a tree lets out fruit.

～ভেᵒ

His grip on the handlebars turned weak. The engine revved, his heart racing at a million rpm. His stomach churned, intestines madly twisting around one another.

"It could be Laxman's child," he said.

Out it came like a great gob of phlegm. He was suddenly very aware of the fact that Kusum's body was touching his. She was leaning into him. His back arched in response.

"It could be," said Kusum.

But it could be his too.

He cursed himself for not using protection, but he hated those fucking raincoats. And he had been careful, he had not come inside her, except once, or maybe twice, and that was beyond his control, to withdraw would have been inhuman, it would have been throwing sand in the eyes of the sublime.

She did not hold his waist as they rode along the beach.

252

Her hands were on the metal carrier. But even if she had held his waist she would have felt the same coldness.

When he saw her at work after that, the deer, the viper—the souls of both were in her. She had tricked him. Inside, she was laughing. She had not tricked him. He had been careless. He had gotten carried away. She was so strong now, walking about *his* farm.

The terrain might be hers, but the farm was his, he told himself.

Just the sheer possibility of it had given her power. And her pain seemed to have melted away, like wax from a candle, and she had conveniently left it on his table, for him to clean.

She even had the audacity to ask him for ginger marmalade.

"That sweet yellow thing," she said to him. "Please get me that sweet yellow . . ."

He brought it for her one day, and she marvelled at the wiggly yellow pieces through the glass. Zairos had to open the jar and offer her some. "Put your finger in," he said. She dug in, licked the marmalade off her finger. The look in her eyes made him think she had seen an angel, or, even better, eaten one.

"I know what you are thinking," she said.

"I'm not thinking anything," he said. "I'm not ready to be a father. It could be Laxman's. When was the time you last had sex with him?"

"The night you came and took me away from him."

After years of trying, perhaps nature had played a final joke on Laxman and Kusum. Conception, and then an hour later, bloodshed and separation, perfect conditions, normal conditions, for the birth of a Warli child.

"I'm not ready to be a father," he said again.

"No man is. Men are cowards. Men are of no use in bringing up a child anyway. Don't worry, seth. I don't want anything from you."

When she said that he wanted to pull her by the hair, choke the viper in her so only the deer remained. He preferred the deer. When she was the deer, the spear stayed in his hand. He left her among the trees and climbed the stairs to his room. But he would rather climb the stars, be far away from this earth, from this woman.

She was right. Men are cowards.

"You should abort," said Hosi. "But Mother Teresa was against abortion. What will your fellow nuns think?"

"The Vatican will be pissed," said Bumble.

The three of them were at the Big Boss Hair Salon, and Hosi was getting a body massage. He was lying on his stomach. His sides were expanding from all the beer and whiskey, and Sharmaji was working on his buttocks.

"Papaya," said Hosi. "All you need is papaya. Papaya can cause a miscarriage. Keep feeding her papaya spoon by spoon like a lovesick Romeo."

It would never work. That was Hosi's specialty. He came up with things that could never be put to use. He was currently making a list of names least likely to be used for women's perfume. The one he was most proud of: Taliban. "It sounds so French," he said. "So exotic."

"If not papaya, then you need to visit Dara Atom," said Hosi.

"Now *that's* an idea," said Bumble.

Zairos protested, but they shoved him into the car. Hosi did not even let Sharmaji wipe the oil off. "My ass feels so smooth," he said.

Before Zairos knew it, they were by the beach, walking under coconut trees on the tiled pathway that led to a wooden door with a large iron handle on it, sketches of which Zairos remembered seeing as a child in the fairy tales of the Brothers Grimm.

The waiting room was large enough to accommodate at least thirty people. The cracks in the wall were so prominent they looked like they had been chiselled. A painting of a dead horse lying on its back adorned one wall. Men, women, and children sat on wooden benches that were lined against the walls, all the patients facing the centre of the room like spectators around a boxing ring. The people there had maladies of every conceivable kind, from arthritis to conjunctivitis, and they sought a cure from Dara Atom. He was no doctor, he was the god man of Dahanu, and the people on the benches were here because they had faith in him.

"What a con man," said Hosi. "I idolize him. It's one thing to cheat the rich. But to cheat the poor, that requires a special kind of being."

"An Irani god man," said Bumble. "I find the concept weird."

The man himself appeared from his inner sanctum. He had put on even more weight since the last time Zairos had seen him at the beach. He was now fatter than Mervan Mota. He trundled along, adjusted the black bandana on his head, breathed heavily, and smeared ash on his forehead with both palms. A child started to cry. Dara Atom wiggled his fingers and scanned the room. This was his way of choosing the next patient. It did not matter how long one had waited. Dara Atom worked on instinct. And ganja. He had a Muslim friend who sat in the mosque next to Anna's all day and made balls of ganja, which he administered to all his patients as medicine. No wonder they swore by him. Just as he was about to pick an old man with a mammoth boil on his nose, Hosi walked up to Dara Atom and spoke in his ear.

The Atom then went into his chamber and came out again with a small plastic bag, which he handed to Hosi. Then he turned to the very child who was crying and said, "I will cure you." He took out a small ganja pill from his shirt pocket and forced it down the child's throat. He then placed his palm on the child's forehead and muttered some prayers.

"The pills he's given you," said Hosi once they were outside, "are not ganja pills. They will cause a miscarriage in no time. I've used them before. It's not a big deal."

"It *is* a big deal," replied Zairos. "This could be my child."

"So what? Do you know how many Iranis have made their servants get abortions? It's common, boss. It's common."

"She doesn't want an abortion. She wants to keep it."

"Who is *she* to keep it?"

Zairos did not know how to answer that.

She was not just another Warli. She could be the mother of his child. And even if she was not, she was something. She was not a mosquito, she was not a pig or horse, she was a woman with a past, present, and future.

All he had to do was crush the white pills and sprinkle the powder in the bottle of ginger marmalade.

He stared at the pills, at the tiny murderers.

She had told him that when the time came, he would not have the guts to claim the child: "Even if it is yours, it will mean nothing. When the time comes, you will not want it. What I don't understand is, if life is about to enter this world, how can you be afraid of it?"

At night, he sat alone on his porch and looked into the wasteland opposite his house. The night insects were out at play, and it was a grand night for them, an opera of sweeping rhythms, dives, and freefalls. He stared into those bushes, into the darkness, and emptied his packet of pills into the cavernous, singing mouths of night creatures.

If only she could tell him whose child it was. A mother would know. Mothers had special radars. They could spot their unborn children among the stars without a telescope.

So Zairos rode towards her hut, not caring if Rami was there.

The motorcycle picked up speed and a beetle hit his face so hard it could have been a suicide attempt. A car approached from the opposite direction, the driver flashing his headlights, afraid that Zairos was a drunken rider. To some extent, he was. He had gulped down three pegs of whiskey at home.

But Zairos was no beetle. He knew exactly where he was going.

She was cooking over a fire, fanning the flames with a paper fan. Rami was not around. Maybe she had gone to relieve herself, far away in the darkness of a paddy field. Zairos took the fan from Kusum and started fanning her face instead. She smiled, but it was a tired smile, a smile that had run thousands of miles.

He could tell that she was disappointed in him. He had withdrawn from her, the days now long and plodding, the sweat on her back heavier than usual.

"My aunt was right," she said. "She said you would lose interest."

But he had not lost interest. He was pausing, slowing down. He was young, and so was she, and something even younger, more fragile, was about to come into this world, and he could not tell if he wanted it to be his or not.

He was lying to himself. He did not want it. He wanted her.

The child would be him *and* her, a mixture that would find it very hard to grow, let alone flourish. He had seen such mixtures before, and none of them were claimed by the Iranis. They were left with their mothers, and the initial lightness of their skin was darkened by the sun, and by the realization that they had been left unclaimed.

Zairos made Kusum sleep on the ground, on her earth, so that its warmth might somehow reach her heart. The earth, in a way, was like tea—it went down your throat and found places nothing else could reach. Soon, he was on top of her and the flames were making them sweat. Her eyes were closed, but he was taking it all in. The brown walls of the hut, the sickle on the wall, the clothesline with Rami's blouses hanging, an earthen pot full of water, and a hand mirror on the ground. His palms were on the thatched floor, and he felt that at any minute the heat would melt the floor and the two of them would sink deep into the earth itself.

"Whose child do you think it is?" he asked.

She opened her eyes, looked directly into his, and the tears came.

For the first time, tears came. But there was no sound.

He got off her. The flames of the cooking fire died down and there was a hiss and crackle, but he was not sure if it was Kusum or the flames. Zairos caught a glimpse of his face in the hand mirror that was on the ground. He could barely recognize himself.

FIFTEEN

ROXANNE THE TOWN GOSSIP was the one who started it. Zairos could tell from her beaming face. On the beach, while Aspi Irani added ice cubes to his whiskey glass, TG added something else. A tinge of the truth for flavour, nothing more.

Along the sand it went, through the pine trees, it circled the white canopy of the Crazy Crab where Zairos and Kusum had eaten, rattled the iron latch on the wooden door of Dara Atom's ganja clinic, created its own language at Anna's, travelled through the telephone line to Anna's wife in Udipi, then came back rejuvenated and hopped and skipped all over the carrom board outside Behrooz's spare-parts shop, on and on it went, a wound-up toy vibrating with an unnatural frenzy, sending a shiver of disgust and excitement through unmarried Irani women, yet managing to tickle their panties, until it finally rested, heavy as a log, stiff as the steel brace on a polio-afflicted leg, smelly as a sock recovered from a swamp, on Aspi Irani's writing table, which had a broken leg that made things slant towards him, so he had no choice but to take notice of what had slid from the table into his hands, this niggling truth, this massive shipwreck, and the juice of the matter was not that Zairos was having an affair with a Warli woman, no, that was not it, what was so tasty was that there was a child involved and that Zairos had bought Atoms from Dara to demolish the poor fucker, just like that, and Zairos, that handsome prick who thought he was too good for Roxanne or any other Irani girl for that matter was nothing new, in time he would be a hirsute creature just like everyone else, and now that this angel was falling from the skies, nose down, the only place he had was the low-life arms of a pregnant Warli.

By bringing this affair, this travesty, out in the open, the Irani women had found their punching bag at last. For years they had tolerated the steaminess of the tribal women, for years they had accepted the fact that no matter how much eyeliner they put on or how smooth they waxed their inner thighs, the Warli women always looked more inviting without even trying. And their husbands went after those women like hungry dogs, but not once did they have the decency to display that same hunger in their own bedrooms, not once did they pant and moan like they were dying, not once did they tear off their wives' clothes with their bare teeth, not once did they writhe in agony like the worms they were when their wives withhold sex from them. Zairos knew he was the poster boy, the crucifixion boy, the molester, the baby killer, he was anything they wanted him to be, and their darts were aimed not only at him but at Aspi Irani as well: now how does he feel, always pretending to be superior, always mocking us, how does that grand patriarch Shapur Irani feel, god only knows how his wife died, he never talks about her death, and what about Mithoo, is she "sweet" now, does she still feel clean as a sparrow, she pretends her marriage is happy, is she clean as a sparrow now?

At home, Aspi Irani had stopped singing. No matter how much the churchgoers wailed, his wail was louder, but silent, something Zairos could not fathom. Even when Aspi Irani cut his apple, it was as though the apple was a dead fruit and he was putting it in his own dead mouth. Mithoo, who in all these years had rarely been anything but chipper, now cooked in silence, her tea was hot but lacked warmth, and when she sat on the swing outside, her cream skirt failed to flow or flutter even a tiny bit.

Aspi Irani put an empty cigarette in his mouth but accidentally bit it and spat out the tobacco. All his habits were becoming clumsy, or disappearing, and somewhere Zairos understood what this meant. His habits were breaking down because Aspi Irani was ashamed of an older habit, the habit of every Irani man, of keeping Warli flesh on the table in the early stages of his marriage. This thought ran through Zairos' mind like a shark streaming through murky waters, biting, flashing the edges of its teeth, then disappearing into the darkness, but one day, after a month of rumours and silences and forks and knives being the only dinner-table conversation at home, Mithoo came out with it, Mithoo, of all people, turned to her son and said in a calm voice, "You have the same disease your father had," and the only consolation Zairos could find in his mother's words was the fact that she used the word *had*, that whatever Aspi Irani had done, he had done in the past and it was dead, or Mithoo thought it was dead until

Zairos reminded her of it like that bastard child whose name was on everyone's lips.

Bitterness had entered Mithoo's sweet voice, turned it sour. Nothing seemed to help her. Not even the warm, love-drenched tongues of stray dogs against her arms.

The only person who remained unaffected by all this was Shapur Irani, but he was so far away from this planet even death could not touch him, or at the most it could move the hair on his eyebrows out of place.

When Zairos went to meet his grandfather, for the first time Shapur Irani got up from his rocking chair, causing the mosquitoes that were around him to break their formation. The flicker of the lantern darted across his cheek as he opened his wooden cupboard. Shapur Irani rarely put on the tube lights in his house. He preferred lanterns. There was no electricity when he lived with Banu so perhaps it was out of habit. He was comfortable with a natural flame because it lit only certain parts of the house, not the whole. Banu lived on in the darkness.

When Shapur Irani was visible again, he had a whiskey bottle in his hand.

"I've not had a drink in very long," he said. "It just shows that what you think you cannot do without in your youth has very little power later on in life."

"Shall I fetch the glasses?" asked Zairos.

"No, you sit."

Zairos sat at the table and watched his grandfather's back—one giant shadow, that's what he was. That's what one became with age. He had also become a collection of sounds: the clink of whiskey glasses as he removed them from the cabinet, the flip-flop of his rubber slippers against the cement floor, the grunt that the old emit when performing the simplest of tasks.

Shapur Irani picked up the whiskey bottle and placed it in Zairos' hands.

"Hold this bottle," said Shapur Irani. "Feel it."

The bottle was quite magnificent, if one could call it that. The glass had a green tinge to it, and its shape was not perfect, it was a bit uneven, as though it was made by a glass blower whose cheerless breath had left it that way. It had no label, just the year engraved on the glass: 1942. The initials RB were engraved in black on the cork.

"When the British occupied India, this is what they drank. At one point, I had thirty bottles of RB whiskey hidden under chickoo trees," said Shapur Irani. "This is the last one left."

"Is there something we are celebrating?" asked Zairos.

"No," said Shapur Irani. "To celebrate anything is to invite trouble, to beg misfortune to come and punch you in the guts. We are drinking this tonight because this bottle existed at a time when your grandmother was alive and all this time I couldn't bear to finish it because it would mean . . . I don't know what it would mean. But perhaps now, with all that is going on, it would be as good a time as any."

He twisted the cork, opened it with his large hands. As he poured the whiskey in the glass, Zairos thought of his grandmother, how this golden stream of alcohol was bottled when she was a young woman.

"Did my grandmother ever drink?" asked Zairos.

"No . . . only brandy when she had fever. I always hoped that someday she would drink with me and in that hope I had kept two bottles of RB whiskey with me, but the other one was lost. I'm sure it was stolen because I never forgot where I hid these things."

"There's one more bottle out there somewhere?"

"The day Banu died, I drank from that bottle, the lost one. That bottle is full of grief."

When Zairos got home, his mother was awake, *The ABC of English* lying in her lap. The book was open to a sketch of a little girl and her dog, the sun shining in the sky, the little girl trying to catch the sun.

Mithoo did not react when Zairos came in. She continued to stare at the open book with a soldier's erect back, and it reminded Zairos of Banumai sitting in a similar position, the pages of her books fluttering about on the floor.

He sat next to his mother on the sofa, hoping that she would talk. Even a scream would do. Clemency could come in the form of screams, ripping through her throat, into his ears, his drums accepting that he had caused her pain. By loving Kusum, he had brought his mother's demons to her.

"You know I never liked Dahanu," she said suddenly.

Her cheeks had become softer in recent days, looser, wider.

"I always wanted to stay in Bombay but your father loved the farm because it was his life . . . It was *his* life, not mine," she said. "I used to feel a crushing sadness on the farm. I don't know what it was, call it depression, call it anything . . . I used to stare at the chickoo trees and wished they would die. I wanted something to come and destroy it all, and I hated myself for feeling that way because the farm was what your father loved. One day, I was travelling alone to Bombay by train. I was to pick you up from school and bring you back to the farm. I thought of getting off that train and never coming back. Not to you, not to your father, not to anyone. I saw an opening and I almost took it."

At breakfast, the crack of the egg against the rim of the bowl made Zairos wonder how long the silence would last. He had lost track of the weeks. They had evaporated in front of his eyes, and it had been ages since Aspi Irani had sprayed mosquito repellent in his room. The mosquitoes had taken over every corner of the house, but even they knew the victory was hollow.

After eating his scrambled eggs, Zairos was about to go to his room when he heard his mother say something, but he was not sure if he had heard right. But then she said it again, as she put the cut onions and tomatoes aside and cleaned her hands with a towel.

"I want to go hunting," she said.

Even Aspi Irani tried to make sense of this odd combination of words from his wife's mouth.

"These people should not shit in the bushes," she said. "If they want to shit in the bushes, they should do it near their own homes. These bhaiyyas should learn from the Warlis. The Warlis never perform their ablutions out in the open."

She strode into the storage room where Aspi Irani's record collection was gathering spiders, and came out with his slingshot.

Sensing what she was doing, sensing that by indulging in people-shooting, a most abnormal activity, she was trying to make things normal again, Aspi Irani rose from his chair with such energy that the chair flipped over.

"Come on," said Mithoo.

She left the door open, not caring who went in. Perhaps their lives had already been invaded in such a personal manner that thief, animal, or wind could do little else. Mithoo walked ahead, fast and purposeful.

The three of them took their position in the bushes and waited. There was no one yet. The defecators were still selling coconuts at the train station. Aspi Irani was showing his wife how to use the slingshot, adjusting the angle of her right hand, telling her to keep her back straight.

"The last time you used it was on our honeymoon, remember?" he said to her.

Zairos did not bother to find out why.

While Mithoo was fidgeting with the slingshot, taking aim and getting accustomed to crouching in the bushes, Zairos began to have minor reservations.

"What if she *does* hit someone?" he whispered to his father.

"That's the point."

"I mean, what if she blinds him?"

"Have faith, son. We live next to a church."

Soon the target appeared, a bald, rotund fellow with his tin can full of water. He took his dhoti off and squatted in the bushes. Mithoo was nervous, but what disturbed Zairos was that when she put that stone in the leather pouch and pulled the black rubber strand back, stretching it to its maximum, her tongue came out of her mouth a little, finding this whole thing very tasty.

"You know many years ago I had written a letter to Indira Gandhi about public defecation," said Aspi Irani. "But she got assassinated before she read it."

Mithoo's hand was now shaking, she was giggling the way schoolgirls giggled on see-saws, except that her giggle was darker. As soon as the man passed one enormous bowel movement, Mithoo let go. He got up, but he was hurt, confused, messy. Mithoo dropped the slingshot. She jumped up and ran, and as she ran, she laughed, and so did Aspi Irani, his chuckle had returned, the imp was back.

In all these weeks, Zairos had not made love to Kusum.

It had happened in stages. First, he had stopped entering her, then a few days later he stopped licking her belly, then the kissing, the holding of hands, even a simple touch or three, and finally distance came, a few breaths, a few days, a few weeks.

She had become a woman near the bathtubs again.

But now Mithoo had propelled her son towards something, and he did not know what that was until he found himself standing outside the Zoroastrian fire temple at midnight.

He parked his motorcycle outside the large cast-iron gate and entered through a smaller one. If he had come during the day, he would have been greeted by red shoe flowers and pink bougainvilleas, but in the darkness only the tall ashokas made their presence felt as they stood grand and respectful.

Two strong pillars on each end of the fire temple had images of afarganyus embedded into the cement, strong flames of faith emerging from the fire holders. But it was the fravashi in the centre of the structure that always welcomed believers, his wings keeping him afloat.

ZOROASTRIAN FIRE TEMPLE. FOR ZOROASTRIANS ONLY.

The moon provided a soft reading light for the sign, which was in English as well as Hindi. Zairos walked up the seven marble steps, each one twenty feet wide, giving the impression that the fire temple was an imposing library.

He took a jug of water from a metal container that was kept outside and washed his hands to free himself of any impurities. Upon entering, he saw the portraits of the dead, the patrons who had built this fire temple, the frames adorned by garlands, angling towards the worshippers. There was a large mirror with the image of Zarathushtra embossed on it, representing the day of his revelation at the age of thirty when he was standing at the edge of a river, and Ahura Mazda and six other Amesha Spentas appeared before him. The light that emanated from Ahura Mazda was so dazzling that Zarathushtra could not see his own shadow on the ground.

In the main hall, long brass chains hung from the ceiling, at the ends of which oil lamps hovered in glass containers. There were at least seventy of these divas, motionless in the air, content with their own light, present not for themselves but for all to behold.

Entranced by their presence, Zairos saw more lights in steel trays on the ground, tiny glasses huddled close to each other, exchanging warmth like it was the only thing that mattered. It was a vast sea of light, a sea that was singing, as if each wave were a note and each note a flicker of light, and the sound was not silence, it was silence made deeper a thousand times by a thousand lights.

He walked between those hanging lights, each one of them lit for a different purpose, or by a different person, each one sending out its own prayer, its own sweet blessing, until he finally faced the Atash burning in a silver vase. He placed his head against the brass bars and longed to get closer, but only the priest could do that when he prayed over it and kept the fire alive.

The priest was in a corner of the temple, seated cross-legged on a white cloth on the floor, performing prayers for the dead. Even through his white mouth-veil, his voice buzzed and hummed with authority, but was still humble. His prayers, mysterious as a maze in a forest, yet gentle and soothing, floated through the room, feather-touching the walls, grazing the photographs of the dead, a gentle reminder to them not to forget the ones who remained.

The midnight oil lamps were a sign to anyone who entered of what was important in the darkness—light was all that was needed. It was all that would be noticed. It could be a small flicker of the diva, or the burning flames of the Atash.

Even a spark was significant.

Even a spark mattered in the afterlife, on the Chinvat Bridge that Zarathushtra said all men had to cross. Based on one's conduct on earth, on how many sparks one had, a man got either a dazzling maiden as a guide or a demonic hag. Both were reflections of a man's own conscience, and perhaps that was why Zairos was here tonight, to see what his conscience looked like, to find out what it wanted him to do.

Each time he tried to listen to his conscience, he heard the voice of both the maiden and the shrew, and he told himself that there might be many voices telling him what to do, but only one of them was true, and he would have to suss that voice out as one selected a single life-giving sprout from an array of weeds.

He needed to nurture that voice because it was the only one that would lead to a good deed. But then again it was ignorant of him to think of claiming his child as a good deed. It was not something that required careful consideration. It was his duty.

The next day, when he could not find Kusum near the bath-tubs, he went to her hamlet. He found her by a stream not far from her hut. The buffaloes in the stream had their heads in the water, which had turned brown in parts because they were causing the mud to shift. On the other side of the stream, red bougainvilleas sprouted, tried to reach as high up as they could.

"You did not come for work today," said Zairos.

He did not know where else to start. He sat by her side, ashamed that he had stayed away from her for so long. He plucked a strand of grass and put it in his mouth.

He glanced at her belly, now clearly swollen.

The unborn child had been unable to ignore the passage of time the way Zairos had.

The buffaloes had finished bathing. They strolled out of the water, went to the other side of the stream. One of them walked into the bougainvilleas and let them brush against its skin.

"Seth, you must be hungry," she said. "You are eating grass."

She took the blade of green out of his mouth and threw it away.

"Even tribals do not eat that," she said.

She was still playful with him. He did not understand how this woman did not want to tear his gums, or break his knees into a thousand beautiful pieces.

She held his hand and led him towards her hut. He liked that it was she who initiated the touch. Maybe it was the child inside. Tired of being concealed, it was making its mother's hands move, its unformed eyes and mouth not being able to see or speak, but its heart sensing with full intensity, the waves of its longing bringing its parents closer.

"Seth," she said. "You had asked me whose child I thought it was."

She swooped in from nowhere, without warning.

"Yes," said Zairos.

She did not say more until they had entered the hut. From the blast of daylight to sudden shade and the smell of cow dung, she made him sit on the ground.

"It is Laxman's child," she said. "I told him that when he came to see me."

"Laxman came near you?"

"He will not harm me. He wants a child. It makes him look like a man."

"How do you know it is his?"

"Seth, it is better if it is his."

She went to a corner of the hut, picked up a large earthen

bowl, and placed it near the hearth. Zairos stared at the sickle on the wall. It hung there at a slant, its arc facing the ground. There was nothing else to look at.

"Kusum," he said. "If the child is mine, I will look after it. And you."

"Seth," she said. "I will not see you after today. I am with my husband again."

She emptied the contents of the earthen bowl on the ground. There were all sorts of things. Bangles, nose rings, a hand mirror, a wristwatch with a leather strap, the twig of a neem tree.

"I want to give you something," she said. "It is from a time when my mother and father were alive. I was happy then."

She tried to keep things buoyant but he could see the pain in her face. Like an evening that knew it faced a losing fight with night.

"Kusum, I will take you with me . . . I will—"

"No. Even if you take me now, someday you will bring me back to this hut. Maybe now you will look after me, but one day you will meet an Irani woman and you will make her your wife . . . and you will realize that you love her, not me."

She had no way of knowing that for sure. He could not promise her a lifetime of happiness, no one could, but he could promise her a morning, maybe a few afternoons, motor-cycle rides that lasted miles, and his hand on her belly when she needed it.

He opened his mouth again, enough for just a purr of words to come through, but she had made up her mind. Something within her was hurrying her up, they were like two countries breaking off, floating away from each other.

She put her palm to his cheek. "Seth, please do not come here again."

Zairos wanted that palm to stay with him forever. Nothing could match the warmth of her palm. But beneath that warmth, he detected something else. There was disappointment, and it was flailing its arms in his face, making it clear that he had let her down, he had failed to fight for her.

He told himself that he had fought, but perhaps it was too late.

She picked up a photograph from the earthen pot, of her as a little girl, standing next to a missionary. Its edges were frayed, as though singed by flames, and she had to pass it on to him before all of it was eaten.

"It is the only photo of me," she said. "It was taken at a time when I used to pluck lilies at your farm, and once I saw you on a cycle . . ."

But Zairos had noticed an object on the thatched floor of the hut. His mind was trying to understand what that object had been doing in her earthen pot.

The cork of a whiskey bottle with the initials RB engraved in black.

"Where did you get this?" he asked.

"It belonged to my father."

"Don't lie to me," he said. "Where did you get it?" He squeezed her arm tight and was breathing hard. "Tell me where you got this from."

"This is the cork I told you about. This is the cork Rami found in my father's fist when he was unconscious as a boy."

Zairos let go of her arm because his grandfather's voice was so loud and clear, Shapur Irani might as well be in the hut himself.

The day Banu died, I drank from that bottle, the lost one. That bottle is full of grief.

After his grandfather, Ganpat appeared: *Many years ago I saw Shapur seth do something terrible.*

And finally, Rami, raspy as ever: *That day, you held a bottle cork in your fist.*

Zairos smelled the cork. It smelled of nothing. It was worn, but it held something.

"Kusum," he said.

His voice contained it all—the pleading of a man who had finally realized he loved his woman, but he was late, like a clock with heavy hands that had failed to reach the mark on the designated hour. He moved towards her, but she did not let him touch her. She pushed his outstretched hand away.

He knew she had every right to, but she was making a mistake.

"Look at me," he said.

If she would not allow him to get through to her by touch, he would do it through sight—the transparency of his eyes, everything she needed to know pouring out of them.

She stared at the ground.

"Please leave," she said.

"Kusum, I . . ."

But the words would not come.

Maybe because what he was about to say to her did not exist. *There is nothing like love.* For years he had read it on his grandfather's cupboard.

He walked away from the hut, from his woman, perhaps for good.

For the first time in his life he had lost something.

At the beach, Zairos watched an army of midnight fishermen. There were at least fifty of them, charging the sea during low tide. They walked through the sticky mud with torches in their hands. They were hunting for squid, directing the flames towards the mud, causing the squid to jump, an attraction for light that led to their capture.

The whiskey was now in him. It was coursing through his veins looking for the finish line. He was ready to face his grandfather. The fishermen went deeper and deeper into the sea, fifty pairs of feet squashing the wet mud, torches flickering in the wind.

Lakhu opened the door.

Shapur Irani was in bed. His bowels were troubling him again. Zairos went to the bed, the solid headboard spreading out behind his grandfather, a dark wall of wood.

"When Banu was alive there used to be a mosquito net around this bed," said Shapur Irani. "After she died, the servant kept making that net until I tore it. After Banu was gone, what could a few mosquitoes do? I pray you never find the woman you love, Zairos."

Each day Zairos heard his grandfather say something different. Each day, it came down to the same thing—the past. Tonight, he would get some answers.

"Pa, did you know that Banumai's fever would eventually prove fatal?" he asked.

It was a starting point. From there, he could move forward, sideways, any way he wished—or was allowed to by his grandfather.

"No," said Shapur Irani. "And even if I did, it would have made no difference. When it comes to the one you love, death is a sudden explosion."

"Were you with her when she died?"

His grandfather nodded. He gave Zairos nothing more.

But Zairos needed to know: Did he hold Banumai's hand as she shivered, covered in blankets, or did he wake up in the middle of the night with the dreaded feeling that even though there were two bodies in bed, only one of them was breathing?

"Pa, we have never spoken about Banumai's death. Even my father does not know much, except that she died of a fever."

"Some moments should be shared only between husband and wife," said Shapur Irani. "Those last moments with Banu . . . it would be wrong of me to speak about them."

"Did you drink a lot after her death?" asked Zairos.

"So much that I cannot remember my sons in the weeks and months after."

"What about the day she died? Were you drunk on that day?"

"Zairos, you are my grandson, but do not think for a moment that you can cross lines."

Zairos tried to soften his approach, but his nerves prevented him from doing so.

"Something happened on the day of her death."

"What do you mean?" asked Shapur Irani. "What makes you think that?"

"This," said Zairos.

He placed the bottle cork on his grandfather's chest, just below his chin.

Shapur Irani narrowed his vision to take a look.

"What's this? Why have you brought this here?"

"This cork belongs to the bottle you drank from the day she died," said Zairos.

Shapur Irani slowly took his hand out from underneath the white sheet and held the cork between thumb and forefinger.

"Where did you get this?" he asked.

"From Ganpat's hut. Ganpat found this cork when he was a boy. He saw you do something . . ."

"I am through with Ganpat. All he wanted was money. And I was right to refuse him."

"That was when he threatened you."

"Threatened *me*? With what will a tribal threaten me?"

Shapur Irani tried to sit up straight but it was not possible. He coughed as he spoke.

"Ganpat asked for money on the strength of something he knew," said Zairos.

"Part of this land belonged to his father. Sometimes these tribals forget they do not own the land anymore. They forget they have lost it. It is now your land, Zairos. It's yours."

"This land will mean nothing to me if I don't know the truth. What did Ganpat see as a boy?"

"Nothing," said Shapur Irani. "He saw nothing."

"Ganpat said you were near a well. Why did Ganpat mention a well? He said something terrible happened."

"By then the torture of the Warlis had stopped . . ."

But even if Ganpat had seen Shapur Irani inflict the worst kind of torture on a Warli, it was not something Shapur Irani could be blackmailed with. That was just the way things were then. Zairos thought of leaving his grandfather alone and going home because what he was about to say next was hurtful. But he could not afford to flinch now.

He held his grandfather's shoulders, put his face so close he could smell the stale breath, the breath of a man who never got sleep.

"Maybe it has nothing to do with the Warlis," said Zairos. "It has to do with Banumai."

"Don't touch me . . ." said Shapur Irani.

He was a child whose bowels were weak, who needed help.

"If you give me this land, give me its truth," said Zairos.

"Zairos, please . . ."

"What happened that day, Pa? What did Ganpat see? Tell me or I am walking out of here, never to return."

"Zairos . . ."

When Zairos looked into his grandfather's eyes, he could tell that something within had moved, some small animal that had been presumed dead.

"How was I to know about the beard?" asked his grandfather.

SIXTEEN

1948

WHEN SHAPUR IRANI woke up, he saw that Banu was not next to him. He was not surprised because he had burned all her books the night before, an act he knew he would regret for years to come.

He rubbed his eyes vigorously, not knowing what else to do. Maybe Banu was in the kitchen making his tea, her morning routine. He hoped that was the case. It would mean she had chosen to ignore what he had done. But when he went to the kitchen, she was not there. Only the tea strainer lay in the sink with two large leaves of mint.

He went to the boys' room next, and they were still asleep. They were purring like cubs. He was proud of his boys. They would become men of the soil, not men of books. He went into the living room where Banu liked to sit at the dinner table and drink her tea.

There was a cup of tea at the table, but it was untouched. The main door was open and through it he saw his wife in her cream nightgown standing amid the charred remains of her books. The soil around her feet had turned black and a lone rooster, full of vigour, failed to dilute the truth of the landscape.

The sleeve of Banu's nightgown was off her shoulder and this troubled Shapur Irani. He did not like the fact that she was out in her nightgown. She was still an attractive woman, her skin was fair, and he did not want any of the workers to have a picture of her in their minds. He saw the way they looked at her—her skin must remind them of goat's milk.

He was about to tell her to come in, but he stopped himself. It felt like an order, and orders were the last thing his wife needed right now because he had behaved like a tyrant the night before. He told himself to stop being dramatic. What he did was an act of love. It was an act of fear as well, but Banu had made him that way with her obsession with shadows.

"Banu," he said, his normally gruff voice trying to find some gentleness. "Please come back in."

She said nothing. She looked at the black soil around her. He noticed that she was barefoot and her feet were dirty. They had picked up whatever the soil had to offer.

"Banu," he said again. "Come inside. The boys will wake up soon."

"How could you do this?" she asked.

He was never good with words. He was a man of physical strength, a man of push-ups. How did she expect such a man to explain his actions?

"I'm sorry" was all he could manage. Even he knew it was weak and insincere.

"It's terrible," she said. "You've killed them all."

"Killed?"

"You've killed hundreds."

She closed her eyes as she said this. Shapur Irani shuddered at the thought that she could not bear to see his face.

"I'll get you new books, Banu. I'll . . . we'll go to Bombay together and buy all the books I've burned, I promise."

"What books? What are you talking about?"

Why did she say that? Did she want him to confess his crime again and again? She wanted him to own up like a disgraced bully, a common thief. He was ready to do that for her.

"You've killed hundreds of people," she said. "You are a murderer."

"What?"

"All those people. They were my friends. Oliver, I loved Oliver. Then the man who sent his shadow out into the world to see what was out there. I understood that man. And that woman who fought with her family to become a writer . . ."

She rattled off names, spoke of events that Shapur Irani had no clue of. After a while, he realized what she was doing. She was telling him about the people in those books. She thought they were alive. If that was the case, they deserved to die. He wanted to hear their fucking screams as they were being eaten by the flames.

He had had enough.

The sleeve of Banu's blouse had dropped even lower. She had no excuse for stepping out of the house in her nightgown. There was an element of purity to her that he wanted to preserve.

"You murderer," she said. There was no rage in her voice. It was cold and clear, a voice that had been cleansed of anger or any form of judgment.

"That's enough," said Shapur Irani.

"How will the boys feel when I tell them? How will your sons feel when I tell them their father is a murderer?"

Shapur Irani's blood swirled around his temples. He reached for her shoulder, the exposed one.

"Don't touch me!" she screamed, escaping his grip.

She bolted through the chickoo trees with such force it made Shapur Irani believe she was chasing all the dead people from her books. She was running after them, pleading for mercy, begging them to come back.

Shapur Irani stood paralyzed. He could not understand how the air around him smelled so good even though his wife was running through the trees, possessed. It was a weird thought to have at that moment, to think about the quality of air.

His boys were alone at home. They were sleeping and the more they slept the better. The door to his house was ajar. Not only the door, everything had been ripped open. His life was one gaping hole. He walked through the trees, slapping branches aside, forgetting the love he felt for his trees.

Even though Banu was out of sight, he did not run. There was no point. He would never catch up with his wife. Today, she had an otherworldly power that gave her strength. It was the power of books, the power of witches, who knows. It all felt the same to him.

He longed for the peace and quiet of the early days of his marriage. The large cups of sweet tea that they would share, the way he would slide his hand up her thigh and she would naughtily remark, "Lately there has been an increase in snakes around here." That woman no longer existed.

He could not tell where she had gone. He noticed one tree with a swelling on its branch, a bump, and just above the bump was a tiny branch, only three or four inches long, one that had stopped growing. He recognized it as the tree under which he had hidden a bottle of RB whiskey. He wished he had the forked instrument he used for digging the soil, but he knew this particular hole was not deep, so he picked up a sharp rock and started.

He needed a shot of whiskey. He thought of how Catholic priests used crosses to fight demons. He had no cross, so he would use whiskey. The whiskey inside him would battle the demon inside his wife. He did not know why, but he felt it was the right thing to do. If she had lost her mind, he would lose his too. Let it all burn. Not just the books. Let it all burn—the trees, the air, the wired fence, his sons . . . He knew that was a horrible thought so he dug with renewed force.

Within minutes the bottle's cork showed its head to him and he did not waste any time. He poured the demon-fighter down his throat with such recklessness that it made him shiver. He had to stop and start again. Stop and start, stop and start, until a quarter of the bottle was gone. He put the bottle in the hole and covered it with mud again. He was wasting time on purpose because he knew it would take time for the demon-fighter to kick in, and he did not want to face his wife without it.

He heard a sound behind him, but when he looked there was nothing. It could be some small animal. But then he saw a little Warli boy. Shapur Irani tried to think of the boy's name.

After a while, Shapur Irani saw her through the trees. She was walking around in circles and the strap of her nightgown was still off her shoulder. He did not want her to see him because she might start running again. He waited and watched. She had a strange pattern—she walked clockwise, took three circles, then walked counter-clockwise and took three more. Then she stopped and examined the soles of her feet. She tried to scrape the book ash off her feet with her hands. Not satisfied with the result, she walked some more towards the well.

Shapur Irani remembered how, when the well was being dug, she had joked that when her water burst the well would be full. After showing much promise, the well did not give water. It was the deepest well in Dahanu, but it was completely dry.

She sat at the edge of the well and used a stone to take the dirt off her feet. She was talking to herself, mumbling in the language of witches. How hurtful her words had become. Someone, some horrible creature, had entered his house at night and swapped his wife's tongue. What wife would call her husband a murderer?

His wife, at this moment, hated him. The idea came to him suddenly. She hated Shapur, the man. What if he transformed himself into something else? A tiger, perhaps? He remembered the game he played with her, where she was lost in the forest and he would pretend to be a tiger, a game that would eventually lead to lovemaking. Sex was not on his mind at this moment, but it might make sense to present himself in front of her as anything *but* himself. Only then would she listen.

He started growling, softly at first, trying to gauge his wife's reaction. She did not move, did not say a word. He walked closer and closer, and his growling increased in volume and intensity. He made sure it was playful, never scary. Her eyes looked above him, as though she was looking through the trees behind him. It was fine. As long as she did not run. As long as she did not move.

"I am the king of this jungle," he said. "What are you doing in my jungle?"

She was still staring at something as he came closer and closer. But whatever he was doing was working because she was now walking towards him. By being a tiger, he was moving from his world into the imaginary, the world in which she was living. He was drawing her closer, and he blessed his stars for inventing this game.

She suddenly stopped. "Stay away," she said, still looking into the distance.

"The beard," she said. "The beard . . ."

Her face was turning pale. She was looking behind him.

Shapur Irani turned to look as well. It was Ejaz the Pathan. He was walking through the trees with a tin of water.

"The beard," said Banu again.

Shapur Irani's brain felt like it was full of wires, and the wires were unconnected, giving off shocks and sparks. He did not like this feeling because things were starting to make sense. And when Banu finally screamed her lungs out and shouted, "The beard!" it was a scream that had a hundred confessions in it.

He looked at Ejaz, at the man who had a long, black beard, and then at his wife.

Then Banu started speaking fast. Shapur Irani could pick up only a few words such as "wooden club" and "Ejaz's breath," and Shapur Irani kept telling himself that these words were completely random and did not mean anything. He went towards his wife, to shut her up, because she was embarrassing herself. But Banu continued, "I'm sorry, Shapur, I wanted to tell you."

"Be quiet," said Shapur Irani. He inched closer to her, and she retreated, went closer to the well.

"I'm sorry," she said again.

"Shut up," said Shapur Irani, and he held his wife's arm.

As Banu continued to speak, his grip on her arm tightened, and when she said, "It's *your* fault, I told you not to trust Ejaz," he hit her hard across the face, so hard that it felt as though she was running backwards, and when she disappeared, Shapur Irani ran too, but it was not really him who was running, it was his heart. He stood staring at the motionless body of his wife at the bottom of the well.

In an instant Shapur Irani turned so cold and grey, ash could have fallen from his cheeks.

He did not even remember how he had walked this far because he was near his house again. How did he get here? He stepped all over the book ash and entered the house not knowing what his steps meant. The cup of tea was still on the table. He sat on the chair and took a sip. It was cold.

The boys were still sleeping. All was well.

After tea, what? What was he supposed to do? He opened his wooden cupboard and took out his shotgun. He loaded it, went into the room where his sons were sleeping. They would not even know. They would not feel a thing. They loved their mother more than they loved him anyway. One, two, three. Three shots and they would be with her again.

Just then, Khodi opened his eyes and stared into the barrel of the gun.

"Papa," he said, the sleep in his eyes preventing his brain from registering the truth.

The moment Shapur Irani heard his son speak, he left the room. He heard his youngest, Aspi, cry as well. He bolted the main door because he did not want to hear Khodi say "Papa" again. More than anything, he did not want Khodi to see his mother at the bottom of a well. He would lock them in this house for life.

The shotgun was still in his hand.

He had told Ejaz not to walk among the trees early in the morning, but the bastard never listened. He trusted the Pathan and the Pathan had let him down. The Pathan was treacherous because he had not followed instructions regarding walking through the trees.

He was now outside Ejaz's shack, hoping that the man would deny everything Shapur Irani suspected him of.

"Ejaz!" shouted Shapur Irani. "Ejaz!"

Ejaz stood in the doorway, imposing as ever.

Shapur Irani could not bring himself to ask any questions. Even the thought of it being true was too much to bear.

"I have been waiting for this day," said Ejaz. "I have waited for this day."

"What do you mean?" asked Shapur Irani.

His hand was trembling, the finger on the trigger so confused, yet so ready. The need to hurt Ejaz was intense, but what he hungered for more than anything was to enter that shack and disappear forever, like a child gone missing.

"I am ashamed of what I did," said Ejaz. "But I had no choice."

"What do you mean?" asked Shapur Irani again.

That was all he could bring himself to say. The question echoed in his brain: *what do you mean what do you mean what do you mean what do you mean.*

"Do you remember that day when landlords went to Dahanu beach and the goons ransacked the villages and raped Warli women?"

Don't use that word, Ejaz. Have mercy on me, please don't use that word.

"That day I stayed here to protect your wife and child because I knew that you would do the same for me. When I told you I had a son in Bombay, you said to me, 'From now on he is my son too,' and I believed you. That day, when you returned after your meeting with the landlords, I told you that I needed to talk to you about my son. But you called me a servant, you humiliated me. My son needed an operation, he was very sick. But that was not why I did it."

Did what did what did what did what.

"The day we went to the fair with your wife and sons, the day you beat Gustad seth with his belt, that very morning I had gotten the news that my son had died. I blamed you for his death. If only you had listened. That night I was drunk and angry in the bazaar and that is when Gustad seth approached me. I was cursing you . . ."

Shapur Irani wondered what that scum landlord had to do with this. He remembered Gustad's smile.

"Gustad seth heard my story and he promised to give me money if I did this thing, this one thing. But I did not do it for the money, seth. If you had listened to me about my son, none of this would have happened."

"There was no one to save your son," said Shapur Irani, finally able to make a pertinent statement. "And now there is no one to save you."

"I have been waiting for this day," said Ejaz. "I could have run away after what I did, but I was ashamed. A Pathan had fallen so low. I did not deserve to stand tall."

Ejaz slowly went down on one knee and lowered the other one as well. But he did not lower his head. He did not even look into the barrel of the gun that was pointed at him. He looked straight at Shapur Irani, and when the bullet entered his brain, his eyes were still wide open.

The sun streamed into the room and illuminated dust, a reminder to Shapur Irani of what he would ultimately become. There were so many cracks in the wall. Each time a line formed on his face, a line appeared on the wall as well. Walls, contrary to what he thought, were not dead things. They absorbed human sorrow, made it their own.

EPILOGUE

2001

They named her Aban.

It was Aspi Irani who chose the name. "It means 'Ocean of Magical Beings,'" he told Zairos. But when Mithoo looked up the meaning in a book of Persian baby names, all it said was "Water," to which Aspi Irani replied, "Those fools know nothing." And from the look in his daughter's eyes, Zairos could tell that Aspi Irani was right. They could not see the magical beings *inside* the water. That was all.

At first, Zairos saw his daughter only from afar. Back and forth he had gone to Kusum's hut, scared at the crying he heard. But he told himself that this little one was a part of Kusum, and if he loved the mother, the child was made of the same substance.

He took a step closer, entered the shade of the hut.

She had her mother's eyes, no question. Brown enough, deep enough, for him to get lost in them. Everything about her was so small, so fragile. Even her breath seemed like a collection of whispers. He caressed her forehead, stroked the small tuft of hair on her head. And when he kissed her cheek, he thought his lips were going to melt.

Seeing Zairos that way, squidgy and speechless, Mithoo picked the child up, cradled it in her arms, and uttered sweet heavenly gibberish. Then Aspi Irani followed, but for some reason he whistled to the child a jingle from a TV commercial for Nirma washing powder, a strange choice indeed which no one questioned, and then he started thinking of names, and once she was given a Zoroastrian name, Zairos knew she was his, and he took her straight to Anna's, where else, and although he had no idea what to say to his daughter, the ones at Anna's knew exactly what to do.

One by one they came up to her and said the most heartfelt—but ludicrous—things. "I feel like eating her," said Merwan Mota, and someone said, "Anna, give this beast an omelette fast!" and Behrooz took a spanner from his spare-parts shop and twirled it above Aban's head as though he were spinning a small cluster of stars. Sohrab Irani announced that Aban would be the only non-gambler ever to be allowed inside the Mobile Casino, and he blew the buffalo horn several times to herald her membership. From his sweltering kitchen, Anna sang a lullaby in Tulu, complete with rooster crows and dog woofs, and Bumble did a wheelie on his BMW for her, which made her cry of course. Hosi, thrilled that the racing season had resumed again, let Aban tug his beard as much as she wanted. Then he passed her on to Anna's dusky, steamy wife, and, in the transfer of baby, he managed to feel Anna's wife's breasts, and the coy look from Anna's wife sent Hosi high as Mount Kanchenjunga.

Thus Aban travelled, away from Anna's, all over Dahanu, to

the giant hands of Chambal the dacoit, who thumped Zairos on the back and called him a mard, a real man, and Aban smelled Sharmaji's homemade massage oils and sneezed repeatedly. At the beach, TG turned away from Aban, still not approving, still viewing the child as a disgrace, and as Xerxes rose in his blue and red glider, Mithoo's excitement rose too, Mithoo gave her stray dogs extra treats because she realized she could finally use her Montessori method of teaching on one of her own, and Aspi Irani, after much heartbreak, decided to throw away his collection of mosquito repellents so as to not harm Aban, but he continued to repel with his own hybrids, duets between Belafonte and Irani, and Aban seemed to love them, and on and on she went from the arms of one to the arms of another, until she finally rested in the lap that had started it all.

Shapur Irani looked at her in amazement and Zairos could feel the iron in this man slowly dissolving. When Shapur Irani let Aban's head rest against his chest, her small fingers uncurled and she caught a clump of his silver chest hair, and, in that moment, on a rocking chair that never rocked, she became Shapur Irani's Juliet, and even though the age gap of over ninety years was a bit vast, neither of them seemed to care, and when she gave a toothless grin and fell asleep, something wonderful occurred: Shapur Irani slept too. For the first time in his life, he wanted to stay on earth, he chose to stay.

With Aban safe in Shapur Irani's arms, Zairos stood at the foot of the Bahrot hills, only thirty minutes away from Anna's. He had parked his motorcycle at the base of a dam, the water spreading out before him, flat and motionless. He walked along the dam wall, a long stretch of grey asphalt that looked like a highway, towards the same hills in which his Zoroastrian ancestors had taken refuge in the fifteenth century.

It was Aspi Irani who suggested he come here.

"Seven hundred years after the first Zoroastrians fled from Iran to the shores of Sanjan, the Muslims hunted us again, when they invaded India," said Aspi Irani. "We seem to have a sweet scent about us that drives them nutty. But this time we did not run. A Parsi commander named Ardeshir gathered a troop of fighters and joined forces with the Hindu king of the region. But they were all slain in battle."

Aspi Irani picked his teeth with a toothpick, as though he was trying to free some truth that was stuck in there.

"The survivors took our Holy Fire, which had been brought from Iran and kept burning for centuries, and fled Sanjan to the Bahrot hills. They hid in its caves for twelve years, tending to the fire, which they called the Iranshah, the Fire of Victory. Son, I thought someday we would climb the hills together, but perhaps it's better if you make this journey alone."

It was a rare serious moment from Aspi Irani.

When Zairos looked at his father, he decided that he would never reveal to him the truth about Banumai. Zairos' stomach churned as he wondered how Aspi Irani might feel if he found out that his own father had once pointed a gun at him. Or that the fever that had claimed Banumai's life was the fevered hand of her own husband, a hand that still shook in horrid recollection of what it had done.

Zairos had also asked his grandfather, hesitatingly, fearfully, if it were possible that Aspi Irani was the son of Ejaz the Pathan.

"No," Shapur Irani had said. "Aspi is mine."

Zairos knew that to be the truth.

It was not only the fairer skin, the full head of salt and pepper hair, and the likeness in jaw structure. There was no doubt about Aspi Irani's lineage because only an Irani would spend his time shooting people with slingshots and blowing buffalo horns outside a nursing home.

As Zairos started the climb, he closed his eyes to the spikes of light and offered thanks to Ahura Mazda for bringing Aban into his life. Since his last meeting with Kusum—the day he discovered the real meaning of Ganpat's story—she had refused to see him. All those months she had carried Aban inside her with Laxman by her side.

During that time Zairos tried hard to forget Kusum, but his longing for her kept on increasing. One night he stood a distance away from her hut, unseen in the dark. All he wanted was a glimpse of her. He waited among some bushes, amid the frenzy of night crickets. He smoked, not caring if she caught the light. She would never think it was him. It could be anyone, or anything—a bug flying into a tree trunk, exploding like a star.

When she appeared, he wanted to tell her how he missed the way she parted her thighs, the way she received him, with lips and curves made of joy, waking up to him in ways he would remember for life. He thought of stepping out of those bushes, into the open for just a moment, to see if she would remain outside upon seeing him. But the moment he tried to do that he felt like an asp, something poisonous coming out of the darkness and disappearing again.

Perhaps staying away was the only option he had.

Worried that no one would employ her, twice he sent Damu to her with a packet of money, but Damu came back on both occasions, the envelope unopened.

So Zairos sent her a brand-new bottle of ginger marmalade.

Even Damu looked at Zairos strangely when Zairos placed this lone bottle in the back of the tractor. The bottle came back too, but when it did Zairos smiled because the cap had been opened and a small chunk, no more than a finger-lick, was missing.

Then one day Damu came up to Zairos and said, "Seth, I think you should see the child."

It had been born on that very day. One of the workers had told Damu.

Zairos knew exactly what that meant. It meant that the child was fair. The child was not Laxman's.

Upon realizing this, Zairos hugged Damu, who turned bride shy and stared at his feet. But Zairos was off by then.

Kusum would surely see him now.

He raced to her hamlet, his heart beating loud enough to echo off mountains, but his hands were steady. That was a sign—of what, he could not tell.

The hamlet was empty. Even the chickens were missing. He stood outside her hut, called out her name, and waited. He waited in the way a man waits in a hospital, behind the white curtains, away from the metal bowls and sweat-soaked sheets.

He called Kusum's name again.

The inside of the hut was dark, but that was always the case.

He looked around and wondered why there was not a soul in sight. It was evening, a time when people should be home, but then who was he to judge. Perhaps there was a festival, yes, he remembered there was a fair nearby and the Warlis must have gone there to buy bangles and nose rings and have their fortunes told.

He took a few steps towards the hut and that was when he saw the first drops of blood.

And why wouldn't there be blood, he thought.

It was to be expected. She had, after all, given birth.

Then Zairos saw her foot, the foot which was unmistakably hers, the soles rough and callused, but the shape dainty, and the anklet she wore he had not seen before, but the foot was hers for sure.

She was sleeping, exhausted.

The inside of the hut was dark, and normally the cooking fire or some sort of flame would be on, but then why would a flame be on when she was sleeping. She did not want the hut to burn. Even the child was sleeping, which is why there was no sound.

In a second or two, he wished he had never entered.

He was staring at her face.

Her face was bashed in, it was her jaw, and there was much blood around, especially on the rock, on the boulder that had caused this.

He tried to lift the boulder, but he had no strength.

It was pointless to do so because it was not on her face anymore. It was next to her face, and there were teeth on the thatched floor, and he looked around for a baby, but there was nothing, there was only this, and he had no idea what he was supposed to do.

He placed his hand on her forehead as though he was checking her temperature. That was all he could do. How Laxman managed to pin her down, how Laxman managed to hurl the boulder on her, how Rami managed to get away with the baby in her arms was beyond him.

He sat by her side and shook.

She was so still.

After a while, even he went still, but around him everything kept moving. The wind, the leaves, particles of dust along the ground, they all moved.

Nothing stopped for her.

Zairos had crossed three ridges and was now on the final ascent of Bahrot. He was in the heart of the reserve forest, and he felt he was being watched by the eagles that sat amid towering trees, resting majestic on the branches that seemed like thrones in the sky. White tree trunks lay on the ground, and he ran his fingers along them, peered into their hollows, hoping to slip into another world.

It had been three months since Kusum's death, and he had still not been able to say goodbye to her. Their daughter had come into his world, promising to find ways into the secret corners of his heart, but one truth still nagged him, made him anguish in the nights. He needed to bring it out into the open, among these hills.

My grandfather and I have something in common, he told himself.

We both killed the women we loved.

A sudden wind came, carrying his failure to protect Kusum the way it carried pollen. It forced Zairos to keep that knowledge coiled inside him tight and secure, and in the years to come perhaps only Aban would have the power to unwind it.

He wished Kusum were alive to witness the sight that he was now beholding. A host of purple karvi flowers, shocking him, a sudden eruption of colour, but stretching upwards, providing a lilt to the path, just as they would have provided to the thirsty eyes of his ancestors centuries ago.

Whatever pain he felt at losing Kusum was only an ounce compared to what his ancestors must have felt, the weight they must have carried up these hills as their loved ones lay on the battlefield in Sanjan—the pillaged homes they had to leave behind, their spinning wheels, their wool, their needles and thread, goats and white bulls, quills and red ink, cutlery, shafts of moonlight, the amorous whispers of lovers that had soaked into the walls of their homes just like the warm soot of the oil lamps they lit, and saris with embroidered designs as intricate as the hymns of Zarathushtra himself.

"There are only a hundred and forty thousand of us left worldwide," Aspi Irani had said of the Zoroastrians. "We are a dying breed, and I fear there will come a day when there is only one Zoroastrian left, fanning the flames of the sacred fire somewhere, half mad."

Our past needs to be conserved, he seemed to be telling Zairos.

And Bahrot was an important part of that conservation. The real fight against the Muslim attackers did not take place on the battlefield in Sanjan. It took place here, among these hills, in the caves where the Iranshah was kept burning.

The preservation of light. That was how the Zoroastrians fought back.

A light men like Zairos would learn to honour.

He kept walking, parting the branches of trees, slipping slices of orange into his mouth, his hair sticking to his wet forehead, the sound of his own breath and the grunt of a wild boar the only things he could hear, until he finally came to the Bahrot caves.

Stone debris, what used to be the outer wall. Stones pressed deep into the earth over time, threatening to disappear. He had reached quite a height, and he looked back over his shoulder just as his people had once done.

Zairos wondered if the karvi flowers were in bloom then.

Bahrot's back, purple with promise, inviting them into its nooks and crevasses, allowing them to stay for as long as they needed to.

There were fissures in the cave walls, the roof being held by large boulders wedged against each other. Three large pillars remained, grey and thick like the old, worn legs of elephants, under which occurred a final act of resistance from his people.

Here, amid the sobs and shudders of mothers for dead sons, the magi fanned the flames of their beloved Iranshah, feeding it sticks of sandalwood, their white mouth-veils preventing their breath from polluting the fire, which remained alive to this day in the town of Udwada, not far from Bahrot, as one of the oldest, purest, most sacred fires known to man. If it was hot in the caves now, Zairos could imagine men sweating underneath their white sudrehs, their sacred vests soaked with the sweat of devotion.

These were the moments that needed to be reimagined and venerated. The moments were holy—not the temples, not the caves, not the places of worship.

It was here that he needed to let go of Kusum.

Knowing that the caves were sacred to the Zoroastrians, the Warlis had built a shrine too, made of karvi twigs, with a small orange flag on the roof.

"We feel it is these hills that have given the landlords so much power," Kusum had said. "So we worship it and hope that it will change our fortunes as well."

To Zairos, it was a meeting place.

The clashing of centuries, two groups of people, both of whom had suffered in the past, one much better off now than the other—powerful, moneyed, with all the hope a ship could hold, the other tribe still lost, suffering less than before, but still losing its young, still sinking.

It was dark inside the shrine, something Kusum would not have chosen.

She had spent too many nights being beaten in enclosures like this one. There were coconut shells and chicken feathers on the ground, red vermillion marks on a cylindrical stone, and an old garland, signs that a Warli witch doctor had performed a black-magic ceremony.

Kusum's ashes could not be released here.

He did not want to send her ashes flying across the grasslands below either, over the painted horns of the grazing cow and buffalo, and the straw roofs of huts. If he threw her ashes over the cliff, they might reach Sanjan.

He wanted her to remain on Dahanu soil.

That was when he heard it. The gushing of a stream down the rocks. When he went towards it, he saw that it was stronger than a stream, the way it rushed along with urgency, to reach someone, or somewhere.

From his knapsack, he removed the small red pot.

The last time he was with Kusum, she had not allowed him to touch her. She had not even looked into his eyes.

For many nights Zairos had dreamt of grace, of being forgiven by the woman he loved—that day would never come.

From the time he had met her, he'd struggled to accept her, to allow her to walk beside him in his world. Now he realized it was Kusum who had accepted him. She was stronger than he was, her love more selfless and powerful.

With that, he let her go.

He sank to his knees as he watched Kusum move, swift and fearless, finding her way around, going underneath twigs, splashing against larger stones in a happy burst.

He could not believe he would never see her again.

She was leaving him so rapidly, it hurt. She was already beyond his reach.

But he had Aban, he told himself.

He thought of how, when he held her face in his hands, it was as though he were holding a baby moon, or the sun before it knew it was the sun. Now it was time to return to her, to listen to her purr and gurgle, to mingle his scent with hers, for father and daughter to exchange whispers and let eyelashes meet.

ACKNOWLEDGEMENTS

My gratitude to God, my spiritual guides the Bhavnagris, and Shiamak for strength and inspiration; Maya Mavjee for her patience, insight, and humour – a true guiding light; Denise Bukowski for unflinching guidance and encouragement; the Canada Council for the Arts and the British Columbia Arts Council for generous and timely assistance; Shaun Oakey for wise and thoughtful copy edits; Kelly Hill for the perfect cover; all the wonderful people at Doubleday, especially Susan Burns, Bhavna Chauhan, Kristin Cochrane, Val Gow, Martha Leonard, and Cathy Paine; Dr. Rooyintan Peshotan Peer of the K. R. Cama Oriental Institute, Bombay, for patiently answering all my queries on Zoroastrian history and religion; Prof. Denzil Saldahna at the Tata Institute of Social Sciences, Bombay, for his time and for providing me with invaluable reference material; my parents for opening up hearts and memories; and finally, a special thank you to my cousin Kaizad Irani for sharing his stories, and for many adventures, few of which can be spoken of.

The following sources were extremely helpful during the writing of this novel: *A Zoroastrian Tapestry: Art, Religion & Culture*; edited by Pheroza J. Godrej & Firoza Punthakey Mistree; *Zoroastrians: Their religious beliefs and practices* by Mary Boyce; *Adivasis Revolt* by Godavari Parulekar; "The Kings of the Jungle" by Winin Pereira; "On Drinking and 'Drunkenness'" and "Tribal Women in the Warli Revolt: 1945-47" by Indra Munshi Saldanha; the thesis by Prof. Denzil Saldanha entitled *A Socio Psychological Study of the Development of Class Consciousness* submitted for the Degree of Doctor of Philosophy in Sociology, Bombay, Department of Sociology, University of Bombay, August 1984.